Praise for *Cures for Heartbreak*

★ "Rabb leavens impossible heartbreak with surprising humor, delivered with a comedian's timing and dark absurdity. Rabb is an exceptionally gifted writer. Readers will cherish this powerful debut." —ALA *Booklist* (starred review)

★ "Black humor, pitch-perfect detail, and compelling characters make this a terrific read. As Mia struggles to make sense of her mother's death and her father's illness, she also sees humor in everyday situations, and her irreverent commentary brings the story to life." —*School Library Journal* (starred review)

★ "This is undeniably a book of anguish; it's also one of raw strength and casual, clever humor in random and surprising places, making it a compelling as well as tearful read." —*BCCB* (starred review)

★ "When the last page turns, four new and fascinating people have been born into the reader's consciousness." —*KLIATT* (starred review)

"Everybody, regardless of age, should read this novel—witty, warm, and gorgeous in its fearlessness." —*The Philadelphia Inquirer*

"Told in the first person with humor and tears, Mia's voice is authentic, and her story of family tragedy and healing rings true. Touching and tender." —*Kirkus Reviews*

"Anyone who has grieved the loss of a loved one will feel an immediate connection to Mia, the narrator of this intimate novel. It gives readers a keenly insightful study of grief." —*Publishers Weekly*

"This novel gets at the blinding ache of grief, while also managing to be very funny, very smart, and addictively readable. This is truly a gorgeous and important book, one I've been pressing onto friends and their teenaged kids." —*Cookie* magazine

"Rabb concentrates not on the brooding and self-pity that can often permeate this type of novel but on an examination of death's antithesis—love—as it touches the lives of her father, her mother and even Mia herself. Each chapter collides and colludes to offer both the familiar and the uncharted with humorous and touching detail, breaking and mending the reader's heart in turns." —teenreads.com

"Intense, poignant but also very funny, Mia's story of the year following her mother's death explores the nature of grief as it is experienced by a Jewish teenager, her older sister, and her father. There is much pain in the story but also much wisdom, not to mention a smart look at school, friendship, and romance."

—Association of Jewish Libraries

"Mia's full of conflicting emotions that are expressed in sometimes humorous ways. She wonders whether it's OK to date shortly after her mom dies; is it OK to wear her mom's clothes; return to school—and how to feel normal when nothing feels normal anymore. It's an experience that will help people understand grieving and know there is recovery." —*Detroit Free Press*

"A powerful debut with unforgettable characters and important things to tell us about family, history, death, love, and philosophy. It's a story that will heal your own heart." —jbooks.com

"In a wry, introspective first-person narrative (sections of which were previously published as short stories), Mia examines the ripple effects of this tragedy, showing how grief and loss infiltrate her life. An artful mix of the poignant and the sometimes comically mundane." —*The Horn Book*

"Humor carries this novel, preventing it from being maudlin. Reminiscent of Mexican milagros, those small religious charms nailed on sacred objects to denote miracles, it is through a series of seemingly small experiences that a shattered heart is miraculously mended." —Ingram Library Services

"A witty, matter-of-fact, and heartfelt look at what grief means to one teenager, and how the relationships and habits Mia acquires help her to accept change. The light, everyday comedy born of a series of disasters prevents the book from becoming maudlin. Peripheral characters are delightfully, even frighteningly, real in their details." —*VOYA*

"If you go to Amazon and limit your search to children's books and type in cancer, you'll get more than 4,000 book titles. With the field so packed with already published books, I thought it would be unlikely for a new book on the subject to be a MUST READ. And now I'm recommending this with all my heart, for teens and adults." —*Marianas Variety*

"*Cures for Heartbreak* is a sad, funny, smart, endlessly poignant novel. Reading it made me feel grateful for my life, for my family, and above all for the world that brings us gifts like the gift of Margo Rabb." —Michael Chabon, Pulitzer Prize–winning author of *The Amazing Adventures of Kavalier & Clay*

"Margo Rabb's story beautifully brings together the intensely personal and the historical, and rings with the authenticity of a bitter, yet illuminating truth."

—Joyce Carol Oates

"*Cures for Heartbreak* is full of sadness, humor, and quirky details that ring completely true. I thoroughly enjoyed it."

—Curtis Sittenfeld, author of *Prep* and *Sisterland*

IN AMERICA

Margo Rabb

HARPER

An Imprint of HarperCollinsPublishers

A brief excerpt of this novel was published in different form under the title "How to Tell a Story" in *Zoetrope: All Story*, 1999.
Lines from "O Tell Me the Truth about Love": Copyright 1940 by W. H. Auden, renewed. Reprinted by permission of Curtis Brown, Ltd.
Millay Estate for "Ancient Gesture" (2 lines) and "Time Does Not Bring Relief."
The lines from Poem XVIII of "Twenty-One Love Poems." Copyright © 2013 by The Adrienne Rich Literary Trust. Copyright © 1978 by W. W. Norton & Company, Inc. The lines from "(The Floating Poem, Unnumbered)" of "Twenty-One Love Poems." Copyright © 2013 by The Adrienne Rich Literary Trust. Copyright © 1978 by W. W. Norton & Company, Inc. The line from "Power." Copyright © 2013 by The Adrienne Rich Literary Trust. Copyright © 1978 by W. W. Norton & Company, Inc., from *Later Poems: Selected and New, 1971–2012* by Adrienne Rich. Used by permission of W. W. Norton & Company, Inc.
"One Art" from *The Complete Poems 1927–1979* by Elizabeth Bishop. Copyright © 1979, 1983 by Alice Helen Methfessel. Reprinted by permission of Farrar, Straus and Giroux, LLC.
"A Letter," from *The Selected Poetry of Yehuda Amichai* by Yehuda Amichai. Copyright © 2013 by Yehuda Amichai. Reproduced with permission of University of California Press Books via Copyright Clearance Center.
"What the Living Do," from *What the Living Do* by Marie Howe. Copyright © 1997 by Marie Howe. Used by permission of W. W. Norton & Company, Inc.

Library of Congress Control Number: 2015935856
ISBN 978-0-06- 232237-1

Typography by Kate J. Engbring
15 16 17 18 19 LP/RRDH 10 9 8 7 6 5 4 3 2 1
❖
First Edition

For Marshall, Delphine, and Leo

PART ONE

LOVE AND GRIEF

Will it come like a change in the weather?
Will its greeting be courteous or rough?
Will it alter my life altogether?
O tell me the truth about love.

—W. H. Auden

I hope your first kiss went a little better than mine did

According to my mother, my first kiss happened on a Saturday in July. The weather: steamy, blacktop-melting, jungle-gym-scorching New York City sunshine. The setting: the 49th Street playground in Queens, good on the sand quotient, low on the rats. The kisser: Hector Driggs, cute but a little bit smelly, like wet blankets and aged cheese. The event: one sopping, clammy-lipped, deranged, lunging kiss, directly on my lips.

I bit him.

I was three.

A mark bloomed on his arm like two tiny purple smiles and he cried for half an hour, but my mother felt no pity for him. In fact, she swelled with pride. "Even at that young age I knew you understood the need for girls and women to fight for our freedom, equality, and personal space," she said when she retold the story. "Plus, he smelled weird. I would've bit him too."

My mom is a professor of women's studies at Queens College. While other newborns were happily drifting to sleep to

Goodnight Moon, my mom read to me in my crib from Simone de Beauvoir, Virginia Woolf, and Audre Lorde. In our living room there's a picture of me in my stroller at a women's rights march in Washington, clutching a sign with my tiny green mittens: *Well-Behaved Women Seldom Make History!*

And so, two years ago, when I was fourteen and began what my mom termed "your ultimate rebellion," she said I chose the worst thing possible. She would've preferred odd piercings, full-body tattoos, or even shoplifting to what I did.

I fell in love with romance novels.

It wasn't even just regular book-love. I was crazy for them, head-over-heels, obsessed. I read them in grocery aisles, on subways, buses, between classes, and most often, curled up in bed. Over the next two years I read one hundred and eighteen of them. (Not counting those I read twice.)

I'd discovered my first romance novel on the shelves of my best friend Annie Kim's apartment—she has two older sisters. Jenny, her middle sister, saw me gazing at the array of colorful spines and handed me *Cowboys on Fire* (book 1), with bare-chested cowboy Destry and gold-belt-buckled cowboy Ewing on the cover. (I'd get to know Destry and Ewing with a passion that bordered on the scientific.) "Here," Jenny said. "You have to read this."

Slowly, my room became plastered with posters of Destry and Ewing on horseback, riding bulls one-handed, and roping calves; of Sir Richard from *Torrid Tomorrow*, who led a double life as the pirate Diablo; and Gurlag, who was raised by wolves and known as *The Wilderness Rogue.*

My mom would come into my room and gaze at the books on my night table, at Ewing on his bronco or Gurlag swinging from a tree, and she'd sigh. "I didn't raise you to worship imbecilic apes."

Other times she'd grow more serious, looking at my books. "I've failed you as a mother, as a woman, and as a citizen of this world," she'd say.

It wasn't true. I called myself a feminist (to her at least—to my friends it would be like calling myself a maiden or some other dusty crusty ancient word). At school I was quick to point out whenever boys dominated class discussions, or girls were excluded from handball games. When a flasher was spotted in our schoolyard three times in one month, I organized a Take Back the Yard march, with forty-five eighth graders parading around the Intermediate School 125 grounds chanting, "Girls on guard! Take back the yard! And dude, put some clothes on!" The flasher was undeterred, but eventually caught and prosecuted.

Still, my books kept bothering my mother. "That happiness only comes from romantic love is the biggest myth of our society," she told me once. "They're selling you a fantasy version of love. It's dishonest. Misleading. And untrue. Real love is a mess. Complicated. Not like *this.*" She picked up *Torrid Tomorrow.*

"But you haven't even read it."

As if possessed by a magic maternal sixth sense, she turned to the worst sentences in the whole book.

> Sir Richard's chest sparkled with man-dew as he whispered, "Lilith, it may hurt you when I burst thy womanhood."
>
> "Hurt me," Lilith breathed. Her rosy domes undulated like the sea as he joined her in a love that vanquished every sorrow known on Earth.

"The rest of the book is filled with a historical portrait of late-nineteenth-century American society, and Lilith is treated as an equal in the relationship—she's at the forefront of the suffrage movement," I pointed out, but my mom ignored my explanations and tried to get me to read *Girls Be Strong: A Guide for Growing Up Powerful* instead.

Girls Be Strong wasn't a bad book. It had some semi-interesting advice about how a boy stealing your scarf may mean that he likes you, but you're still entitled to tell him to get the hell out of your way. And it included a funny piece by Gloria Steinem called "If Men Could Menstruate," which said: "Guys would brag ('I'm a three-pad man') or answer praise from a buddy ('Man, you lookin' good!') by giving fives and saying, 'Yeah man, I'm on the rag!'"

But it wasn't exactly a romantic book, either.

To my mother, my real problem was that I believed in love, in great love. I had this trickle of hope, always, that the future would be filled with romance. I didn't expect to meet a Sir Richard or a Destry exactly, but it didn't seem entirely impossible.

My mom says that the events of last summer all started because of those one hundred and eighteen romance novels percolating in my brain. I don't think so, though. I think everything started when I met Will and told him about my father.

I sang in my chains like the sea

The first thing Will ever said to me was: "Tell me the truth." Then he plunked several pieces of crumpled notebook paper on my desk.

It was last September, in the tutoring center in our school's crumbling north tower. Our high school was a charter school in a city-owned former mansion in the Bronx; it featured a faded fresco in the auditorium, gilt moldings on the first floor, and entire wings of the building that were never renovated or used. The north tower overlooked Van Cortlandt Park. Iron bars covered the windows, as if someone was afraid we'd be tempted to hurl ourselves out.

When Will appeared at the door, Mrs. Peech, our faculty adviser, read his form and announced, "William Freeman," as if everyone didn't know who he was already—he was like a part of the school you learned your first week, along with your map and schedule. "You're with Eva."

Seventeen faces watched him sit down. He barely fit in the small chair.

I felt like I'd stepped onto a shaky subway train. I'd had a

8

crush on him for over a year, since I saw him my first day of high school. Now I tried not to stare at him. He had dark, wavy, unkempt hair like Gurlag, Destry, and all the wind-blown men on my romance novel covers, but he was different. He always carried books around—James Baldwin, Joseph Heller, Kurt Vonnegut—and while his friends were laughing and talking on the 1 train home, sometimes he'd just read. He managed to be weird and popular at the same time. The trophy case on our school's second floor displayed a shelf of his swim team awards (he was the captain), and his photo. I glanced at it every time I walked by: his brown eyes and his smile that always seemed partly sad and partly amused, as if he was thinking of some dark, mysterious joke.

I picked up his pages and the words swam before me. I glanced across the room at Annie; we both tutored at the drop-in center every Friday afternoon. She raised her eye-brows.

Focus. *Focus.* Do *not* think of man-dew.

I smoothed his rumpled pages and read. It was a college application essay about a swim meet, with descriptions of but-terfly strokes and buzzers ringing, and it was achingly boring.

"This sucks," I said.

"Don't hold back now."

"You said to tell the truth."

"Because I thought you'd say it was *good.*"

"There's no punctuation."

He pointed to a period.

"A period is the wallflower of punctuation. And you only have three."

"Three good ones," he said. He gazed right at me, practically through me.

Rosamunde Saunders, author of *Torrid Tomorrow*, would describe him as having *cheekbones as big as apricots* and *café mocha skin*. I glanced at the pale scar on his chin, like a tiny river. He sat so close to me that I could smell soap and something else—was I imagining it?—like sugar. His leg, in his dark jeans, brushed mine.

He picked up Dylan Thomas's *Selected Poems* from my desk. I'd been reading it before he got there; he'd arrived forty-five minutes after tutoring hour had started. "He looks startled," he said, staring at Dylan Thomas's face.

"It's startling to be reinventing the English language," I said. "I mean—dingle starry!" I blurted, quoting from the book. *The night above the dingle starry* . . . I took a breath and tried again. "I mean, in the book, um . . ." Why was I babbling? What was wrong with me? It was like an evil spirit had overtaken my body. I couldn't believe I was talking to Will and we were talking about Dylan Thomas, and the sheer magnitude of it all turned my brain to goo. All that was left was Rosamunde Saunders's voice. *He's looking at you with liquid velvet eyes. Eyes that know how to love a woman and—*

The bell rang. Someone called his name. A girl who stood

in the doorway, a swim team girl. Vanessa Valari. She and her friends bought entire pages in the yearbook to fill with photos of themselves in their bikinis on Rockaway Beach, their hands on their hips, laughing at the camera.

Will stood up, still holding the book. "Can I borrow this? I'll bring it back next Friday."

I nodded and watched him leave with the bikini girl.

The door closed behind them. "What's a dingle starry?" Annie asked me.

I took her phone—it was faster than my own Crapphone—and Googled Dylan Thomas's "Fern Hill," and showed it to her. "Fern Hill" was my father's favorite poem. He'd bought the book of *Selected Poems* for me one summer day after he phoned in sick to work (playing hooky, he called it), and we took the train to the Strand and picked out a whole pile of books, then went uptown and bought so much food at Columbus Comfort Kitchen that we could barely carry it all—fried chicken and fluffy biscuits and fried apple pies, still warm in tinfoil, and chocolate malt shakes smothered in whipped cream. We walked through Central Park and sat by Turtle Pond, and all afternoon we ate and wrote and read. I'd never heard the words *dingle starry* before, but I could see the stars dingling and sparkling, the sun dappling hidden lakes and magical trees, everything feeling easy and light, and though I wouldn't be able to say exactly what it meant to *sing in my chains like the sea*, I knew that I'd felt it, that I hadn't known that feeling existed until I saw the words on the page. After we read the poems, we wrote in notebooks—small spiral-bound college-ruled ones from the drugstore—he never saved his, but mine were stashed in the back of my closet. I hadn't looked at them since he died.

"You let Will take your dad's copy of the book?" Annie asked me, in shock.

My insides dropped—why had I done that? What if he spilled something on it or lost it? All week I watched him in the cafeteria and schoolyard, but I never had the guts to say, *Hey, by the way, please be careful with my book!*

On Friday at tutoring, he brought the book back to me, in perfect shape.

"Good book," he said.

I'd hoped we'd have time to talk, but he was late again, and we had only fifteen minutes. Mrs. Peech kept glancing at us; we got right to his essay. He'd rewritten it. I read it quickly. "The punctuation is great now, but I think the swim team topic has got to go," I told him.

"Why? That's what I *do*."

"Everyone does a sport. Maybe if your sport was, I don't know—calf roping—that might be interesting, but they're going to get a million essays about swim meets."

"I've got nothing else to write about."

"I don't believe you. Dig deep," I said.

"How do I know you're giving me good advice?"

"My mom has been coaching me on my college application since I was a fetus. Plus Mrs. Peech makes all the tutors read a book about college essays."

The bell rang. The bikini girl waited in the doorway again. "See you next Friday," he said.

The week crept by. Annie and I studied—sometimes I felt like all we did was study: we studied on the 7 and the 1 trains (the 1, when it reached the Bronx, was quieter), at the Woodside Library, the Sunnyside Library, the 42nd Street New York Public Library, and at Athens Diner, which was halfway between our apartments, and where they let you sit with a hot chocolate for three hours and never kicked you out. At night, before we fell asleep, she texted me updates about *Dancing with the Stars* and all her favorite reality shows, and I texted her quotes about Gurlag's manroot.

I couldn't wait to see Will again. When the day arrived I kept watching the door, expecting him to appear, which he did, only ten minutes late this time.

His new essay was about his dog, Silas.

"The college essay guide said no dogs," I said.

"What's wrong with dogs?"

"They get so many pet essays, they usually toss them right out. Instant reject."

"My dog isn't a normal dog. He has three legs."

"I know. Silas sounds like a great dog. Still. Four-legged dogs, three-legged dogs—the book said they get tired of reading about dogs." I tapped his essay. "Also, the voice here doesn't sound like you. I mean, it could've been written by anybody. You want something that could only have been written by you."

I scribbled in the margin of his essay: "More you." He took the pen from me and put it down, and then touched my finger.

"You have a callus from writing so much," he said.

No one in my books ever pointed out a callus. *"I love your callus,"* Sir Richard said. *"What a beautiful callus."*

He ran his finger up and down mine. My face warmed; a flicker traveled under my skin. He let go as the bell rang. The door opened and there stood the bikini girl, as always.

He left without a word. I stared after him. I told Annie what happened as we packed up our things and walked down the hall.

"He touched my finger. He told me—he actually told me, *'You have a callus from writing so much.'*" I said it in a husky tone.

Annie squinted. "What's wrong with your voice? You sound like you have a throat disease."

Annie was a romantic only up to a point. She liked watching *Anne of Green Gables*, *Pride and Prejudice*, and even the occasional Lifetime Original Movie with me, and she loved her reality shows, but she drew the line at reading romance novels, or having a real-life romance right now. "We've got plenty of time for all that crap in college," she'd say.

In college. That was Annie's mantra. She always knew

she'd wait till college to fall in love. Her sisters, Jenny, who was a junior, and Lala, who was a senior, got straight Cs and wasted all their time thinking about who they hoped to hook up with, or regretted hooking up with. Annie said they were on a fast track to folding sweaters at American Eagle for the rest of their lives.

Our wait-till-college plan was easy since no boys were interested in us anyway. At our nerd-heavy school, the boys rarely had the guts to speak to us, except when asking to borrow math notes or to pass a beaker in lab. The only guy who'd ever asked me out was David Dweener, who had oily hair and liked to a wear a T-shirt from the musical *Cats*. Will belonged to the good-looking elite, a small, ultracool crowd. I never thought in a million years that he'd ever speak to me.

Annie and I walked toward the subway. "Maybe next week you'll get lucky and he'll ask to touch your bunion," she said.

"That would be wonderful. Except I don't have a bunion."

"*Sadly, it was a short-lived romance, since Lady Eva's dead skin was not yet thick nor copious enough to satisfy Sir Will,*" Annie said.

Laughing about it made me feel a little less nervous when I thought about him, but the next Friday, my heart banged away when he walked through the door of the tutoring center.

He had a completely new essay:

The last time I saw my brother he looked perfect. They made his skin pink. His lips were bright red.

He wore a fuzzy blue sleeper that had been given to him as a gift, but he'd never worn it while he was alive. My mom wanted each of us to give him something to be buried with, to take wherever he was going. My dad gave him a tiny telescope so that he could always see us on Earth. I gave him one of my stuffed animals, an orange monkey. My mom gave him a gold necklace that said "Mother" on it, which she'd been wearing the day he was born.

I was seven.

When people ask my mom how many children she has, she says two. For a while, if someone asked me how many siblings I had, I said none. She got mad when I said that. She likes talking about him. It gives her comfort. *I had another son, a baby who died in his crib. They don't know what caused it. I put him to bed on his back. I didn't have a blanket in the crib. I didn't do anything wrong but it happened and you have to learn to live with it. It never gets easier.*

It doesn't bother her that people cringe and look away when she talks about him. They don't want to hear about it. She talks about him anyway. She takes out the album and looks at his photos, and she remembers his birthday every year and thinks of how old he would've been. Eleven now. He'd be eleven. My mother tells me *He will always be your brother. He was born, he lived, he died. Don't erase his life from yours.*

My mom says that if my brother hadn't died, she never would've known who my father really was, that he was the type of man who would leave when things got hard. After my brother died, my dad started drinking, staying out all night, stopped coming home. Then one day he left for good. I didn't see him again for ten years.

So I guess this essay is supposed to be about what's influenced me the most, but I think sometimes the biggest influence isn't what's present in your life, but what's absent. Those missing pieces that shape you and change you, the silences that are louder than the noise.

I was quiet for a long time. "It's good," I said. "Really good." My voice was soft. "I'm sorry about your brother and your dad."

I couldn't stand how lame *sorry* sounded. "I hate *sorry*—I mean—my dad's dead—he died almost two years ago. I've never figured out what the right thing to say is. Or to hear."

I knew what the next question would be before he even said it.

"How did he die?" he asked.

Truth

When people ask how my dad died, I lie. I say he died of a heart attack, in his sleep.

When I used to say the truth, when I used to say plane crash, there was always this look. This flash as their mouths opened, this unbearable hungry eager excitement. They'd want to know what kind of plane, how big it was, where it was going, what went wrong. They wanted more of this freakish thing that didn't happen to real people, not in real life, not to anyone they'd ever met, it didn't.

I understand the curiosity. I mean, I do it too—who doesn't click on links to accidents and scary things, kids falling down wells, burn victims, serial killers? People always ask bits and facts about the plane, but what they really want to know is how it would be to die like that, to fall from the sky, how it would feel.

The heart attack happened in his sleep so he never felt a thing, I tell them. Peacefully. *Rest in peace.* I can never stop thinking about those words *rest in peace.*

The airline officials asked my mom for items so he could

be identified. Hairs from a comb. Toothbrush. She gathered these specks of my father, specks because there might be nothing of him left from the impact, nothing but other matching specks.

"You'll feel relief when they identify the remains," said the grief counselor lady assigned to us. Her chest was the size of a jumbo loaf of Wonder bread. I called her Wonderboob. Wonderboob liked to tell my mom and me things like "You need to make the time to do your grief work," as if it was something I could add to my homework list after algebra and English. She led group sessions for the families; she belonged to a team of therapists who'd donated their services. During these weekly sessions she'd yawn and periodically check her texts. She recommended vanilla scented candles and Be Relaxed herbal tea. The plane had crashed deep into the ocean, and only a small amount of remains and wreckage had been recovered from the surface. As the search and DNA analysis continued, Wonderboob ended all our sessions by saying, in a businesslike tone, "I'll keep you updated on the status of the remains."

Remains. She really liked the word *remains*. You'd think that adults—social workers, grief counselors, people whose job it is *to make you feel better*—you'd think they'd come up with a better word than *remains*.

My mother attended all the sessions with me, but she never said a word during them and never seemed to hear anything anybody else said, either. She'd gaze into the distance, emotionless.

I never said a word during the sessions either, but I listened to everything. Back then, during those first six weeks after the crash, I was certain my dad was still alive, that he'd never gotten on that plane. I saw him everywhere around the city. I followed a man in a suit into a subway car, thinking it was him. I saw him in a taxi whizzing over the 59th Street Bridge. In a booth at McDonald's. It was never him.

I tried not to think about it. I didn't think about it, I'd be okay not thinking about it, and then I'd see a girl my age with her father and it was like someone was pulling my intestines out with their teeth.

There's a KFC on my walk home from the 52nd Street subway station, and sometimes I glance in the window and see them. Girls and their dads doing the tiniest most boring thing like sharing chicken wings (and I don't even like chicken wings), and I watch them through the window, wanting to soak up all this fatherness, this luxurious fatherness they don't even appreciate. Usually they're not even talking to their dads, they're texting or playing a video game in their laps. Don't they know? I want to shake them. Don't they know how lucky they are to sit in the KFC with their fathers?

Six weeks after the crash, they confirmed my dad's remains. They'd found a small part of his body.

Three months after that, my mom got rid of his stuff.

His clothes, his shoes, his papers all went in the trash or in a Queens Thrifty-Thrift truck. The only things that she approved of me keeping were our photo albums, his books, and presents he'd given me—a horseshoe necklace for Hanukkah, a silver bracelet for my birthday, three turquoise rings, pens, and notebooks.

I snuck some other things away before she could throw them out, though. I hid them in a large purple shoe box in my closet.

Things I kept:

> spare glasses with brown plastic frames and
>   scratched lenses
> Brooklyn Bridge paperweight
> eight postcards he sent from business trips
> soft white Hanes T-shirt
> collar he bought for our cat, Lucky
> two blue handkerchiefs
> striped silk tie
> a receipt from Popeyes for 5 TENDER,
>   1 BISCUIT, SM PEPSI with his signature
> six Toffee Crisp wrappers I found in the pockets
>   of his coats

I take these things out sometimes; I touch the paperweight and T-shirt and candy wrappers and I lie on my bed, holding them.

A year after he died, my mom said our apartment was too big and expensive, so we moved to a smaller place nine blocks away. That's when I began saying *heart attack* to our new neighbors and the owner of the corner grocery store and any stranger who asked.

A heart attack. In his sleep. At the hospital. He went into the hospital with chest pains and had the heart attack there, in a comfortable hospital room with yellow walls and a striped curtain separating the beds. (I've only been to a hospital once, when my aunt Janet had fibroids removed, and that's what I pictured.) It was a quiet room with a flower painting and a window with an East River view. The caring nurses comforted my mom and me, and we held his hand and said good-bye and I kissed his forehead. I knew the whole scenario. I almost believed it myself. I called it *his passing*. I heard someone say this one time, *his passing*, about their father who had a heart attack in his sleep, and I envied it. I was actually jealous of how someone else's father died. The *passing*, the peaceful transition between life and death. Rest in peace. That's how I wanted it to be.

Funny grief

The heart attack was so sudden that he never felt a thing. People say it's lucky to die that way," I told Will. Around us, in the tutoring center, people talked in quiet voices; someone clapped a book shut.

He nodded with a sad and intense look.

I paused. "I always wish they had cartoons—sympathy cards with cartoons, you know? That would capture all the crazy messed-up feelings." After my dad died, we'd received a mountain of cards featuring footsteps on beaches, silhouettes staring out rainy windows, and bare-branched trees. Annie and I decided that someday we'd come out with our own line of funny sympathy cards. I drew one with a cartoon on the back of my English notebook: *The Stages of Grief: (1) Cookies. (2) Candy bars. (3) Bed. (4) More cookies.*

"I'm sorry about your dad. I'm sorry for saying *sorry*. I wish I had some cartoons." His voice was gentle and quiet, patient and kind.

I'd never had a conversation like this with anyone, not even Annie. Her parents were together. No one close to her had died.

There was something in the room, something new between us this Friday. An understanding. He knew what it was like to lose someone, to be in that dark and awful space, to have your family changed forever.

"My mom never talks about my dad," I told him. "She's the opposite of your mom. She kind of pretends he never existed."

"Even around you?"

"Especially around me." A year after he died, my mom said she was done grieving, that was all, it was over, like a roast cooking, a timer went off, *Aha! All better now!* She gave me a book called *The Stages of Mourning*, which was much worse than *Girls Be Strong*. *The majority of mourning will take place in the first year*, it said. *After that, it will be easier.* I kept thinking, When? When does it get easier? I felt like I was two different people: happy at school, laughing with friends, smiling on the subway reading *Torrid Tomorrow*; then I'd go into Sunshine Market and see the Toffee Crisp bars, his favorite chocolate bars, next to the gum and Tic Tacs, and I'd stare at their orange-and-yellow wrappers as my eyes began to sting. This other half of me would take over, my stomach would fill with wet rags, and I'd think how hardly anyone even knew this about me, this piece of my dad buried in me.

One day, I bought a Toffee Crisp and left it on the kitchen counter, and when my mom thought I wasn't looking, she stuffed it in the garbage. She did the same thing with the newspaper whenever any subject remotely related to his death appeared there.

Lulu, my mom's best friend, had explained my mom's attitude to me once: *She's coping differently than you are. This is her way of grieving.* She said my mom's practical, thick-skinned, stuff-the-feelings-away-and-get-it-done approach came from her parents, especially her mom, who'd been born in Germany and survived the war. "People do what they have to do to get through," Lulu said. "She's doing a good job as a single mother. You two are different, but she really, really loves you."

My mom said "I love you" every night—"Good night, brush your teeth, I love you"—like an item on a to-do list. My dad used to say it with a soft voice and a kiss to the head, and I told my mom that once: "Daddy said *I love you* differently." She looked stricken. She told me she had a headache and she went to bed.

Now, most of the time, she looked like I was giving her a headache.

I turned to Will. "When I talk to my mom these days, she pretty much always looks like this." I imitated her, scrunching up my face and clutching my forehead with one hand.

"This is what my mom looks like when talking to me." He made the exact same pained expression.

I laughed.

"They're singing in their chains like the sea," he said.

I paused. My ears felt hot. "You liked it. The poem."

"He breaks the rules. Made-up words. If I turned something like that in to the Undead, she'd faint. I mean, if she was capable of human reactions." The Undead was what everyone called his AP English teacher, Mrs. Saddler. She was a stickler for rules and looked approximately 150 years old.

He liked the poem. His quoting from it had the same effect on me that Sir Richard telling Lilith *I will give you all the world's riches* had on her. Of course he liked poetry—he already seemed like a poet. A loner. *A bit odd* was how Annie described him once. Occasionally at lunchtime he'd go off by himself and wander to god knows where. (I'd suggested to Annie one day that we should follow him. *That would be stalking*, she'd said.) He told me he rarely checked his email, and he was barely online at all. He only posted photos a few times a year—artsy pictures of subway tracks and his three-legged dog—and he had an ancient flip phone that belonged in a museum (it made my Crapphone, an old, basic smartphone, look almost fancy).

I loved his oddness. Poetry was sort of odd, which was why I thought—I hoped—he'd like it.

"My dad used to say that giving someone a poem is like gifting them a feeling. Everything will change from black and white into color," I said.

"Your dad was a writer?"

"No, not really. His day job was in corporate communications, but he had a PhD in English—his thesis was on Dylan

Thomas. He scrawled stuff in notebooks, but he always threw out everything he wrote."

"But you write," he said.

I paused. I hadn't written anything since my dad died.

"I used to write poems and stuff." I shrugged. "I don't really anymore." When I tried to write after my dad died, nothing came out. I'd open a notebook and stare at the blank page, but it hurt too much to put anything on it. It felt like staring at a giant slab of pain. Go away, I'd tell the feelings. Go away. I don't want to talk about you. I want you gone. I'd stick the notebook back in my closet.

The bell rang. He stood up and stared at the doorway. A new bikini girl waited for him this time: Gia Lopez, who had giant boobs and looked about twenty-five years old. She was the most beautiful girl in our school. I saw her on the subway sometimes and men always gawked at her. Rich-looking guys in suits handed her their business cards.

He said good-bye, then picked up Gia's backpack and slung it over his shoulder. I watched them leave. His sure-footed, confident stride, a cowboy-like walk.

Annie came over to me. "You have this really weird expression on your face," she said.

I buried my head in my arms. "I love him," I muttered to the table.

She sat down. "I think what you're feeling is *limbic resonance*."

I looked up. "My limbs are vibrating? You know, they kind

of are a little, every time I see him."

"No. Limbic resonance is the ability to feel someone else's feelings. Girls and women are really good at it. It's part of evolution, so we can sense what babies feel even though they can't speak. When you see him, you're feeling that resonance." Annie's favorite beach read was *Behavioral Endocrinology*; by sophomore year she'd already taken two AP science classes and gotten the highest grade in each.

"Maybe," I said. "Or maybe I actually love him."

She shrugged. "If you're sure, then you should tell him."

I zipped my backpack closed. "What planet do you live on?"

Annie rooted around in her bag, which contained, in addition to her textbooks: a TI-89 calculator; Sephora Magnetism lipstick; Quarky, her stuffed subatomic particle (her good-luck charm, a birthday gift from me); three issues of *Us Weekly* (she liked to read about "Stars—They're Just Like Us!" and molecular biology simultaneously); and chocolate fudge Pop-Tarts, which she preferred to eat cold.

"In the animal kingdom, they don't fake it or hide their feelings," she said. "Baboons' backsides turn bright red and swell when they see a male they're interested in."

"Thank you. That information is hugely helpful. I'll be sure to drop my pants and shake my red ass at him in the middle of lunch tomorrow."

I didn't drop my pants. I'd think of Will during English

and Spanish and chemistry, picturing us floating from medieval Europe to Antarctica to the Tahitian islands in our romance. Friday couldn't come fast enough. I sent out pleas to the universe, hoping he'd come back to tutoring again, and all week I imagined things to say to him. Funny things. Smart things. Things that would make him dump Gia Lopez and travel across South America with me, by vine.

Then, the next Thursday, I saw Will and Gia kissing in the hallway outside the cafeteria, all lips and hands and shiny hair. They could've been a couple from a perfume ad, glossy and passionate and perfect. They could've been the cover of a romance novel.

I couldn't get the image of them out of my head. Gia was a foot taller than me and a million times prettier, and all day my brain kept watching Will's hands roam over her shoulders and behind her neck, again and again and again.

The next morning, when I woke up, my stomach turned. My legs hurt. I tasted something sour in the back of my throat. The longing for Will rolled into my old grief like a mudslide, growing and gaining speed. I felt *griefy*. I wished *griefy* was a word. I thought about my mom and how she worked all the time now. She worried about money. She taught extra classes and on weekends spoke at conferences about women and economics. Sometimes she'd fall asleep with her head on her desk after grading papers. Other times she'd be buried in writing lectures and then suddenly look up and remember

I existed. I'd seen two new books on her bookshelf: *How to Talk to Your Teenage Daughter* and *Living with Your Teenage Daughter and Loving It.*

My dad wouldn't have needed a book to talk to me. He never needed instructions.

Almost two years had passed, but I missed him just as much—sometimes I missed him *more.* How was that possible? How could it get worse? Junk mail still arrived in his name (despite my mom haranguing the postal service); telemarketers asked for him; when I went to the grocery store, I bought the stuff that only he ate. He was born in London, and our cupboards used to be filled with tea and Jammie Dodgers, Lyle's syrup, Heinz baked beans, Colman's mustard, orange marmalade, and jars of Marmite. I'd always thought Marmite was gross, but a month ago I bought it, shut the door to my room, and ate tiny tastes of it with a spoon.

Now, before my mom left for work, my stomach began to feel worse. I felt this gnawing inside me, a hollow ache. I felt like I might throw up. My mom leaned over my bed with a worried frown. She took my temperature. Normal.

"It must be another stomach bug," she said. She rubbed her forehead.

For the past two years I'd been getting stomach bugs once a month or so. She'd taken me to the doctor after the first few times, and they tested me and said I might have some bacteria and put me on a course of antibiotics. "Sometimes these drugs work. Sometimes they don't," the doctor said.

The drugs didn't work. My mom worried that something really bad was wrong with me. She talked to her best friend, Lulu, about it on the phone. Lulu had gone to graduate school with my parents; she'd lived three blocks from us for years, until she moved to Arizona, where she was an English professor.

"Depression and grief can make you physically ill," Lulu had told my mom. "If you push those feelings away, they're going to come back and bite you in the ass. Or the stomach," she said. "Let her have her sick days, her days off. She needs them." Lulu suggested my mom and I see a therapist, but we'd had such a bad experience with Wonderboob that my mom didn't want to try that again. After our last group therapy session, Wonderboob's parting advice to my mom was that we should get a cat.

Now my mom muttered about trying a new antibiotic, and then glanced at her watch. She didn't want to be late. She said I could stay home from school and made me promise to call her in a couple of hours to check in.

I tried to sleep. I couldn't. I turned on my Crapphone. And then I did the thing I sometimes did when I felt this crazy crushing pain in my chest—I went to a website my mom forbade me to visit.

It was a private forum for the crash victims' families. Visiting always made me feel better—maybe only a millimeter better—but at least it made me feel like I had company.

Fran Gamuto, the forum's moderator, had told my mom about the site over the phone. Fran called every family personally to let them know about it. She wanted a place where we could keep in touch about the investigation, the lawsuit against the airline, and the ongoing search for the wreckage. The fuselage and black boxes still remained somewhere on the ocean floor. Three major searches had been attempted over the last two years, and Fran and the other families lobbied for a fourth search to begin in the late spring. Three underwater robotic vehicles were going to search a new area of almost two thousand square miles. Without the black boxes, none of the theories of what caused the crash were ever proven. Fran was convinced that someday there would be proof.

My mom had visited the site once and established a password (she used the same one for everything), and then she decided it was ridiculous. "They're not talking about the lawsuit. They're talking about their *feelings*. Why would anyone want to go on here and do that to themselves?" she asked.

I wanted to do that to myself.

I went on it sometimes at the laundromat, in the computer room at school, or at night after my mom was asleep. Other times I'd be waiting for the subway and I'd be thinking about Fran Gamuto and Nancy Johnson and Jill Bluelake and the others who posted. Some people had signatures that appeared after their names on every post:

Fran (husband Frank, daughter Lisa, Seats 22C, 22D)

Jill (Jacques Bluelake, 14A)

Nancy Johnson (Adam, Robert, Adam Jr., 11C, D, E)

I never posted myself but I loved lurking, reading what other people wrote. In the Wonderboob group sessions we went to after it happened, people were stunned and sometimes cautious and hesitant when they talked about their feelings. Online, everyone was more honest. One day, a year ago, Fran started a new thread. She asked what everyone was most afraid of. The responses came quickly.

I drive 10 miles out of my way to avoid going by the airport.

The depression. Wallowing. Sometimes I get stuck in this pit of grief and bad feelings and I don't know how to get out of it.

I always thought I had some control . . . exercise, drive safely, get checkups, wear a seat belt, and now I laugh that I ever thought it was that easy. I'm afraid maybe I'm marked for disaster. I'm waiting for the other shoe to drop.

It's the guilt that gets me. I should never have let him go on that trip.

I ran my finger down the screen of my Crapphone—it loaded each message slowly, as if it were clogged with sand—and I watched its reload symbol struggle to get unstuck until I finally fell asleep. When I woke up, I read romances and ate cookies till my mom came home.

The next Friday, Will asked: "Hey, where were you last week?"

"Oh—I was sick. A stomach thing."

"I had to meet with Mrs. Peech," he whispered. "She's got bad breath."

I needed to forget this crazy crush. I had to push it out of my mind, which I tried to do over the next month as we kept working on his essay. Each week I learned more about him: that his mom owned a bakery in Manhattan, and his dad was an artist and lived in LA now. He told me that his mom was black—her family from Saint Lucia—and his dad was Scottish and Italian. People could never guess what race Will was—black people guessed he was Latino. White people thought he was Jewish.

One chilly fall afternoon, Will told me the story of how his dad came to New York last year for a gallery show, and Will agreed to meet him for the first time since he'd left. Will's mom was okay with them getting together, but she wouldn't say his dad's name. She called him Jerkface. "Jerkface called you," she'd say. "Jerkface sent you a check." Jerkface was getting remarried next summer to a woman who was twenty-seven. Will's mom called her Mrs. Jerkface.

My mom had met a guy herself a couple of weeks before. She'd been out with him twice. Apparently, she did have time for one thing besides work. "His name is Larry," I told Will now. "He's the first guy she's gone out with since my dad. She won't admit they go out on dates. She calls him her 'acquaintance.'"

"What do you think of him?" Will asked.

"Annie and I call him the Benign Fungus. He's not awful. Just mildly annoying and might be hard to get rid of."

He laughed. "You should tell your mom that."

"I can't tell her she's going out with a fungus." It felt good to laugh about it. It was either laugh or scream.

"You told me I sucked—you can tell her anything." He paused. "You're really honest. You're one of the most honest people I've ever met, you know."

I glanced at my lap, thinking of all the ways I'd lied to him. I'd told him my dad died of a heart attack. I was lying to him even now, not telling him how I really felt about him. I'd been tutoring him for nine weeks. An eternity. Longer than he'd seen Vanessa Valari or Gia Lopez. It seemed forever.

He finished his essay. He applied to colleges. I thought he'd stop coming to tutoring, but he signed up for next semester, too. The Undead had told him that he needed a good grade on his AP English test if he wanted to place out of freshman English in college. He said he needed help. I tried not to read more into it.

I knew he wasn't interested in me, but I couldn't stop daydreaming.

Will showed up for tutoring hour on time. He loped toward the window and tore off the bars with his bare hands. "I never loved Gia Lopez. I only want to reach the zenith with you," he said as he grabbed a vine, enfolded her in his manly arms, and swung with his beloved out of the north tower and into his jungle love lair nestled in the trees of Van Cortlandt Park.

I dwell in possibility

In January, on the first day after winter break, the news coursed through our school within hours: a big modeling agency signed Gia. They'd flown her to Europe for a fashion shoot in a wilderness preserve. School had given her a leave of absence. She'd be back in three weeks.

That Friday, at tutoring, I waited to see if Will would show up. I'd caught a glimpse of him at lunchtime as he wandered off by himself, but I hadn't seen him since.

Mrs. Peech sat at her desk marking papers. Outside, it began to snow. Aside from the two of us, the tutoring center was empty. Annie was at Science Club; all winter her project group met every afternoon.

I shivered in the freezing room. Frost laced the windows and clung to the iron bars.

I hoped he'd come. I'd woken up at six that morning and spent an hour getting ready. I'd tiptoed around the apartment—if I woke my mom, she'd squint at me and ask why I had on eyeliner and had straightened my hair, but I couldn't tell her about Will. My mom's concept of feminist freedom didn't include freedom in love. "I trust you," she told me once. "I just don't trust boys under eighteen. Or under thirty, actually."

Over break, I'd kept daydreaming and feeling so anxious about this endless hopeless crush that I called Lulu for advice. Lulu was kind of a second mom to me—she never judged or criticized, and I could tell her things I couldn't tell my own mom. During the blurry weeks after my dad died, Lulu had stayed with us. She grocery shopped, she did the laundry, she sorted the mail, she cooked. Homemade mac and cheese. Lasagna. Pot roasts. Tortilla soup. She slept on our couch at night and opened our blinds every morning—she was probably the only reason my mom and I survived those black-hole days.

Now she told me not to worry. "Don't be so hard on yourself. It's okay to have a big crush. When you're around him, just be yourself," she said. As if I knew who that was. Which self? Should I tell him I had stomach bugs and ask if he wanted to eat an entire pack of Chips Ahoy cookies with me in my twin bed?

I looked up—Will appeared at the door. My neck prickled. He walked over to my table and took out his essay. It was his AP lit assignment from over vacation. An essay about Edna St. Vincent Millay. The Millay topic had been my suggestion—I'd lent him a book of her poetry and a biography of her that had been my dad's. I stared at the paper but I couldn't absorb the words. *Gia is gone* echoed in my head.

He leaned close to me; his knee touched mine. I shivered again. My hands went cold.

"Do you need this?" He took off his maroon scarf and put it around my neck and shoulders. It smelled like him, like soap and sugar. I wished Annie could see me in the scarf. Even she had to admit that scarf lending was much better than touching a callus. Or a bunion.

After a while, Mrs. Peech stood and picked up her bag. "I'm leaving early before the snow starts coming down hard. You two better get going, too—they're predicting three inches."

Will put his hand on his essay. "Could we stay a few more minutes? It won't take long."

"All right." She smiled at him. I think she loved him almost as much as I did. "Just a few minutes. Lock the door on your way out."

She left. Will and I were alone. I felt a sharp stab beneath my ribs. I picked up his essay. It was typewritten. "Where'd you get the typewriter?" I asked.

"I found it. Someone left it on a stoop near the Strand with a Free sign on it. Carried it all the way back uptown." I'd mentioned the Strand bookstore to him once before—he'd never been—and told him that my dad and I used to go there all the time, and now Annie and I loved to go there together.

"You liked the Strand?" I asked.

"I want to move in there." He took a book out of his messenger bag. "I found this there too. On the dollar cart."

Mansions and Manors of the Bronx. He flipped to page twenty-three, to a picture of our school. *Brookhill Manor.* "Look." He pointed at a photo of our auditorium, which used to be a private theater. A woman dressed in white read on the stage. The caption: *Poetess Edna St. Vincent Millay addresses the audience.*

"I can't believe it. Our school is famous." I paged through the other black-and-white photos. They showed our cafeteria when it was a ballroom, and our school's roof: a spectacular garden covered the whole place, with a giant stone table, trees, fountains, and a view of the city. I'd heard rumors before that our school had an abandoned roof garden (or a forest, or a colony of escaped convicts, depending who was telling the story). People also said the moldings on the first floor were made of solid gold, which was proved wrong when Evan LeDuff chiseled a chunk off and plaster crumbled out.

"I can't believe it's true," I said. "What's up there now?"

He shrugged. "Who knows. Dead bodies maybe. Ghosts."

"I've always thought this building was haunted." The pipes always clanked, the radiators hissed, the floorboards on the stage creaked. "Maybe Edna's the ghost. If people called me a poetess, I'd come back and haunt the place too."

"Poetess," he said, and stared at me. Then he took out a colorful flyer that had been tucked into the back page of the book, under the jacket flap. "I saw this in the Undead's classroom today. You should enter it."

URBANWORDS: A CITY-WIDE POETRY CONTEST AND FESTIVAL. STUDENTS, SUBMIT YOUR POEMS BY JANUARY 31ST. WINNERS WILL BE ANNOUNCED IN JUNE.

"I don't have any poems to submit," I said.

"Write one. I'll proof it for you. It better have good punctuation."

"It will be all punctuation. A blank page with question marks."

He stared at me a little strangely. Then he said, "I missed seeing you over the break."

My heart flipped. I wanted to say *I missed seeing you too*, but the words caught in my throat. I touched the typewritten pages again.

Out the window the snow came down harder.

"I can't talk about this kind of stuff with anyone else," he said.

Obviously Gia would never talk about writing and books. It was probably a big deal when she read the entire J. Crew catalog.

"The guys on the team are not exactly into reading," he said.

"I'm shocked."

He shook his head. "They already think I'm weird."

"You *are* weird."

He smiled. "So are you."

"Exactly. Welcome to the club."

My dad used to tell me: *All good writers are weird. Proudly weird.*

I always sort of wondered what he meant. I knew it was kind of strange to lie in bed at night and grasp thoughts and feelings and memories and corral them into lines and verses. Was that why I'd stopped writing, too? Because it was a strange thing to do, without my dad here to encourage me, and to share that strangeness with me?

Will's strangeness, and his mysterious and elusive thing, somehow made me like him even more. In December, I'd mustered the guts to ask him where he went on his solo lunches—any good delis he knew of? He hadn't answered. "I need a lot of time alone" was all he'd said. He was always forgetting to charge his flip phone, and he used a pay-as-you-go plan that kept running out of minutes. Gia had yelled at him one time when she picked him up from tutoring: *Why don't you get a new goddamn phone?*

I glanced out the window at the snow.

"We better go or we'll be stuck here all night," he said.

I felt a buzzing beneath my skin. We gathered our things and walked down the winding staircase toward the main floor. Girls stared at him as we walked by, as they always did, though he didn't notice, or ignored it. "How long does it take you to get home?" he asked.

"Over an hour usually. Today will be longer, if the trains are running."

"Let me give you a ride. I've got my mom's van. It's parked around the corner."

My mom told me once that if a guy ever asked me into his van, he was probably a serial killer, and I should only say yes if I wanted parts of me scattered across the tristate area.

"Sure," I said, and got in.

Mad love

Will's van wasn't a typical choice for serial killers: a giant chocolate cupcake rotated on its roof, and the words "Sugarland Bakery" curled down its side.

As we drove, we passed broken-down cars and kids throwing snowballs; traffic crawled along. A woman pointed at our roof and squealed, "Cupcakes!" A kid shouted, "Yummy yummy yeah yeah *yeah!*"

Will sighed. "The guys on the team refuse to ride with me in this thing."

"I like it. Every car should have a cupcake on its roof."

He turned the heat on high, and I took off my coat but kept Will's scarf on. Everything felt different, being alone with him in the van, in the seat beside him where a girlfriend would sit. *I missed seeing you.* We talked about Mrs. Peech and whether her bad breath had improved (it hadn't), and Edna St. Vincent Millay—how she'd traveled around the country and read poems to packed theaters and giant crowds, like a rock star—and we talked about our fathers.

He told me how over Christmas his dad sent him lots of

gifts—a watch, a wallet, a tie he'd never wear, and a check for $600 to buy a new phone. His mother couldn't watch him unwrap them without muttering "Jerkface" and "guilt money."

"What kind of phone did you get?"

"I never got it. I gave the check to my mom." He said his mom's bakery was in trouble—they were losing money and she had to lay off most of the staff. He'd spent the whole break working there, in between meeting with the swim team to practice. "We're behind on rent, and our landlord's really nice, so we'll see what happens." His tone had a harsher, darker edge. "I'm actually glad school started."

"Me too."

He paused. "Christmas must be hard without your dad."

"We're Jewish, so we never celebrated it, but—you know. It's like the world is made for families with two parents and lots of kids. Not for measly families of two," I said.

He nodded. "I know."

I felt a surge of sympathy for him about his mother's bakery, and his father who'd abandoned him for all those years, and his baby brother, and at the same time I reveled in these things, that we both had this in common—tragedies. Did he talk to Gia about his lost brother and his dad? Did he only talk to me about it? There was no way he could talk to Gia like this. What tragedies had she survived? A snag in a cashmere sweater. A slight redness after a mustache wax.

"Holidays kind of suck," he said.

"I used to like them. I remember the winter before my dad died, we used to go to this coffee shop he liked in the West Village—it isn't there anymore—where they had crepes and huge cups of hot chocolate. We'd sit there by their fireplace for hours and write in notebooks."

"You stopped writing because it was something you only did with him?"

I shrugged. "I guess." That wasn't entirely true, since I used to write on my own also, at night before I went to sleep. Now, instead of writing before bed, I read romances. It was a painless way to escape.

"So are you going to send a poem in to that contest?" he asked.

"No."

"Are you afraid?"

"I'm not afraid." My voice sounded more defensive than I meant it to. Why was he bugging me about this?

"I just don't think talent should go to waste," he said. "Maybe you just need company. Sometime we can go find a café and write."

"We should." Did he mean it? Would we do that?

He peered over the windshield. "Sorry this is taking so long. Takes them forever to plow."

"It doesn't matter." I felt so happy, inching toward the Triborough Bridge, happier than I'd felt in ages. The sun began to set, sitting on the horizon like a butterscotch candy. Orange light bounced off the windshield, and everything became quieter as the snow sugared the streets and parked cars. I loved the city in snow, the hush and slowness. And I liked looking at him as he peered over the steering wheel. I saw things I'd never noticed about him before: the tiny red birthmark on his neck, and the crumbs and little moth holes in his black coat. I listened to the van's motor humming and the voices on the radio, which he kept turned down too low to really hear. The faint voices rose and fell in waves, and I wanted to freeze that time in the van with him, to keep it forever.

The happiness stayed with me the whole drive, and when we finally reached my apartment building, he exhaled.

"We made it," he said.

I asked if he wanted to get something to eat, but he said he should get back, it would be a long drive back to his apartment on 114th Street. I thanked him. I still couldn't believe he'd driven so far out of his way. I started to take the scarf off.

"Keep it," he said. "Stay warm."

He drove off.

As soon as the lobby door closed behind me, I called Annie.

"*He drove me home.*" My voice dropped about ten octaves. I sounded like a dying werewolf. I had to repeat myself twice before she understood.

"Wow. He's a really nice guy," she said.

"He said he missed me over break. Does he like me? Do you think he likes me?"

"Of course he likes you. You're *friends*. He has a girlfriend in case you've forgotten."

I reminded her that Gia was in a European wilderness preserve and hopefully had been eaten by bears. "Why did he drive me home if he doesn't *like* me?"

"Because he wanted to show you his liquid velvet eyes and his manroot."

"Ha ha ha. Funny."

"Because he can't stand the thought of you waiting, cold and alone, on a subway platform. He's a genuinely good guy."

"But he said 'I missed seeing you.'"

"He could've meant it as a friend." She paused. "I don't want you to get your hopes up."

"I'm not getting my hopes up." *Friends.* Friends was good. Friends was great.

Except we weren't exactly *friends*, not like any friends I'd ever had. It didn't feel like friends when he stared at me, or the way he said my name sometimes, *Eva-a*, a little too slowly, a little sarcastically. Or that electric feeling between us, like we were always balancing on a high wire.

Maybe I was imagining the whole thing. Maybe it was just limbic resonance. During the school day he was with the swim team crowd and the seniors, a distance so far it could've been another country. Maybe we were a different type of friends: Friendish. Friendesque. Someone needed to invent a word for it.

The next Friday morning I felt hyperawake, the afternoon lying ahead like an unopened present.

Then came lunchtime.

"What are you staring at?" Annie asked me, and followed my gaze. "Uh-oh," she said. "Gia's back."

I felt this crumpling inside. At tutoring, Will explained that Gia's parents changed their minds. They didn't want her missing so much school. (A rumor I'd heard that afternoon told a different story: she'd been fired from her modeling job for getting drunk. I didn't ask him about that.) When she picked him up that afternoon, her legs seemed to have grown even longer, her hair thicker and shinier. Her eyebrows looked like skinny black licorice.

I blinked back tears the whole subway ride home, wishing I was in the van with him. I felt this huge ball of shame in my stomach, too, at this crush that never seemed to go away. At all this doomed yearning and useless hope. What a waste. "Pour all that energy into school," Annie said when I called her that night. "That will help you forget about him a little."

It didn't help. I had a stomach bug day the next Friday, and the Friday after that. I knew I had to stuff the crush away again, to stop it from growing and flowering. I thought about quitting tutoring, but Annie said that was a mistake—I needed a good recommendation from Mrs. Peech for college. Anyway, quitting tutoring probably wouldn't make a difference—whether I tutored him or not, the crush still simmered beneath everything, like a fluish misery.

"Just wait till summer," Annie said. She'd heard a rumor that Gia was going to Greenland over the summer. "It'll be different then," she said. Lulu agreed with the wait-till-summer plan. "See what happens," she said. "Let the feelings be there, without judging them. Everything is always changing. This will change, too."

Will started his final term paper, and the warm weather arrived early—the school yard sprang alive with Frisbees and thumping basketballs and backpacks on the ground like colorful sleeping cats. One afternoon, he came to the north tower holding a letter. He'd gotten accepted to UC–Santa Cruz, his first choice, with a scholarship.

Will took off his cowboy hat. As the moon rose into a perfect crescent in the indigo sky, he told her, "I know everybody supposes I'll head off to Santa Cruz, but I ain't goin'. I'm stayin' here with you, Miss Eva. Now get over here and lie down with me by the creek on this bed of moss."

Our friendish friendship continued but the crush never disappeared. It just lay buried, like an underground spring.

Little things he said in passing encouraged it.

We should hang out at the Strand over the summer.

I'm supposed to write an essay for college freshman English in August. You'll have to help me. No one else will tell me the truth about how much I suck.

We exchanged phone numbers, though he never used mine. (I'd texted him once when he missed tutoring:

`Hope you're ok—are you coming today?`

but he never wrote back.) He didn't find small things important: returning texts, charging his phone, being on time, punctuation.

I brought him a brochure of summer classes that the Poetry Society was offering for free to high school students— I planned to take a three-week one starting in late June. He signed up also.

The end of school wasn't the end but the beginning. Gia would be gone and things would start over. Start new. Annie still said that after Gia left for the summer, I should tell him the truth about how I felt about him, but I knew I could never go through with it. Loving someone seemed like offering your soul on a plate—*Here you go! You can have me!*—and they could so easily say, *No, none for me. No thanks.* If my dad hadn't died, if my insides weren't filled with quivering Jell-O, maybe I could handle the rejection. But his death had scrubbed off a layer of my skin. It made me feel scared that at any moment the world might throw something else at me that I couldn't take.

I loved romances because when you opened the first page, you knew the story would end well. Your heart wouldn't be broken. I loved that security, that guaranteed love. Sure, a minor, usually unlikable character might drop dead from typhus or consumption or starve to death in the brig, but bad things were only temporary in those books. By the end, the hero and heroine would be ecstatically in love, enormously happy.

In real life, you never knew the ending. I hated that.

I knew if I told Will how I felt about him and he said *no thanks* I'd have a stomach bug day that I'd never get out of. It would become a whole stomach bug life.

I measure every grief

'd taken Will's advice: I wrote a poem, the first poem I'd written since my dad died, and submitted it to the contest.

(It wasn't exactly "writing"—I'd scrawled it really fast on the back of a Fresh Direct receipt while I stood at the kitchen counter at midnight. It was the night after Will asked, "Are you afraid?" *I'm not afraid*, I told myself. Then I ate an entire package of Chips Ahoy.) I hadn't written anything else since.

It didn't win the contest, but in June I found out that it received an honorable mention.

"They're printing it in a book and giving me a certificate," I told my mom. "At this festival held at our school. It's called Urbanwords. It's next Friday."

We were sitting at the kitchen table on a Saturday morning, eating breakfast. We lived in an old brick building with peeling green paint and cracked mirrors in the lobby, and hallways that smelled like overcooked cabbage and Mr. Clean. Out the kitchen window, the pink neon sign of Mega Donuts blinked on and off, though the "n" was broken. Mega Douts. *Mega doubts*, I always thought.

I had *Cowboys on Fire* (book 8: *Cousin Bryce*) propped in front of my fried eggs and potatoes. The *New York Times* lay in front of my mom's spinach omelet.

My dad used to be the cook in our family—pastas, roast chicken, and eggs were his specialties, and I was his assistant. Now I was the cook. My mom had never asked me to (for a long time, we'd order takeout when she came home from work, and scarfed down cold cereal for breakfast every morning), but I liked cooking. I liked going to the store and stuffing the fridge and cupboards full of fresh bread and cheese, eggs, ripe peaches, berries, cantaloupe, and other delicious things to eat, and standing over the stove with the recipes my dad had torn out of magazines. I even liked placing the Fresh Direct order, ordering bagels and whitefish salad.

"The ceremony starts at five o'clock," I said.

She looked up from her newspaper and pressed her lips together. "I have a conference at Brooklyn College that day. I'm giving a keynote at five and I have events till late at night."

I shrugged. "It's not a big deal." But I felt this emptiness just the same.

She seemed angry—not at me—but she stared out the window at some uncertain point in the distance and seemed almost teary for a second. "Sometimes I get so frustrated that I can't be in two places at once," she said. "Can you bring back extra copies of the book for me?"

"I'll get extra copies if you promise to read it."

"Of course I'll read it."

I didn't believe her. She'd glance at the poem, her face as blank as when she read her students' papers.

She put her hand over mine. "I'm sorry I can't be there." She paused. "I hope the ceremony won't go too late. I don't want you taking the subway from the Bronx after eight."

"I'll be fine. It won't go late."

Ever since my dad died, my mom had been worried that something bad would happen to me. A year ago she signed me up for a Self-Defense for Women class where each week I repeated the phrase "I want I need I deserve" and practiced sticking my fingers into a dummy's jugular notch. She worried about muggings, crazy people on the street, kidnappers, and every crime that she read about in the paper.

Even now, the thought of me riding the subway at night set something off in her, and she passed her newspaper to me. "Read this." She pointed to an article about pedestrian deaths. Kids who had been killed while crossing Manhattan streets.

"These people crossed with the light but the drivers turning didn't see them. When you cross, you have to make eye contact with the drivers. Make sure they see you," she said.

I rolled my eyes. "I'm always careful." I stood up and put my dishes in the sink. I glanced at the clock. "I'm meeting Annie to go study. I promise I'll make eye contact with drivers when I cross the street."

"I'm not joking," my mom said.

"You be careful too, then," I said. "You're spacier than me." My mom was always doing her work on the subway and missing her stop.

"I will," she said.

As I walked to Athens Diner to meet Annie, I thought about how my dad used to say that when he looked at me, he felt like he'd re-created himself in girl form. "You're both gooey lovecrumbs," my mom had agreed. Now I wished she was a little bit of a gooey lovecrumb. A smidge of a lovecrumb. She used to be, before he died. When I was younger, we'd go to the park, and from the swings I'd watch my parents kiss. On weekend mornings, I climbed into bed between them, and the three of us read books together. We stopped doing that after he died.

It was like my dad was the glue between my mom and me, and the glue had been washed off.

Annie waited in a booth. We ordered hot chocolates with extra marshmallows and I told her about the poem.

She squealed and hugged me. "Did you tell Will?"

"Not yet. He hasn't been in school the last couple of days, and there's no point in texting him—his phone doesn't work half the time." I'd never even told Annie or Will that I'd written it and submitted it—I wanted to spare myself the humiliation if it didn't get picked.

She propped her head on her chin. "I heard a rumor this morning about why he was absent. Jill in my lab group is in

AP English with him, and she told me he was out because his dog died. The Undead was not sympathetic."

"Silas?" I pictured the three-legged, sixteen-year-old dog that he'd had since he was two. I couldn't believe Silas was dead. I thought of everything he'd told me—how Silas slept at the foot of his bed every night, and how even when Silas lost his leg—he was hit by a car—he just went on so happily as if nothing was ever wrong. He was able to walk and run again, though a little strangely, and he slept with his head in Will's lap while Will studied. Will had told me that without Silas maybe he'd never have gotten over his dad's leaving them, his brother's death, everything.

I stared into my mug. "I should go see him. Today. I should stop by the bakery. He told me he works there on Saturdays."

"Really? To say you're sorry about his dog?"

I nodded. "It's what you're supposed to do. Like a shiva call." We'd never sat shiva for my dad—we'd barely survived the funeral, and my mom decided sitting shiva would be too much. We never even went to synagogue anymore. My mom didn't want to see our rabbi and be reminded of my dad's death and funeral every time we went.

"People sit shiva for dogs?" she asked.

"I don't know. They should. If it had been my dog, I'd want him to come."

She looked skeptical. "Are you sure it's a good idea? What about Gia?"

"She leaves in three weeks. She'll be doing her photo shoot in Greenland." In my mind, I watched Gia drift away on an ice floe with a crowd of hungry walruses. "Anyway, I'm not going to *do* anything with him. I just want to tell him I'm sorry."

We studied a little while more, but all I could think about was going to the bakery. I'd visited the bakery's website dozens of times but never had the guts to go in person before. Finally, I gave up studying and told Annie I was going to head over there.

"Maybe he'll give you some free cupcakes. You can pretend you like them," she said.

I'd never liked frosting—I loved cookies and chocolate, but cake and cupcakes with their thick layers of too-sweet buttery goo weren't my thing. Still. "I know I'll like his cupcakes," I said.

"And his man frosting," she said.

I hesitated. "I don't even know what that is."

"Me neither."

"Well. I'll tell him that you asked about his man frosting."

"He'll love that. Thank god you have me here to give you romantic advice," she said.

I packed up my backpack and stopped at home—my mom was grading papers, and barely noticed I was there—and grabbed a copy of an Edward Gorey book called *Amphigorey* that had once belonged to my dad. Not cartoons exactly, but dark and funny and perfect. I said good-bye to my mom and told her Annie and I were headed to the library—but she just nodded and went back to work.

The whole subway ride I could barely focus on anything but seeing him. I couldn't read. I kept staring out the window of the 7 train and the 1 train, into the dark tunnels, and dreaming.

I got off at the 96th Street station. I walked a few blocks. I froze for a second when I saw it on the corner.

Sugarland. Its polka-dot awning fluttered in the breeze. A little blue bench sat in front. Inside, its turquoise-and-chocolate-brown walls were decorated with framed black-and-white posters of old New York. I was the only customer. A chime rang when I stepped on the front mat.

Will poked his head out from the back.

"It's you," he said, and smiled. He was hauling a sack of flour. "Just one sec." He stacked it in the back room and dusted himself off.

Will's muscles glimmered with a light coat of man frosting as he placed a forty-pound bag of flour in the corner.

He looked sincerely happy to see me.

"I heard about Silas," I said. "I'm so sorry. And I'm sorry for saying sorry." I reached into my backpack. "I brought you this."

I showed him *Amphigorey*, and I told him my dad had gotten it for me during one of our trips to Gotham Book Mart before it closed.

He opened the cover and read the beginning. "Can I keep it for a few days? I'll give it back to you in school this week."

"Of course."

He pointed toward the tiny marble tables. "Have a seat," he said. "I know it's hard to find one, what with the swarms of customers."

I sat down. He grabbed a plate from behind the counter. I gazed around, taking in the surroundings, trying to imprint them on my memory. It was decorated so elegantly—an antique crystal chandelier hung from the pressed-tin ceiling, and the glass case holding the cupcakes was trimmed with aged, polished wood with brass hardware. Stacks of turquoise gift boxes sat on the counter, tied with brown ribbon.

"Which would you like to try?" he asked. "Chocolate? Red Velvet?"

"I can't decide."

"Here." He put four cupcakes on a china plate, grabbed two blue napkins, and sat at the table with me.

I took a bite of the chocolate. I even liked the frosting. I let it melt on my tongue and bit into the cake—dark, rich, delicious. "I love it," I said.

"Judging from the crowds, you're the only person in the city who feels that way." He didn't take a bite himself.

"Don't you want one?"

"After working here, I never want to eat another cupcake in my life."

I glanced at the chandelier and the photos on the walls. "It's so pretty here, though. Maybe it just hasn't been discovered yet."

"The problem is my mom opened this place at the same time as a thousand other cupcake bakeries were opening. It's kind of a brutal business." He ruffled the corner of the Edward Gorey book and shrugged. "Thanks for coming, though." He said each word slowly, then lowered his voice. "It means a lot."

"Of course. I mean—well. Was the end—with Silas—okay? Did you get to say good-bye?"

He made a sort of laugh. "Yeah. I appreciate your asking. The vet was great—he died in my arms. It was okay. Peaceful." He paused. "No one else wants to hear you talk about your dead dog. Even my mom. I missed two days of school over it. I told my mom I was sick. I don't think she even got it, why I stayed home. For a dog."

"I've done that. I mean—feeling sick over grief. Missing school." I'd never said it so plainly before. Sick with grief. "In my head I call it a griefy feeling."

"That's exactly what it is. A griefy feeling."

I told him about my cat, Lucky, who died when I was ten. She was a stray; my mom was allergic so I couldn't officially adopt her, but I fed her every day and snuck her into my room whenever I could, and she slept in a little plastic house on our fire escape every night. "A few weeks after my tenth birthday, I saw blood in the corner of Lucky's eye," I said. I told him how my dad and I took her to the vet and they diagnosed her with squamous cell carcinoma. The tumor had started in her mouth and spread toward her brain, creating pressure that made her bleed. I snuck Lucky into my room each night, and we paid the vet hundreds of dollars to do surgery—we never told my mom what it cost. Lucky never woke up from the surgery.

"That's awful," he said.

"I cried on and off for two months. My mom said that was too long to mourn a cat. 'Try not to be so thin-skinned,' she said." It was a phrase she repeated when Joey Braga started calling me "Jewfro" in fourth grade, after a bad haircut, and more recently when I cried at the end of *Roman Holiday* and *An Affair to Remember*.

"I spent more time with that dog than I did with my dad. Than I have with either of my parents," he said. He looked down at the cupcakes on the table. "Gia hated Silas. He drooled on her. When I told her he died, she seemed relieved."

"That's terrible."

"We broke up," he said.

"Oh."

"It wasn't just the dog."

I tried to process what he'd said, but it was almost too much to absorb. I wanted to text Annie and tell her.

We were quiet for a minute, and then I said, "I took your advice. I wrote a—thing—and I sent it to that poetry contest."

I told him about the honorable mention. "It didn't win but, you know. Thanks."

He smiled, seeming the happiest I'd seen him yet today. "I knew you had it in you." He folded his arms and leaned back in his chair. "I'm coming to the ceremony. So it better not suck."

"Oh, it sucks. It totally and completely sucks."

I felt warm all over, a hundred different kinds of warm.

He stood and put my plate back behind the counter. "Come in the back a sec—I have a couple of books to return to you."

The back of the shop was brightly lit with long stainless steel tables, concrete floors, a giant sink, stand mixers, ovens, and stacks of metal trays. In the far corner were two large, messy wooden desks. One had to be his mother's—covered with files, a vase of dried flowers, a desktop computer, account ledgers. Two framed photos hung on the wall above it. One was Will at about ten years old—he looked like a tiny version of the way he looked now. The other was a baby, swaddled in a blue blanket in his mother's arms.

"Your brother?" I asked.

He nodded.

I touched the frame. He was so tiny—pink-faced—and all you could see of Will's mom was the back of her head leaning toward him, kissing the top of his head. I sent out a silent hello to his mom and the baby, and I thought of his telescope, staring down through the universe.

Will riffled through the stacks of mail and school papers on his desk. "Here they are." He pulled out a Millay book and one of e. e. cummings's collections that I'd lent him. "I didn't mess them up. I promise."

I walked over to his desk. It held his typewriter.

"This is where I write all those goddamned essays," he said.

A blank page was rolled inside the typewriter. I typed Hello!, getting a feel for the keys. "It's nice," I said. I typed: I am griefy.

Beside the typewriter, on top of the stack of mail, was a wedding invitation. Will picked it up. "Mrs. Jerkface's wedding," he said. "I'm just going out there for two nights. My mom wants me to bring moldy cupcakes as a wedding gift."

I noticed something else next to his typewriter—a little white tin box decorated with black paw prints.

I picked it up. "What's—?"

"Silas," he said.

"Oh."

"I had him cremated."

"I'm sorry."

"He was sixteen. That's like a hundred and ten in people years."

"Still."

"It cost four hundred and fifty dollars for the ashes. I paid for the rush service. This place is probably going under and I paid four hundred and fifty dollars for the ashes of my dead dog. Well, I asked my dad to pay for it, actually."

"It's worth it."

He sighed. "I can't exactly explain why it's next to my type-writer. Inspiration?"

"Very inspiring. I mean, who wouldn't be inspired?"

"I'm glad you finally got to meet him."

"Me too. I think it's nice having him near your typewriter. Kind of like a muse."

"I can sprinkle him on the keys for good luck," he said.

I put down the tin of ashes and he placed his hand over mine. I couldn't speak. He laced our fingers together. He pulled me to him until our waists were touching. My throat dried up. Everything in the room gleamed bright.

The phone rang. Loud, shrill. He rolled his eyes. "I better get that. Hold on."

I almost had a heart attack. What had happened? What had almost happened?

"My mom," he said when he'd hung up. "I have to go meet her in a half hour—we're checking out a new apartment to see if we can afford it. We can't pay the rent on the one we're in anymore."

"Oh no, that sucks," I said.

"We'll figure it out." He shrugged. "She told me to lock up the bakery for a couple of hours. Not that anyone will care if it's closed. We've had about four customers all day." He picked up my hand again naturally, as if it was no big deal at all. He kept holding it. "I'm glad you stopped by. I'll walk you to the subway. It's on the way to where I'm meeting her."

He picked up the books he'd borrowed from me, and we went to the front of the shop and I put them in my bag. He slung my bag across his shoulder and we walked up the street, still holding hands. On the way to the subway we stopped at a Rite Aid—he'd promised his mom he'd pick up one of her asthma prescriptions. I never enjoyed being in a Rite Aid so much. I loved this Rite Aid. I loved the bright lighting and shiny rows of gum and shampoos, and how the entire store pulsed with life, and even the shaving cream and soaps seemed happy.

We left the Rite Aid, still holding hands. His fingers were softer than I'd imagined, his grip gentle. I was floating. The sidewalk sparkled in the sun.

And then, just before we reached the station, he stopped walking.

He swooped down and kissed me. I was in his arms, suddenly, without warning, leaning back, I couldn't believe it was happening, I melted into the sidewalk and became two people at once. The person who was kissing him and the person who could barely think and absorb and believe that I was kissing him. Time stopped. The world stopped. There was only the kiss.

It seemed as natural as breathing—the kiss, good-bye, thanks for the book, thanks for stopping by, and I was off into the subway, sailing through Manhattan and back toward Queens.

The whole subway ride home, I couldn't read, I couldn't do anything except replay the kiss, the whole afternoon, in my head again and again and again—I could have replayed it forever.

When I got off the 7 train, I called Annie.

"We *kissed*." I repeated it three times. I told her about the bakery, the typewriter, the ashes.

"Only you would have a romantic moment over the ashes of a dead dog," she said. She didn't sound sarcastic—she sounded impressed.

"It was perfect," I said.

At his touch, the scabs would fall away

In romance novels, nobody ever asks, "Hey, what's going on here exactly? Why did you kiss me? What kind of relationship do you have in mind? Are we going to be together or what?" Instead, there are three hundred pages of cholera, explosions, amnesia, stabbings, natural disasters, and misunderstandings keeping the couple apart.

I can handle cholera, I thought. I can handle typhus, tornadoes, and packs of wild homicidal javelinas if it means getting to kiss him again.

It felt like he was still kissing me as I ate fried eggs for breakfast, washed the plates, and waited for the 7 train. He was still kissing me while I studied, grocery shopped, and as I fell asleep.

He texted me on Monday:

```
Apt hunting w my mom—out of school today &
maybe this week—see you Friday at festival tho
```

His first text to me. I wanted to bronze that text. I wanted to say back: *I love you come here now kiss me again please I can't wait till Friday.* But I wrote instead:

```
Ok—see you Friday!
```

"What do you think?" I asked Annie for the third time before I sent it. We were riding the subway to school. "I want to sound confident and not needy, you know? I mean instead I could say—"

"Send it or I'm going to kill you," she said.

He didn't write back, and he didn't return to school. On Friday I didn't see him in the hallways, or in the cafeteria at lunch, or anywhere. At tutoring that afternoon—the last tutoring session of the year—I waited for him to show up. Annie wasn't at tutoring that day either—she had her own awards ceremony that afternoon at Hunter College, for the winners of the Schilling Science Prize. Her parents, her grandfather, and her sisters were going.

Mrs. Peech had brought juice and popcorn to celebrate the last session. I crammed handful after handful of popcorn into my mouth and watched the door, waiting for him to arrive. I pretended to listen to the other tutors talking about summer jobs and classes and TV shows, but all I could think about was Will. I glanced at the clock. Thirty minutes till the festival started.

Twenty minutes.

Ten.

My stomach dropped.

He couldn't miss this. It wasn't possible. I couldn't go to Urbanwords alone.

There was a reason, there had to be a reason why he wasn't here. Cholera. A car had struck him like in *An Affair to Remember*.

It was four thirty. "Let's clean up and head to the festival!" Mrs. Peech chirped.

I helped pack up the leftover juice and wipe down the tables and then picked up my backpack and followed everyone else out the door.

The Urbanwords festival had been set up in the lobby of our school—I wandered past tables representing literary magazines and poetry organizations from around the city. I kept watching the front doors, waiting for him to come, and when the ceremony started, I sat in the auditorium in a back row, alone.

The room was packed with kids and families, everyone hugging and picking lint off each other's clothes. All I had to do was walk across the stage and pick up the award. I stood behind the other kids, got the award, and followed along, but my knees felt wobbly. I returned to my empty row.

I could sneak out and leave, but where would I go? Home alone? I fingered the certificate in my lap. I touched its raised letters. "Honorable Mention." Whoopee. Maybe if it hadn't been a "mention" but a real prize, my mom and Will would've come. There had to be a reason why he wasn't here. There had to be. I clung to the belief that something had happened. A subway delay. Or something simpler: he'd gotten the time wrong. I checked my phone to see if he'd texted me.

Nothing yet.

I felt paralyzed. Glued in place. I checked emails and voice mails—nothing—and then went to the message board. I hadn't been on the message board for a week, not since the kiss. I hadn't needed or wanted to. I hadn't even thought about it.

Normally there was a slow trickle of new messages, just a few new ones a day. Now there were 114 new ones.

Fran Gamuto had started a new thread. I clicked on it. She'd posted a link to a newspaper article. From this morning.

Freedom Airlines Flight 472 Wreckage Is Found
By HUMPHREY COLES

Investigators announced that they have located the wreckage of Freedom Airlines Flight 472, which crashed in the North Atlantic two years ago, renewing hopes that the flight data recorder and cockpit voice recorder can still be located and may explain what caused the plane to crash.

A team from the Woods Hole Oceanographic Institution led the search. Three REMUS 6000 autonomous underwater vehicles helped investigators locate the

71

wreckage nearly one and a half miles below the surface.

"It's a happy discovery," Frank Longbrown, the chair of the National Transportation Safety Board, said at a press conference. He noted that it could take weeks before specialized recovery vehicles can reach the site and begin bringing the wreckage to the surface.

The flight crashed in a thunderstorm while traveling from New York to Paris. All 228 passengers and crew members were killed.

My chest tightened. I felt dizzy and began to sweat.

I had known they were starting the search again, but I figured it would be just like the other searches—*like a needle in a haystack*, someone had written on the message board. *We shouldn't get our hopes up*, other people had said.

Try to breathe.

Was I dying? I wasn't dying. I'd felt this before. A panic attack. I'd felt exactly like this two years ago, when I had my first panic attack, before they identified his remains, when I was sure he was still alive. I was supposed to give an oral presentation about dolphins for school that day. Long-beaked, short-beaked, white-beaked, bottlenose, Indo-Pacific hump-backed. I'd researched almost every dolphin in existence. All the parents stood in the back of the room—my mom couldn't make it, of course, since she taught a class at the same time—and I kept watching the door. I knew he was going to come.

He'd never missed a presentation, school play, or anything. I went last—I'd asked the teacher if I could go last—I got up to speak and my dad still wasn't there, and everyone stared at me with this weird look. My chest froze; it felt like it was slowly filling up with cement. I woke up in the nurse's office.

I kept reading the message board.

> Even if they find the data and voice recorders, the data might not be intact. As much as I want to finally put an end to the questions and misery and uncertainty, we have to accept that we still might not get any answers.
>
> Tim (wife Beth, 3B)

> I don't want to know what the recorders say. I'm at peace now and I don't want to know any more about it. I wish things had been left alone and this had not happened. I'm not sure why it was important to everyone to lobby for the search to continue all this time.
>
> Jill (Jacques Bluelake, 14A)

I couldn't absorb it. I couldn't move or think or do anything but read message after message.

I didn't even notice when someone sat down beside me until I felt a squeeze on my shoulder.

"Hey—I'm sorry I'm late, I've been—" He saw my face. "What happened?"

I couldn't speak. I didn't cry—I was too stunned—I felt numb.

"What happened?" he asked again. When I didn't answer, he said, "Let's get out of here." He took my hand and picked up my bag, and we walked out of the auditorium.

He led me toward an empty, quiet stairwell. We sat down. I was shaking.

"Are you okay?" He held my hand. "Should I call someone? Or—"

"It wasn't a heart attack." I spoke quickly, and somehow, saying it aloud, telling him I lied, cracked the numbness and made the tears slide out for the first time.

I took out my phone and showed him the article.

He read it and held me for a long time, until I caught my breath and calmed down, and then I told him everything. I told him how there had been different theories—from the small amount of wreckage they'd recovered two years ago, at first some people thought the plane had broken up in midair. Then they decided it had hit the water intact. My eyes focused on a piece of old gum that had turned into a black spot on the stairs. "I always thought—I decided—that he didn't know it was coming. That he was sleeping and they fell into the ocean, and he was never scared or terrified or felt anything. That's what I've always thought. Hoped. That he didn't suffer."

"I don't think he was scared," Will said. "I know he wasn't scared. He didn't suffer."

I loved that he said that. I loved that he wanted that to be true, that he knew how incredibly important it was for that to be true. Something relaxed inside me, like an unwinding coil.

He looked at me like I was the only thing he saw, not the stairs or the window or the trees swaying outside. He understood, without judgment or surprise. It was like our surfaces were peeled off and it was just our cores. He didn't ask for details; he didn't show the eager hunger. He just listened.

"What bothers me most of all is that I don't know what he felt in those last minutes. What happened to his body. Sometimes it upsets me more than even the fact that he's dead—that I don't know if he passed out and died peacefully, or if he felt pain . . . or if he was sort of asleep . . ." I had to stop and speak more slowly and keep my voice level. "It matters for some reason. I don't know why. But it matters."

"Of course it matters."

Once I started telling him things, I couldn't stop. "My mom got rid of all his stuff after he died, but one of his ties was hidden in a ball in the corner of their closet. She made this horrible groan when she found it months later, like she was so mad that he still had stuff in our house. She threw the tie in the garbage."

He stared at me, listening.

"After she went to bed, I fished it out of the trash. I had to wash coffee grounds off it and egg and tomato sauce and it took me forever, it was silk, so I bought this special silk cleaner and spent three days getting the stains out. It actually looks pretty good now. I keep it in my shoe box. I only have a few things of his, and I hide them in my closet in a shoe box."

I'd never told anyone, besides Annie, about the shoe box. It had seemed too weird, keeping his receipt and candy wrappers and stuff hidden in my own closet. But Will was looking at me, not judging or anything, just staring at me patiently— it was okay to tell him; he was nodding like he understood exactly why I spent three days washing that tie.

"I wish I could've met him," Will said.

"I can show you some candy wrappers. It sort of brings him back."

I took a tissue out of my bag and wiped my nose. We were quiet for a while, sitting on the stairs.

Will said, "I almost killed myself—not on purpose—when I was a kid. We lived on the second floor of a brownstone, and one night I sat on the fire escape and I just jumped. I was eight. I guess I thought if I hurt myself really bad, it would make him come back."

I asked if that was where the scar on his chin was from. He nodded.

"I also kind of thought that if my brother was dead, maybe I should be dead too. Or that maybe I could bring him back. I barely even remember my brother, but I still think about him all the time." He paused. "I guess you never stop missing them."

You never stop missing them. It was a simple thing to say. But I'd never heard anyone say it before. Not the grief counselors. Not my mom. Everyone seemed to think the opposite: you moved on, you forgot, it was impolite to keep talking about it. My mom had stopped missing my dad years ago.

We stayed on the stairs for a long time. I sat quietly in his arms until he said, "I want to show you something." He picked up my bag again. He started up the staircase. It led to the south tower, the closed-off part of the school.

"Where are we going?"

"You'll see."

We kept climbing the winding steps, higher and higher. At the third floor he stopped by a black door. "My coach came up here to propose to his fiancée two days ago. I snuck the champagne up here for him. He forgot to ask for the key back."

He opened the door.

The walled garden looked like a surreal kingdom: birds fluttering, a blanket of weeds and tall grass and spindly dark trees sprouting from clouds of ferns and wildflowers. How was it possible that this place existed? A stone path wound through the terrace. Beyond the wall, the sun was setting, and the buildings around the park glowed like a bracelet of lights.

"Listen," he said.

The wind whispered through the trees. We were in another world.

I saw the giant stone table from the photo book. Will went over to it and brushed off the dirt, dead leaves, and branches, clearing a spot for us to sit. Its surface was cracked, with grass growing in the crevices.

The sun dipped behind the buildings in the distance. He picked up a leaf and tore the stem off. He reached into his bag. "Here—I got these for you." He handed me five copies of the Urbanwords book. "They had them stacked on a table outside the auditorium. I read your poem."

This was my poem:

Fathers

My father died two years ago.
My mother met her new friend Larry
at a Children of Holocaust Survivors
social in the back room of Meredith's Restaurant
in Bayside, Queens. Apparently it's a regular
meat market at these things. They laughed
and drank and flirted over cocktail knishes
and cheap wine and shared familial genocide.

No one actually discussed the shared familial genocide.
It was just there, I guess, like the wine
and the desperation. My mother never talks about her family's
history. Her mother escaped Poland during the Holocaust.

But she never spoke of it either.
Not once. I called my grandmother
Bubbe 409 because she had a bottle of Formula 409
permanently attached to her hand.
She died when I was eight.
My mom's dad died when she was a teenager.
Larry's father survived Dachau.
My dad's parents survived the war in London. They died
*   before I was born.*
My father's grave is in Westchester but we never go see him
*   there.*

A bad poem. It wasn't even a poem really, just a bunch of sad and depressing lines chopped up into verses. I wondered why I'd even wanted my mom to come today. She'd probably keel over when she read it. I'd published private details about my dad and generations of our family. She'd murder me. What had I been thinking? Well, I knew what I'd been thinking: if she read the poem, maybe she'd be forced to talk about him again.

"I know it sucks," I said. "I wrote it on the back of a Fresh Direct receipt."

"It sucks beautifully," he said.

The air felt chilly now. He took a fleece pullover out of his backpack and offered it to me. I pulled the soft navy sleeves over my arms.

We were quiet. I kept thinking: as long as I'm with him, everything will be okay. I remembered catching my parents kissing on the bench in the park, how happy they were back then, a happiness I'd always wanted and that I finally felt now, for the first time.

The trees swayed. There was a gentle sound, a bird, maybe an owl. We were in an owl-filled castle, a mansion that had been used for waltzes and parties a hundred years ago. Up there on that roof, it suddenly seemed that anything was possible. The world was literally at our feet. The sky turned the strange orangey-gray color it often was on city nights. I used to hate that color and wish for a deep velvet or indigo sky, a romance-novel sky. Now I loved this sky.

He sat on top of the stone table and looked toward the park. He knit his hands together in a way I'd never seen him do before—his fingers touching each other, then moving apart.

"What is it?" I asked.

"We didn't find a new apartment," he said.

"Oh no. How long will you keep looking?"

He shook his head. "We're not looking anymore."

"What do you mean?"

He gazed at me again, that intense stare. "We're getting evicted from our old one. I didn't think our landlord would actually go through with it, but he is. We've looked for a new place nonstop, but there's nothing we can afford. My mom finally decided to move in with her best friend, into her one-bedroom apartment. She doesn't have another choice. She wants me to move in with them too. I can't. It's crazy. That's why I was out of school this week. We're trying to figure all this out."

He rubbed his forehead. "My mom's declared bankruptcy on the bakery. We're getting evicted from there, too. I'm not moving into her friend's place." He shook his head.

"Then where will you go?"

"Only place I can go. My dad's."

I froze. "What?"

"I'm moving in with him," he said quietly.

"I thought he lives in California?"

He nodded and stared out toward the park. "I'm taking a red-eye tomorrow night. I'm sorry. I didn't know how to tell you." His voice was soft.

He told me his father's wedding was this Sunday—the wedding I'd seen the invitation for, but I hadn't looked at the date. Mrs. Jerkface. He was supposed to go for two nights and come right back, but now he was going to stay and live with his dad until his freshman year started.

I couldn't look at his face. Everything I'd imagined us doing this summer—taking the poetry class, going to the Strand, reading books in cafés, writing—evaporated.

"It's not such a big deal. I'll be back soon to see my mom," he said.

"Really?"

"Of course."

My eyes focused on a light blinking in the park. I thought of cholera and typhus and tornadoes. *It's not such a big deal.* It could be worse. Annie and I always said *Could be worse* whenever we didn't do as well on a test or a paper as we'd hoped, or didn't win an award we thought we might get—it was a joke between us, but there was something real to it, too. Whenever I said *could be worse*, I thought of my dad. It had been worse. The worst had happened. Nothing else could be that bad again.

Will wasn't dead. He was just going to California. It would be okay. He'd be back soon.

He touched my wrist. Slowly, his fingers stroked my arm, my elbow, my collarbone, my neck. My skin felt like it could slip off my body.

He kissed me. His hand crept up my back, his fingers wound through my hair, my mind danced and catapulted and shouted HE'S KISSING ME and MORE. My brain no longer felt connected to the rest of me. I looked at him but felt almost afraid to look at him—his hair, so thick and dark as chocolate, the pale scar on his chin. I was scared to look in his eyes, that he might see what I was feeling. That he might see the love that had been there all along, waiting so many months for this.

Every bad feeling I'd ever had, the stomach bugs, the

griefy grief, disappeared. Each kiss removed the bad things from the past—erased them, brushed them away.

We spent the night in the roof garden. Later, when Annie asked me, I said nothing happened. I meant no clothes had come off. But everything had happened. Everything had changed.

After the sun came up, he drove me home. He parked two blocks away from my building; I didn't want to take any chance that my mom might see us. I'd texted her last night before my ten-o'clock curfew and told her I was spending the night at Annie's.

"When will you be back?" I tried to sound normal, my voice even, casual.

He smiled. "Soon." He said it factually, without a doubt.

Soon.

"When?"

"I'll be back in New York in December."

December wasn't soon. It seemed five thousand years away. There was no way I could wait till December.

He saw the look on my face and said, "Come see me in California." He said it so matter-of-factly, as if I could pop out there in a second, any time I wanted.

"Okay," I said. "Sure."

At that moment, even though we only had a few more minutes together, his leaving didn't seem real. Our night together, our kiss on 96th Street, our whole friendship, had lasted a million years. Of course we'd see each other in California. Soon. We had to. Because this was so rare and strange and happy, there was no way it could end when we said good-bye.

We kissed again and my mind blurred, and I thought how until now I'd never known what it was like to be kissed. Spell-casting kisses, kisses that take off layers of your soul, that split you open.

There's no way you can be kissed like that and not have it change you.

It was like his kiss took a part of me into him, and I had to go find him to get that part back.

Or to let him keep it, and to give him more.

I wished that grief group had been led by Rosamunde Saunders. She would've told the truth. She would've told me: *What you need to do, Eva, is find someone to love you. Not a parent—that's not replaceable. We know that. Nothing you can do about that. What you need is one goddamn romantic dude who will love you like you've never been loved before. When you've found that person, someone who understands your secrets and sadness, don't let him slip away.*

Go get him.

PART TWO

THE SMARTEST GIRL IN AMERICA

if i were a poet
i'd kidnap you
—nikki giovanni

47,500,000 ways to get to California
when you have no money

Will sent letters. Real letters, just like Sir Richard, Lord Ellis, and Gurlag did (though Gurlag's were written on birch bark in ink brewed from blackberries).

We'd only spoken once since he left two and a half weeks ago—he'd called on his ancient phone and we got cut off when his minutes ran out, and he hadn't called again since. He'd given me the number to his father's landline, but I'd called it once and a woman said, "Jim Freeman's line, how may I help you?" and I'd been so nervous, I hung up.

I remembered how he'd told me that Gia complained about his phone not being charged or prepaid. "I hate being interrupted. I don't always want people to find me." He'd said the words *find me* as if they were a punishment.

"If I didn't have a cell phone, my mom would probably implant one in my head," I'd told him.

In some ways, letters were even better, though. I sent him the reading list for the Poetry Society class we'd planned to take together, and he'd look up the writers' work online and copy out a poem he liked, sometimes by hand and sometimes on his typewriter. So far he'd sent three letters with poems: Yehuda Amichai's "A Letter," Nikki Giovanni's "Kidnap Poem," and Marie Howe's "What the Living Do." Today I'd received this:

> Hi from the land of sunshine and plastic surgery. The wedding gifts for my dad and his wife (I can't say stepmother—it sounds like she'd be ordering me to sweep the floor) keep coming. You wouldn't believe what rich people buy. Someone sent a "gardening kit"—three bags of soil, compost, and fertilizer. No joke. They sent fertilizer. I couldn't have come up with a better gift myself.
>
> I miss New York. Miss you.

I felt the paper, soft as cloth, and could almost smell soap and sugar. The thought of him hovered behind everything now, like a shadow.

I hadn't had a stomach bug day since our night on the roof. I wrote back to him:

> I'm coming to see you. I'm not sure when I'll get there yet—still working out the plan—but hopefully it'll be really soon.

I clipped out the latest newspaper article about the wreckage. There was little progress. We'd been waiting for the specialized recovery boats to reach the site, and they'd finally arrived, but the robotic submarine they used to travel to the wreckage took twelve to sixteen hours from the surface, and they'd been delayed by bad weather and storms. More waiting. I wrote:

You were right—you never stop missing them.

I always debated every word, writing and rewriting it.

"You should send some of your own poems back to him," Annie suggested.

"I haven't been writing any poems," I said. I hadn't had the urge to stand at the kitchen counter and scrawl on another Fresh Direct receipt. It was easier to pack those feelings away and read romances instead. After that night with Will, when I showed Annie the article about the plane crash being found, she'd said exactly what I wanted to hear. "'A happy discovery,'" she quoted when she finished reading the newspaper report. "*Happy*. It's nice how people always know the right thing to say."

I'd laughed.

"The NTSB should send you a giant balloon that says *Happy Discovery!*"

One of the reasons Annie is my best friend is because she understands how funny and absurd all this is. My mom of course didn't find the whole thing funny at all. When I got home from seeing Will, I'd asked her if she'd seen the news. Her lips were thin and tight. "Yes," she said in the high-pitched voice she used when she wanted to pretend something wasn't happening, and then changed the subject. Afterward, she went to her office. On a Saturday.

Now, after we finished our summer classes in the morning, Annie and I worked at her parents' laundromat all afternoon; her mom paid us to do the wash-and-fold for the drop-off service. Outside, a heat wave had struck the city, and even the blacktop seemed to melt. Inside the laundromat, the gas dryers made it even hotter.

I glanced at the row of framed academic prize certificates Annie's mom displayed behind the cash register—Annie's sisters, Jenny and Lala, called it the Annie Shrine, with a roll of their eyes. Jenny and Lala were always calling Annie "14C." (14C was the apartment where their neighbor, a retired, never-married scientist, lived alone with her six cats. She rarely appeared except to welcome delivery boys carrying groceries and kitty litter. Nobody knew she'd died until the hallway began to smell and Animal Control came and took away the cats.)

Jenny and Lala worked weekend shifts at the laundromat, which they hated, and weekday shifts at American Eagle in

Queens Center mall, which they loved. They were happy to let Annie shoulder all their parents' hopes.

Annie never complained about the pressure from her parents, mostly because academics came naturally to her, and she was the most ambitious person I knew. She wanted to do big things. It rubbed off on me—I wanted big things, too. I didn't know what I wanted to do with my life exactly, but I definitely didn't want to stay in Queens forever, watching the Empire State Building looming over 43rd Avenue in the distance, as if it were taunting us.

Annie tossed a bag of men's clothes into a washing machine and tugged at her latex gloves. That day, a woman in her seventies had dropped off a giant bag of G-strings; a tall guy handed over a sack of lace lingerie, size 44W, and he had no wife or girlfriend that we ever saw; and when a woman with a baby came through the door, we wanted to hide. I had no idea what a little baby could do to clothing. It was terrifying.

If I did write Will a poem, it would sound like this:

Seeing you is the only thing
keeping me going while washing and folding
old G-strings
man undies
and stinky onesies
with rubber gloves on
and if it wasn't for you

I'd read the newspaper articles
about my dad
over and over and over
feeling worse
and worse
but I don't
because I think of you.

I couldn't send that. It was bad, it was too much, and I wasn't that brave or that crazy.

We finished the folding while the dryers thumped and the washers whirred, and then we took a break. Annie studied, poring over her *Animal Behavior: Mechanisms, Ecology, Evolution* textbook, and I did homework and Googled. Every day since Will left I searched:

> free bus New York to California
> free train cross-country
> must get to LA broke

I had no idea how I was going to get to California. I couldn't fly—just the thought of getting on a plane almost gave me another panic attack. My mom had been afraid of flying even before my dad died, and she hated to leave New York. When he was alive, we never even visited our cousins in London because she couldn't stand the idea of getting on a plane; my dad visited them alone on business trips. "New York has everything," my mom always said. "Why would you need to leave?" I'd only left New York the handful of times my parents took me along to visit their friends in New Jersey and Connecticut. I didn't think it even counted as travel if you'd never left the tristate area.

I kept Googling, and I fantasized about finding a bag of money on the street. I saved all the money I made, but it would still take me the entire summer to save enough for the bus fare—it was cheaper than the train—and food along the way. By then it would be time to go back to school.

I couldn't ask my mom for the money. Her elbows tensed whenever a bill arrived, and she often said how much she hoped that I could go to the Honors College at Queens College, where she taught, for free. Though even if we did have the money, she'd never let me go see Will. How could I even ask her? *Oh, by the way, I fell in love with this guy, so I'm going to travel to LA by myself, don't you love that idea ha ha ha ha ha ha ha ha ha ha ha ha ha ha ha ha ha ha?*

I had to find a way to get there. I kept thinking that if I could find a last-minute internship out there, or some reason that my mom would approve of, then I wouldn't even have to mention Will to her.

There had to be a way. Buried in the internet, there had to be something.

I kept Googling.

need job internship student free travel LA no flying
desperate now PLEASE

There were contests sponsored by travel agencies (but you had to be eighteen to enter), sketchy-sounding real estate brokers, and some particularly skeezy-looking sites that sounded like they were abducting girls into slavery.

My legs stuck to my plastic chair as I waded through www.be-a-courier.com, www.freestudenttravel.com, and sites casting for reality TV.

Are YOU a Female Athlete Who Has Overcome a
Devastating Illness?
Are YOU a Promzilla?
Do YOU Own Lots of Cats and Need a Boyfriend?

And then I read this:

Are YOU the Smartest Girl in America?
Are you taking college-level courses as a high
school sophomore? Do you read math books for
fun? Do you feel like your academic achievements
are worlds ahead? How would you like to earn a full
college scholarship worth $200,000? Reel Life, Real
Teenz Productions is looking for the smartest teens
across the country for a new game show that will
crown the Smartest Girl in America this summer.

I clicked links; it sounded like an ordinary quiz show taped in Burbank, except it featured teen girls vying for scholarships. The show would be broadcast on a new cable network; the scholarships were funded by various corporations and a nonprofit called Girls Strive (their mission statement: "Fostering Female Academic Achievement.") Casting calls were taking place right now in cities all over the country, including New York.

I answered the Sample Test Questions. "What are the names of the Brontë sisters?" Easy: Charlotte, Emily, and Anne (I read *Wuthering Heights* and *Jane Eyre* in English class, and they were basically romances). But "What scientist and peace activist discovered the concepts of orbital hybridization and electronegativity?" "Which Nobel prize winner is also the mother of another Nobel prize winner?" and "One hundred people are in a room. How many handshakes can take place between any two people?" I had no idea.

I touched Annie's elbow and asked her the handshake question.

She thought for five seconds. "Four thousand nine hundred and fifty," she said.

"What scientist and peace activist discovered the concepts of orbital hybridization and electronegativity?"

"Linus Pauling." She answered instantly, with a yawn.

"Which Nobel prize winner is also the mother of another Nobel prize winner?"

She glanced at me as if I was a bit dim. "Marie Curie and

her daughter, Irène Joliot-Curie. Marie Curie is the only woman to have won the Nobel twice, and the first person to win in two different fields. Her daughter won for chemistry in 1935 for discovering artificial radioactivity."

I wasn't the smartest girl in America. But Annie was.

If Marie Curie would do it, you should too

I t's not happening. No way." Annie shut the dryer door with a clang.

"Think of it as an honor. Marie Curie would've kicked ass on this show. And every quiz show on the planet."

"No self-respecting intelligent person would go on a show produced by people who spell *teens* with a *z*."

At least I hadn't asked her to be on *Promzillas*.

"You love reality shows though," I said.

"Because they're like rubbernecking at a traffic accident. I don't want to *be* on one." She opened another dryer, removed a load, and dumped it into one of the huge rolling metal baskets. "They're not looking for the smartest girl. They're looking for the girl who's most willing to flash her underwear or make out with someone just to get on TV."

"That's not true. Look. It's sponsored by Girls Strive. They're fostering female academic achievement."

She wheeled the basket to the folding table. "I can't believe you want me to go on a crazy show just because you've got a crush on some guy."

"It's not a crush on some guy. It's Will. It's the real thing. I have to see him again. We have limbic resonance. He resonates my limbs."

She pointed at me. "Dopamine. Your brain is flooded with dopamine and norepinephrine every time you think of him, which makes you act kind of nuts. And by the way, those are the same brain chemicals associated with falling in love and with drug addicts and people with OCD."

I folded a fitted sheet. "I'm not a drug addict and I don't have OCD. I just want to see him again. I have to."

She shook her head. "'Smart girl' and 'reality TV game show' should not be in the same sentence."

"The grand prize is a two hundred thousand dollar scholarship."

"Two hundred thousand dollars for whoever strips naked on TV."

"It's not like that." I went back to the computer and read more of the site, in case I'd missed a sentence requiring everyone to be naked.

An hour later, I'd read everything. There was nothing about being naked. In fact, the more I read, the better it sounded. One of the show's sponsors was the Mirabelle Resort, an oceanside hotel that was offering three nights' free lodging to contestants and their companions. When I clicked a link to the "Companion" page, it said that contestants were allowed to bring a friend, sibling, or parent who would serve as their lifeline, offering help whenever they floundered on a question. "Every time the companion successfully answers a question, they will receive a ten thousand dollar cash prize," I read aloud. "The companion will have the opportunity to earn up to fifty thousand dollars."

With $50,000 I could *move* to California.

"We have to do this," I said.

Annie had been collecting scholarship information for years—she had folders full of applications for grants and loans. She dreamed of going to MIT; she drooled over pictures of their laboratories and had lists of all the classes she wanted to take. But MIT cost an insane amount of money.

"You told me once that the only way to make sure you get a scholarship is to apply for as many as possible," I said. "Just read it. Read the site. Please?"

She put down the laundry, sat in front of the computer, and squinted at every page of the site like she was expecting it to reveal a diabolical darker purpose.

I stood at the table matching socks. "You're a shoo-in," I told her. "If you win, you'll have college completely paid for. You can go to MIT and study brain chemicals and chromosomes and animal behavior for four whole years and not worry about financial aid or loans or anything. What's there to lose?"

"My self-respect? My pride in not having anything embarrassing about myself on the internet?"

"You were thinking of trying field hockey just so you could get a sports scholarship. This would involve a lot less pain and humiliation." And with our athletic abilities, the only sport we qualified for was the Scrabble team.

She tilted her head and studied the site for a long time, reading every page and sidebar and pop-up window. Eventually, her face began to soften, and she got that dreamy look she often had when gazing at the pages of *Population Genetics and Microevolutionary Theory*.

"It says, 'Professors from Princeton and Cornell are developing the quiz show questions,'" she read aloud. "They've even linked to the professors' websites." She read their bios. "I guess this is legit," she whispered. "It says, 'The grand prize winner will also have the opportunity to attend a summer program at the National Science Foundation, the Princeton Laboratory Learning Program, or'"—her voice thickened—"'*the MIT Research Science Institute*.'"

Her face flushed. She looked the way I did when I read about Gurlag or dingle starries.

"Do you know how hard it is to get a spot in MIT's RSI program?" she asked me.

I shook my head.

"It's almost impossible."

She stared dazedly at a dryer for a moment, then started typing. I set down the socks and peered around the computer screen. She'd typed her name and address into the online form. She paused. "This is crazy," she said.

She bit her lip. Her fingers hovered over the Enter button.

"*Two hundred thousand dollars*," I said.

She sat still.

"An internship. *And* four years at MIT completely and utterly *free*."

She pressed the button.

Reel life

The waiting room of Reel Life, Real Teenz Productions on West 23rd Street swarmed with girls. One stared at the book on her lap so hungrily, it looked like she wanted to eat it; another listened to her earphones and chanted mathematical theorems. In Latin.

Annie had been in the audition for over two hours. I was getting worried. We hadn't told our moms we were coming—we'd decided to tell them only if we got picked, since Annie's mom would probably expect her to get chosen, and my mom would freak out and find a million new things to worry about.

Would they pick us? They had to pick us.

She stood beside Will on the deck of his ship, the Black Dawn, *off the coast of California. She smelled the wind and sea and his wild manly tang.*

"I waited a fortnight until word came that I was to see you again, dear Eva. But I'd wait an entire lifetime for you." He kissed her with a fiery, ancient need and carried her to his love grotto.

"You okay? You look dazed," said the curly-haired girl sitting beside me. She wore a navy skirt, white knee socks, saddle shoes, and a navy blazer embroidered with "Lillian

Birch School" in gold thread, even though it was a Saturday.

"I'm okay," I said. "Hey—good move, wearing the uniform."

She shrugged and scratched beneath her sock. "My friend I'm here with wanted me to wear it in case it helps. No uniform at your school?"

I shook my head. "Nope." If my school had uniforms, they would be orange jumpsuits, since the powers that be seemed to try to re-create the experience of prison as closely as possible. Guards at the front doors, metal detectors. ID numbers. I sometimes thought that we were part of some disturbing psychological experiment being performed on New York City public school kids. I thought again of the photo book Will had showed me, and the roof garden. The other world on top of our school, that barely anybody but us even knew about— I hoped that the next time Will was back in New York, we could somehow sneak up there again.

"At least you don't have to wear white knee socks and saddle shoes every day," the girl said. She adjusted her matching navy headband.

"True," I said, but I wondered if we'd be any match for the private school set.

A few minutes later her friend returned. She was about six feet tall and wore the same uniform. A blond version of Gia Lopez. She smiled and held up a golden envelope. They both squealed.

"Good luck," the curly-haired girl said to me as they headed out of the waiting room. "Maybe we'll see you in LA."

"Maybe," I said.

I drummed my fingers on my lap and then turned on my phone. The Wi-Fi network was named ReelTeenzDrama-Queenz. That didn't bode well. As always, my Crapphone took an ice age to connect.

Sitting there in the waiting room alone, with the fate of my future in the hands of some TV game show producers, I felt my chest beginning to hurt.

Don't panic.

Annie would get chosen. We'd get to LA. We had to.

The anxiety always built slowly, simmering. I was afraid everything could change again in a second. Someone could die. Someone could stop loving you. Tragedy was always peeking around the corner.

I tried to ignore the pain in my ribcage. I needed company. I opened a new window on my phone and went to the message board.

There were 102 new messages.

> The recorders have been recovered. It will be announced to the media tomorrow. It will take a week or more to examine them and see if the data is intact, and then several more weeks to transcribe and analyze it. We've waited this long to know. It will only be a month or two longer. The bad news is they still can't retrieve the second part of the wreckage from the ocean floor. He assured me they'll keep trying.
>
> Fran (husband Frank, daughter Lisa, 22C, 22D)

I'm relieved that after years of waiting, we'll finally have answers.

Erin Farwell (Malcom, 19E)

I read the messages one by one. My blood pounded in my ears. I wanted to know what the data said—what had happened, how he died, what he felt—but I was scared to hear the answers, too.

In a grief group session after the crash, a girl had asked Wonderboob if she thought her mother and little brother, who'd been on her mom's lap in the back of the plane, had been afraid. Wonderboob said no. She said it was common for passengers to fall unconscious from the sudden change in cabin pressure. They wouldn't know what was happening. They wouldn't be afraid.

It was so swift, they never felt a thing, she said.

I ask you: How did she know that? Have they done studies, dropping people at hundreds of miles per hour and tearing their limbs apart, then asking them how they felt? How could they possibly know this? How could they know?

On the message board a year later, the subject came up again. Fran said the unconscious theory wasn't always the case. Unfortunately the passengers might have felt the plane's violent lurching movements and have known what was happening. Or so Fran said.

I wanted, more than anything, for Fran to be wrong, for them not to have known the plane was going down, for my dad not to have been scared. "He didn't know, he never knew, he didn't feel a thing," my mom had said. "We're lucky it wasn't a long, painful, drawn-out illness." I'd asked her about that a few days later, after the words had sunk in. *Lucky?* She shook her head and never mentioned it again.

In my first letter to Will after he'd left, I'd told him how nervous I was about the recorders being recovered. He'd written back:

> The recorders will confirm what you already know: he wasn't scared. I'm glad you're coming out here. It will be great to see you.

He sounded so confident, so sure, and I thought of how he walked down the halls of our school, fearless as a cowboy, as if he knew what was out there and was ready to face it. Unlike me. I was always shrinking back, peering around corners, trying not to panic. My insides felt like a mushy mess, and the part of me that loved him also wanted to soak up his strength and fearlessness and become like that, too.

The door to the waiting room opened and I looked up: Annie stood in front of me, holding a golden envelope.

Because my mother is about as likely to let us take the bus
to California as she is to let us travel by donkey

Annie cradled the envelope. She didn't seem to believe it herself.

My whole body felt warm and cold at the same time. She told me about the audition, the screen test, the interviews, the exams, the mock quiz rounds, and the endless forms to fill out. *We were going to California.*

I caught my breath. I couldn't get too excited yet: I still had to figure out how to pay for the trip. And I had to convince my mother to let me go.

We walked toward the elevator. I knew that as soon as I mentioned the word *bus*, my mom would recite all the bus accidents that had happened in the last ten years. She didn't even like the idea of me crossing the street, not to mention crossing the country.

I thought of my mom's research papers and the talks she gave about women and economics. The only thing that might convince her was the hope of winning the money.

"I don't have enough saved for the bus fare, though," I told Annie.

"I can lend you the money. Then when we win, you can pay me back. Even more motivation for us to kick some ass."

"I love you," I said. "I'll pay you back with interest. Unless my mom locks me in my room forever, which will probably happen after I tell her this whole plan."

I spent the next twenty-four hours memorizing passages from *Women and Economics*, by Charlotte Perkins Gilman ("The troubles of life as we find them are mainly traceable to the heart or the purse"), which was the subject of my mom's PhD thesis. Annie helped me put together a spreadsheet about what the $50,000 might mean for my future wealth, success, happiness, and achievement (especially if, according to Annie's calculations, it accrued interest at an annual 6 percent rate).

The next night, I practiced what I'd say to my mom as I cooked dinner. I chopped garlic and parsley, and stirred the tomato sauce. The kitchen was my favorite room in our house. When I cooked, I forgot about school and Will and everything for a little while.

When my dad cooked, he'd hum or whistle and enter this happy sort of trance. Sometimes, what I missed most about him was this secret well of joy he always had, how he made everything fun. Whenever I had a bad day, he'd say, "All is not lost, is it?" He'd make tea (he only liked Tetley, sent from his London friends—he said the kind sold here wasn't the same) with sugar cubes on the saucer, and there would be Toffee Crisp bars cut into small pieces, and Jammie Dodgers and Rich Tea biscuits on a tray. On cold nights—our stingy landlord always kept the heat low—he'd fill up a hot water bottle and put it in my bed, so the sheets were warm when I got inside. Once a week, he bought my mother flowers from the bodega on our corner.

Tonight, as we ate dinner, I twirled and retwirled the spaghetti on my fork. My mom seemed distracted; she kept glancing out the window. She always seemed in her own world lately. She'd leave little Post-it notes all over the place—*Tuesday: department meeting, pick up dry cleaning, pay electric bill, committee report, grades due*—and forget about them. I'd find them and stick them in her bag. Or she'd forget that she'd left the iron on, and I'd have to turn it off. She had insomnia, and sometimes I'd hear her up at three thirty in the morning.

I took a breath and finally told her, "I've been reading Charlotte Perkins Gilman. She's amazing. The best part is when she says—"

My mom wasn't listening. She stared into space and tucked a gray strand of hair behind her ear. She'd stopped dyeing it in the last year. She touched the edges of the faded, worn Pucci scarf around her neck. She used to love to hunt through thrift shops in the bowels of Queens and Brooklyn and unearth vintage Lanvin skirts and Yves Saint Laurent shoes for dirt cheap. When I was little, I'd hide in the middle of the clothing racks and squeal when she found me, and she'd always let me pick out a little treasure—a glass heart-shaped box or a wind-up toy.

We never went shopping together anymore, and she hardly went out for fun at all now, except for her weekly dinner with Larry at Meredith's restaurant in Bayside (if you could call that fun).

Now, my mom took a deep breath, looked up from her plate, and met my gaze. "Larry and I've decided to get married," she said.

"*What?*" I almost spat out my iced tea.

"We started thinking about it when he got laid off. He needs insurance . . . and it seems like the right time for me to consider marriage." She said the word *marriage* the way one might say *back surgery*.

"I don't want to worry you, though," she added. "Larry and I will keep our separate apartments and assets. Our lives won't change much."

"You're freaking kidding me." I put down my fork. It clanged on the table. Annie and I still called Larry the Benign Fungus, or sometimes the Sad Fungus, because he was a disaster magnet. He kept losing things: wallet, keys, library books, his job—recently, the accounting firm where he worked laid off Larry's entire department. If someone threw a soda can out a window, it would hit him on the head. Birds aimed at his bald spot. Ceiling leaks dripped only onto him. He'd met my mom when he accidentally dumped an entire glass of kosher wine on her thrifted vintage shoes. He tracked down a replacement pair on eBay and hand-delivered them to her office, along with a first edition of Anzia Yezierska's

Bread Givers, her favorite book.

I couldn't think of anything to say. It wasn't that I hated Larry—it was that I knew she'd decided to marry him because it would be the final, most permanent way to forget my dad.

"Do you even *love* him?"

"He's a good person. I like him very much."

"You hardly know him." I should've seen this coming, that they were getting serious. A month ago, Larry's mother, Irma, had flown from Texas to New York to meet us. Irma's hair was whipped into a frothy golden swirl; her teeth looked as white and thick as bathroom tiles. She'd taken us to dinner at a barbecue place in midtown where you could drop your peanut shells on the floor, and kept smiling at me somewhat creepily and saying, "Isn't she cute?" as if I wasn't actually there.

"We know each other well. Really well," my mom said.

"You said *like*. You didn't say *love*."

"Not every relationship involves sunsets and pirate ships."

We left most of our dinner on our plates.

In my parents' wedding pictures, my mom literally had stars in her eyes, bright glints in the photos. They'd gotten married at City Hall and then walked across the Brooklyn Bridge in the rain. In the pictures (taken by Lulu) my mom wore a vintage white short dress and carried a white umbrella; my parents' faces glowed beneath it, beaming.

When my mom looked at Larry, her eyes said, *Please don't spill that on me.*

Now my mom washed the dishes while I hid in my room.

Sunsets and pirate ships. She was always saying things that squashed little bits of my soul. She'd see me wearing one of Annie's sister's old miniskirts and say, "Where'd you get *that*?" Or she'd look at my romance covers, or walk in while Annie and I were watching a Lifetime movie, and make scoffing noises. Annie and I even had a hand motion for it: we'd mash an invisible flea with our thumbs. It had become a joke, but it was telling the truth, too: every time she said these things, she crushed tiny little bits of me.

I decided to call Lulu and ask for advice. She told me, "This trip to LA is perfect timing for both of you. You each need some space right now. You can give her some time alone with Larry, so she can be sure she's making the right decision. And maybe time away will help you wrap your head around it, too. Remind her of that and she'll let you go."

I hoped she was right. My mom had to agree that it was a good idea for me to go away right now. And I was sure the uninterrupted time with Larry would make her come to her senses and call it off.

My mom knocked on the door. I was still talking to Lulu on the phone, so I said good-bye and passed the phone to her, and they talked for a few minutes.

"What were you and Lulu talking about?" she asked me after they hung up.

"Nothing," I said. "School stuff."

I knew Lulu wouldn't tell my mom what we spoke about. They had sort of an agreement—my mom liked that I had "another female role model" to confide stuff in, and so she let us talk without making Lulu share it with her. It was good that Lulu lived in Arizona, since otherwise my mom might make her crack under pressure.

I decided to tell my mom about the trip the next night. After our shift at the laundromat, Annie helped me put together an entire file folder of stuff about the show, and when my mom walked in the door at six o'clock—Larry followed behind her—Annie and I stood up. I handed the file to her, and I told her about the $200,000 scholarship for Annie and the $50,000 bonus for me.

"I need to make a brave choice and take this economic risk. This opportunity could change the course of my future. And you and Larry need time alone right now. So Annie and I are going to leave threeweeksfromThursdayonabus." I said the last phrase really fast, hoping she wouldn't notice the last word.

"On a what?" she asked.

"On a very, very safe"—I said it quietly—"bus."

She glanced at the pages we'd printed out. "On a bus. And where is this bus going—where's this show taking place?"

"Los Angeles," Annie said.

"Two sixteen-year-old girls alone on a bus? Cross-country?" My mother laughed. She looked stunned that I'd even asked to go, as if I'd just asked if I could perform brain surgery on her with my fork.

"My daughter, my only child, is not taking a bus trip across the entire country with no adult supervision," she said. "The bus is for society's underbelly. For sex criminals and moral degenerates and psychotic rapist-murderers."

I shook my head. "This is all Aunt Janet's fault. She's poisoned your mind." When my aunt Janet lived in Syracuse, she'd take the bus to see us once a month and always arrived with stories of the crazies on board. One time she sat next to a recently paroled man from Auburn. The man wore an eye patch and proceeded to slowly eat his hair; he'd pick out a few strands and then munch the hairs in his gnarled paws like a squirrel. His patchy head resembled a checkerboard. Then he asked Janet on a date. *Tonight's yer lucky night. I'm gonna take ya out and buy ya an ice cream.* She'd told him: *No thank you.* I'd thought it was a funny story. My mom and Janet hadn't laughed.

Now my mom shook her head. "It's not just Aunt Janet. You remember that beheading in Canada." Years ago, a crazy person had stabbed and decapitated a young guy on a Greyhound. I knew my mom would file that story away and use it against me someday.

"We could take the train instead," Annie suggested. "Though it's more expensive."

My mom shook her head. "It's no safer."

"They could just fly," Larry said brightly. "It's an easy hop to LA—I did it lots of times for my old job. Unaccompanied minors get special treatment." He had a large yellow stain on his button-down shirt; it was a rare day when he appeared stain-free.

He glanced at my mom and me and suddenly remembered why we didn't fly. He picked up the newspaper and hid behind it, as he always did whenever anything remotely relating to my father came up. My mom's face hardened and she looked away.

She asked, "Annie, is there someone else you can take with you? Your mom, or another friend?"

Annie shook her head. "My mom can't take off work. Eva has to come. She knows the most about my weakest subjects, like literature and women's history. I can't do it without her."

My mom seemed unconvinced. She glanced at the file we'd given her. "I just don't think it's a good idea. I'm sorry." She handed the folder back to me, then turned and went into her bedroom.

"You have to let me go," I called after her. "Charlotte Perkins Gilman says all troubles are traceable to the heart or the purse, so this could save me from a lifetime of trouble—"

My mom's door closed with a thud. I heard perfume bottles clinking. Whenever my mom had a bad day, she'd stand beside her dresser, remove the little crystal stoppers of Coco and Opium, and inhale. She guarded them Gollum-like and forbade me to try them on, since she didn't want me wasting or breaking them.

I returned to the kitchen and stared at Annie. "What now?"

She shrugged. We sat down at the table. Larry busied himself in the kitchen. He took a package of pistachios out of the cupboard and cracked one nut with his molars.

"I was in the Academic Bowl in junior high, but we only won gift certificates to McDonald's," he said between chews. He rolled up his shirt sleeves and scratched his elbow; a bandage covered his fleshy arm.

"What happened to your arm?" I asked.

He rolled his eyes. "I was turning the corner on 42nd Street and a hot dog cart ran right into me. Gouged a hole here. Scratch on my leg too."

"Larry," Annie said with a sigh. Everyone always said *Larry* with a sigh.

He picked at his bandage. "Maybe I can help," he said. "I can talk to your mom for you. The chance for that kind of money doesn't land in your lap every day."

I doubted that it would help—it might even make things worse, knowing Larry. "I don't know," I said.

Annie was more optimistic. "It's worth a try."

I touched the dented edge of our kitchen table and looked at him. "Just please don't make her more angry. Don't make her ground me for the rest of the month."

"I won't. I promise. Here goes." He tossed his red pistachio shells in the trash and wiped his hands on his shirt, leaving pink streaks. "Wish me luck." He disappeared into the bedroom.

"I think she'll come around. She has to," Annie said.

I wasn't so sure.

Our bathroom shared a wall with my mom's bedroom; Annie and I perched on the edge of the tub, listening to my mom's raised voice.

"I'm not going to let them travel alone, with no adults to watch over them on the way," she said.

"Maybe you can take some time off work to go with them," Larry told her.

Oh god. There was no way I'd get to see Will if my mom was with me.

"You know I can't afford to do that. I'm teaching all summer," she said.

They were quiet for a few minutes. "What if she's not alone on the way?" Larry asked. "They can stay with family. There's your sister in Cleveland, and my mother in Texas, and Lulu in Arizona . . . they'd watch out for the girls. And she can keep in touch by cell phone and email. We'd know where she is at all times."

"It's not safe for her. She's never traveled. She's never been anywhere," my mom said.

"She's a good kid. Got a good head on her shoulders. In two years she'll be in college. This is exactly what she needs, to try out being on her own. And think about us. The wedding. This will give us time to take care of everything."

They whispered something I couldn't hear, and they were quiet again.

Kissing noises. Ugh. I frowned and moved away from the wall. We went back to the kitchen.

Annie checked her watch; it was time for her to go home and study. Her parents worked until nine o'clock, and her sisters were out with their latest boyfriends—she loved the few, rare hours when she had her apartment to herself to read and be alone.

"I bet your mom will change her mind," she said.

I shrugged. "I hope."

We said good-bye; two hours later my mom came into my room. She'd been sitting on the fire escape talking to Aunt Janet and Lulu on the phone—our fire escape was like a little deck, with a chair and a spider plant; it was the only place in our apartment where you could actually have a completely private conversation. Larry had gone back to his place.

She stood in my doorway. I'd been reading *Torrid Tomorrow* (book 6: *Torrid Tears*) but had shoved it under my pillow when she knocked on the door.

She perched on the edge of my bed and stared at the collection of historical teddy bears sitting on my bookshelves. She'd bought one for me every year until I turned twelve: Amelia Bearhart, Florence Nightingbear, Ida Bear Wells, Elizabear Cady Stanton. She loved those bears. Sometimes I think she liked the bears better than me. The bears achieved great things in the world, and they were perfectly dressed, always smiling, never wallowing, never emotional, never wearing too-short skirts or disappointing and bewildering her by joining the Romance of the Month Club, or turning on *Pride and Prejudice* just to watch the kissing part.

I kept thinking: *Please let me go.*

She picked at an unraveling corner of my quilt. "Aunt Janet and Lulu really want to see you. Larry talked to his mother, and she said they'd be thrilled to have you stay with them." She used her high-pitched voice, her conflicted tone.

"Does this mean . . . I get to go?"

She sighed. "I know I'm overprotective. I just . . . I worry about you. I don't want anything bad to happen to you."

"Nothing bad's going to happen to me."

She put her hand on my arm, and I resisted the urge to pull away. She always wanted to be close to me at the exact moments when I didn't want to be touched. I most needed to talk to her on the nights she worked late or sat huddled at the kitchen table, hidden behind a fortress of her students' papers. During the moments when we got along well, like when we watched a TV movie together last Saturday night on the couch, a wall still stood between us. During a funeral scene at the end of the movie, I couldn't escape the rushing memory of my dad's funeral. I felt a surge of anger remembering that day, the worst day, the day that we never spoke about. I stopped watching and went to bed.

I knew I was harsh on her sometimes because she was here, and my dad wasn't. But we couldn't go back to the way things were before he died.

Now she moved her hand away. "It's not that I don't trust you . . . it's all the crazy people out there who I don't trust. The world isn't what you think it is."

I wanted to tell her that I knew this—that I understood, just as she did, that the world was the kind of place where your father could leave on a business trip and never come back. But we never said these kinds of things to each other.

"It's a long time for you to be away," she said.

"It'd be two weeks. You wouldn't even notice I was gone."

She sighed. "Larry and Lulu think it's a good idea. *A once-in-a-lifetime opportunity*, Lulu said. And Janet really wants to see you. She told me you'd be even safer with her than with me."

"Definitely true, knowing Janet." Janet was so neurotic that she made my mom look almost mellow. "It's not such a big deal," I said. "We'll be back before you know it. Safe and sound."

"You'll promise to be careful?"

"Of course. I'm always careful. And I'll be with Annie. The most responsible person on the planet."

She walked over to my bookshelves and straightened Margaret Thatchbear's hat. Below the bears, I'd stacked *Women and Economics* and *Girls Be Strong* beside my romances. A pile of the Urbanwords books lay on the shelf underneath. I'd never given a copy to her, and she'd never asked.

She sat on my bed again and brushed my hair away from my forehead. She had absolutely no idea who I was.

Lately I had this feeling, sitting in our apartment in the melting summer, of wanting to shed it. To shed our apartment building with its two hundred residents piled on top of each other like rats; to shed riding the 7 train every day with its smells of garbage and BO and strangers smushed together like cattle; to shed Larry with his broken glasses and bird-poop-attracting bald head; to shed my mother and her worries and expectations and refusal to talk about my dad. Sometimes I wanted to shed my whole life.

I had this constant sense of yearning, and I wasn't even sure what I was yearning for.

It was for Will—but for more, too. Maybe it was yearning for another life—for that dream life, that sublimely happy existence it seemed a few people had, that I wanted.

On the subway every morning I watched the crowds of strangers in their suits and dresses, jeans and sweatpants, and I'd wonder sometimes if I'd become one of them. When I grew up, would I stay in Queens? Who would I be? Where would I be?

"So . . . can I go?" I asked her.

She was quiet for a moment.

"Yes," she said finally, reluctantly. "You can go."

PART THREE

IT FEELS SO OLD A PAIN

I measure every grief I meet
  With analytic eyes;
I wonder if it weighs like mine,
  Or has an easier size.

I wonder if they bore it long,
  Or did it just begin?
I could not tell the date of mine,
  It feels so old a pain.
                    —Emily Dickinson

Love, love, love, love, love, love, love, love, love, love, love,
love, love, love, love, love, love, love, love, love, love

The morning we had to leave, I scurried around our apartment making sure I had everything: my favorite jeans, my red sneakers, my soft blue pajamas, my dress and shoes for the show, and my books. It was so early, it was still dark outside; my mom and Larry sipped giant cups of coffee at the kitchen table. They showed me the heavy artillery they were sending me away with: an iPhone (a discounted floor model, courtesy of Larry's cousin who worked at AT&T) to replace my Crapphone, pepper spray, and a Swiss Army knife. And they handed me a map of the country marked up with our route, and a red dot to show every person's house where we'd be staying—Aunt Janet's in Cleveland, Annie's cousin Grace's in Tennessee, Larry's mother's in Texas, and Lulu's in Tucson.

"You have the dress and heels carefully packed, too?" My mom had let me borrow one of her vintage dresses—black with white piping—and a pair of red patent heels (they fit perfectly after I stuck two gel liners inside them) to wear on the show. "Please be careful with them," she said. "Please don't get them stained."

She'd never recovered from the time I was twelve and borrowed a blouse of hers for a school dance without asking. It had gotten splattered with fruit punch and she'd nearly killed me. I'd asked my dad why she was so angry, and he said, "Your mom didn't have a lot of nice things as a child. They had no money. These things are important to her now." I thought of my mom's mother, Bubbe 409, who worked at the Swingline stapler factory in Queens. Lately, my mom seemed to hoard her nice things more than she actually wore them. She liked to keep her dresses in perfect condition in her closet, like it was a museum.

"I won't stain the dress. I promise," I said.

Larry seemed most excited about the pocketknife, which he'd owned since he was ten. He showed me each of the twenty-one attachments.

"Now look at this doohickey over here." He maneuvered a gray piece of plastic. "A tiny magnifying glass. You could start a fire with that if you needed to."

"Why would I need to start a fire?"

"You never know," he said. "It's all about being prepared."

"That's why I'm glad I had you take that Self-Defense for Women class," my mom said.

"I want I need I deserve," I said.

"Don't be sarcastic. Now come here. I got you this." She

reached into her bag and handed me an orange whistle on a matching string. "Please put it on and don't take it off."

"You're kidding." It was the ugliest thing I'd ever seen in my life. It was like wearing a tiny traffic cone around my neck.

"It's not a fashion accessory. It's for your safety."

I put it on. There was no way I was wearing this thing in public.

Larry hunched over the iPhone and beckoned me closer. "I wish I understood half the things this gizmo does. Let's see." He squinted. "Your mom added a Locate My Kids app so we always know where you are, but I haven't figured out how to—uh-oh. What did I press?"

The screen turned black.

"Here—let me help," I said. He didn't want to fork it over, but eventually relented. I turned it back on.

"Don't forget the gifts," my mom said, and brought out a bag of things we'd picked out for everyone: Murray's bagels for Aunt Janet (her favorite, from Manhattan); lipstick for Grace from a boutique in the West Village and a New York City cookbook for her parents; chocolates for Irma; and a letterpress print of an Elizabeth Bishop poem for Lulu, made by one of my mom's colleagues. My mom had rolled it up carefully into a cardboard tube.

I checked the time on the phone. "We're running late— there are still a few other things I need to pack, okay?"

My mom stared at the whistle swinging against my stomach. "Hurry back though, so I can show you how the pepper spray works."

I went into my room and shut the door.

I pulled the purple shoe box out of the back of my closet.

I opened it. I emptied it onto my bed.

I held the gold horseshoe necklace my father had given me. The chain was so delicate, the horseshoe tiny, the size of my fingertip. It had a pink stone in the center. I'd always been afraid to wear it because I might lose it, so I kept it in the shoe box. Now I didn't want to leave it here.

I fastened it around my neck, under my shirt so my mom wouldn't see it and give me her *Let go of him* look.

I picked up one of the postcards, from a business trip he took to Chicago four years ago. A picture of the Tribune Tower, with rocks from the Parthenon and Edinburgh Castle and the Taj Mahal embedded in its side, brought back by journalists from their travels.

I stared at the signature:

Love, love, Daddy

That was how he signed all his postcards, so many loves that they curled up the edge toward the address and around the stamp—there was never enough room.

I kept staring at it. This happy string, this happy endless string of loves.

I picked up the Toffee Crisp wrappers. When we'd cleaned out his office, we'd discovered a Toffee Crisp treasure trove: he'd hoarded them in his desk, filing cabinets, and even inside an old flower vase.

I snapped the cat collar closed. He'd taken me to Petco to pick it out for Lucky. He helped me choose the purple collar, and Fancy Feast Wild Salmon Florentine and Marinated Morsels Beef Feast. ("Lucky eats better than we do," he'd said.) We both felt sad seeing all the cats in cages at the store, waiting to be adopted, especially the ten-, eleven-, and twelve-year-old ones who looked forgotten and forlorn. "Someday we'll come back and adopt all the old fogies," my dad had said. "We'll turn our apartment into a nursing home for old cats."

Try not to be so thin-skinned, my mom had said after Lucky died. But she'd never said that when I cried about my dad. For three months after the crash, I spent every night in her bed. I'd wake at four in the morning and not know why I was in her room. Then I'd remember. The tears would roll out like water as I watched the green numbers on her clock. She'd press me to her stomach, which was warm and soft, holding me like she did when I was six years old. I'd think of how I used to climb into their bed on weekend mornings, to cuddle and read, and how different this was—not snuggling at all—it was more like she was trying to save me from drowning.

We never talked about it in the morning. We pretended everything was fine.

She never really wept in front of me; she only did it in the bathroom, running the water so she'd think I couldn't hear. When she came out, I always wanted to ask if she was okay or wanted to talk, but she'd give me this withering look that said, *Don't ask. I don't want to talk about it.* I'd look away and pretend I couldn't tell she'd been crying.

Sometimes she had fits of anger, too. One day soon after they confirmed my dad had died, I stood outside our apartment door, about to put my key in the lock, when I heard her scream my father's name. Then she smashed a ceramic pitcher. It had been my grandmother's pitcher, Bubbe 409's. I'd hovered outside the door for a long time, and when I finally came inside, she was sweeping up the shards. She said it had slipped from her hands. An accident.

Now I picked up the pillow from my bed, took off the pink pillowcase, and put the postcards inside. Then I folded the tie, handkerchiefs, and white T-shirt and put them in also. I stuffed in the paperweight in the shape of the Brooklyn Bridge, his glasses, the cat collar, Popeyes receipt, Toffee Crisp wrappers, and the bracelet and rings he'd given me, and tucked it all inside my backpack.

After all this time, even to take them out of the box hollowed out my stomach. He was in these things. They were him. They were a part of me, as much myself as my arms and legs and eyes and blood.

You can't keep weaving all day and undoing
it all through the night

Annie's mom picked us up in her laundry van to drive us to Port Authority; Annie talked so fast I could barely keep up. "I had the hardest time choosing which books to bring—I couldn't decide what my weakest subjects were, so I packed *Silver's Scientific Miscellany*, *The Eberson Review of American History*, *Complete Mathematical Theorems*, and . . ." She named ten other books. She loved her rare, beloved books from the Strand better than anything you could download or read online. "My mom wants to kill me. We couldn't lift my duffel bag, so we had to ask our neighbor Mr. Rigamonti to help, and he got it in the van but he threw out his back. My mom had to offer him free wash-and-fold for a month. Did you bring the lit books?"

I nodded. "*Reader's Encyclopedia*, *A Complete History of English Literature*, and a lot of poetry." My dad's books. I'd fit all my stuff into my backpack and a rolling suitcase I'd borrowed from Larry.

My mother and Larry sat in the row behind us; my mom gazed out the window as the city blurred by. She sighed, one of the long, heavy sighs she'd been making the entire ride.

"This is good for both of us," she said, as if she were trying to convince herself this was true. "It's good you're going to see the country a little. Really good."

She put her hand on my shoulder. Her fingers were trembling.

"They'll be okay," Larry said, and patted her on the back. "They're staying with friends and family every night. They have pepper spray, an iPhone, and the best pocketknife."

"And a whistle." I held up the orange monstrosity.

"And I have a can of Mace. My sister Jenny got it for me," Annie said brightly.

"Some people would think it's odd that New Yorkers are this worried about *leaving* the city," Larry pointed out. "Most people are afraid when they *come* to New York City."

We all turned and stared at him.

He shrugged. "It's true."

Larry was the only one among us who'd spent most of his life outside of New York. His mother had been married four times, and he'd lived in New Mexico, Kentucky, and Texas—places that seemed as exotic as Fiji to us. Places that we were now going to see.

"When you say you're from New York, people think you live your life dodging muggers and bullets and thugs every day," he said. "You'll see. They'll be shocked that you think you need Mace and pepper spray to survive your journey through the cornfields. The Midwesterners, Southerners, and Texans will probably be afraid of *you*."

Annie and I exchanged looks.

"I'm serious," he said.

At Port Authority, we waited outside the turquoise-and-silver Go Blue bus. My mother glared at everyone on line as if they were all ax murderers. She clutched her elbows; she looked like she wanted to grab me and yank me back inside the station.

"You sure you want to go?" she asked me as the driver took Annie's ticket. Her voice wavered. "Because you could change your mind right now. It would be completely fine." She looked like she might cry.

"It's only two weeks. I'll be back really soon. Please don't worry." I was so embarrassed. Was she upset because she'd miss me, or because she didn't want me to have any freedom?

Larry put his arm around her.

We gave our bags to the luggage worker. Larry gave me a quick, awkward hug. "Godspeed," he said. "And good luck."

"Good luck!" Annie's mom echoed. She waved at us, looking thoroughly unworried about the impending trip—she looked excited, in fact. "Bye-bye!" she said. "Come back with the two hundred thousand dollars!" She grinned.

Annie sighed. "I'll try."

We boarded the bus. I watched my mother's gaze scan the windows, though they were tinted so darkly there was no chance she could see me anymore.

There is no music like this without real grief

What no one ever tells you is that riding a bus can make you feel rich. The key is the front seat, the view out the wide grand window, perched high above the traffic. As we emerged from the dark station and into the city, I thought that I'd never seen Manhattan like this before. You were always stuck in subways and on crowded sidewalks, in the backseats of smelly taxis or standing inside packed city buses. It never looked like this, so bright and open, the road and the river flowing out the window.

Annie cracked open *People*, *EW*, and *In Touch*. She speed-read them before she took out a textbook and a folder. "We only have six days till the show, so I made a schedule," she said, unveiling an elaborate spreadsheet. Today said *Math* in her column; in my column she'd typed: "Prep Annie for lit q's!!!!"

Aside from being her Official Literary Consultant, I was also our Travel Coordinator. I'd checked out guidebooks from the library and read tons of travel sites, and decided what we couldn't miss: the Rock and Roll Hall of Fame, the Grand Ole

Opry, the Fort Wells rodeo, Sabino Canyon, Universal Studios, Venice Beach, and the Santa Monica pier, which wasn't too far from where Will's father lived (I'd Google mapped it).

The bus driver caught my eye in the rearview mirror. "Big trip?" he asked.

I nodded. "We get off in Ohio today. Cleveland." Almost nine hours from now. I couldn't believe I was finally traveling for the first time in my life.

"Ohio is the best. You gotta eat at City Chili," he said. "Chili on top of spaghetti. The chain started in Cincy. They got them in Cleveland too now. First time I ate there, I come home and I says to my wife, I says, 'Let's put the chili on top of spaghetti for a change.' She says, 'No way. Chili? Spaghetti? No can do.'"

I elbowed Annie. Why was he telling us this?

"Most people you know, they want to stay in their little house and not change nothing. But when you hit the road— and do I hit the road, I been to every state in this country, and you know what? Everything you ever thought about the world is wrong. That's why you gotta travel. I'm telling youse two this cause you're young. You got time. You gonna eat chili on spaghetti, right? You gonna see the world, right?"

The world seemed a bit overzealous, considering we hadn't even gotten to New Jersey yet, but I said "Right" anyway.

We sped toward the George Washington Bridge. I half expected a taxi to follow us, my mom's voice on a bullhorn:

I changed my mind! She'd send out giant mechanical pincers to pluck me up and hoist me away.

I stuffed my whistle into my backpack. Sunlight bounced off the cars below us, their paint shimmering. My stomach quivered. I took out *American Poetry* and opened the cover. I'd stashed Will's letters inside it. I'd gotten seven of them in the six weeks since he'd left.

I loved seeing where he'd written Eva at the top of the page, or sometimes just E—, and once: To the Poetess. I loved the feel of the paper and the envelopes, reading my address in his handwriting, the postmark dates. I touched where he'd written Miss you. And once, instead of his name, he signed it Griefy in LA.

Eight days until I'd see him. We'd be traveling for over two weeks—one week to get there, three days in LA, and then five days to return home.

Annie glanced at the letters in my lap. "Don't you wish sometimes that you could just text him? With no waiting?"

"Lord Ellis, Sir Richard, Destry, and Gurlag didn't text," I said.

"Gurlag wouldn't know how to text. He couldn't read," she said.

"Only because he was raised by wolves and without a formal education. When Penelope started teaching him in book three, he picked it up really fast."

Even though I said this, I still kept checking Will's photo

stream every day, though he hadn't posted anything in six months. I Googled him daily, too, though nothing new ever appeared, and I'd practically memorized the small amount of info about him already online—three photos on school web pages from swim meets, a picture of him from last November that Gia had posted (ugh), the website of his mom's bakery (still up, though the bakery had closed now), and his dad's website. That was all. Still, I clicked on this stuff all the time, with the magical hope that something new might appear.

Letters were better, though. You could hold letters in your hand. Yesterday, I'd received a small package from him with a mix CD. Songs for our road trip. He'd burned it on his dad's computer, and used a CD that looked like an old vinyl record. He'd typed up the song list on his typewriter. I felt a thrill every time I looked at the CD, with its antique-looking surface.

1. The Littlest Birds - The Be Good Tanyas
2. Chicago - Sufjan Stevens
3. Petoskey Stone - Dana Falconberry
4. The Only Living Boy in New York - Simon & Garfunkel
5. I Don't Know - Beastie Boys
6. On the Road to Find Out - Cat Stevens
7. Everyday - Vetiver
8. Drowning in the Days - Old 97's

9. A-Punk - Vampire Weekend
10. Swim Good - Frank Ocean
11. I'm on a Roll - Over the Rhine
12. What I Got - Sublime
13. The Way I Am - Martin Sexton
14. Star Witness - Neko Case
15. Tape Loop - Morcheeba
16. Walking on the Moon - The Police
17. America - Simon & Garfunkel
18. California - Joni Mitchell

I'd loaded it onto my new phone and listened to it over and over. I'd played it so many times that I kept hearing the songs even when my phone was off.

The CD also held a snippet of a poem, typed on a white label and stuck on the case:

i like my body when it is with your
body. It is so quite new a thing
--e. e. cummings

Every time I read it, I felt like I'd inhaled too much air. Floating, inflating, my face felt hot and my stomach felt full. I was back in the roof garden again.

In two of his letters, Will only sent poems—just the poem and nothing else. Not even romantic poems—he'd sent one by Langston Hughes and another by Philip Larkin. As I read them, I kept thinking of what my father once said: *Every poem is a love poem.*

Sometimes I sat by the window waiting for the mailman to reach our building—I'd race for the elevator, run down the hall, turn the mailbox key, and see the long skinny envelope, the familiar handwriting. In my last letter to him, I'd included the dates of our trip and the addresses of where we'd be staying on the way, hoping I'd keep hearing from him, keep receiving the letters and poems. I never wanted it to stop. I'd told him about each person we were staying with— Aunt Janet in Cleveland, Annie's cousin Grace in Tennessee, Larry's mom in Texas, and Lulu in Tucson. I wanted him to be a part of the trip, to share it with me.

Last night, while his mix played, I'd sat on my bed and arranged his seven letters on the quilt in front of me, organized by postmark date. Somehow it made it all seem more real that way. Holding them in my hands, they were undeniable. The letters, poems, and eighteen songs were proof.

Proof of us. Proof of love.

We flee to the Cleve

As our bus approached Cleveland, something rose inside of me. I liked the way the city looked—the small cluster of buildings, the river, the sky. There was so much sky. In New York you had to brace yourself before you went outside, muster the courage to face the crowds and subways and noise. Here, we'd passed farmland less than an hour ago. The sun shimmered on baseball diamonds, emerald lawns, and pretty, quaint houses.

We'd arrived, our trip was real, there was no turning back now.

Outside the window, Aunt Janet stood in the parking lot. She wore green pants that sat high on her skinny waist, and a green blouse buttoned to the neck. Her hair frizzed out sideways. She looked like a stalk of broccoli. Broccoli with glasses. She was eight years older than my mom; she'd always been part older sister, part second mother to my mom.

We gathered our bags, and the bus coughed us out onto the street.

"You made it." Janet hugged me and Annie tightly. As we

waited for our luggage, Janet squinted at the phone in my hand. "May I see that, please?"

I handed it to her. She cradled it like it was a hand grenade. "Your mother's put parental protections on it, right?"

"Um . . . I don't think . . ."

"Do you know what this is?" She held it up.

I hesitated. "A phone?"

"It's the most convenient, direct conduit between pedophiles and sexual predators and *you*. This is the best thing to ever happen to those people."

"But I don't talk to pedophiles or sexual predators."

She slipped the phone into her pocket. "I'm going to put controls on it, some safety measures."

I glanced at Annie. I'd warned her about Janet—I'd told her that Janet had moved to Cleveland from Syracuse five years ago for a guidance counselor job at a private Jewish school, which she eventually quit to start her own business. Her company, Safety Solutions, instructed parents about infant CPR, babyproofing, and children's and teens' health issues, and in recent months she'd begun leaving creepy messages on our home voice mail. "Gonorrhea," she'd said. "I'm very worried about gonorrhea and teenagers. Please sit down with Eva and discuss the risk of gonorrhea with her." When she visited us for Passover in the spring, she left pamphlets about herpes and gonorrhea on top of my desk. I called her Aunt Gonorrhea for a long time, until my mom made me stop.

The three of us dragged Annie's duffel bag through the parking lot, a slow and excruciating process. Eventually, we got all our luggage into the back of Janet's gargantuan white Honda Odyssey.

Janet pumped Purell into our palms. She'd gotten her germ phobia from her mother, Bubbe 409, who used to stay up all night long scrubbing the kitchen floors, behind the refrigerator, and under the stove. Bubbe 409 had been my age when she survived the war. To my mom and Janet, just the mention of *the war* explained everything about Bubbe 409. Whenever I asked my mom about her, my mom would clam up. She'd say, "Your grandmother lived in very dirty conditions during the war"—and that was all.

Janet glanced at my legs as I climbed into my seat. "Have you gained weight?" she asked me.

"No." I looked down at my body. I didn't think I had, but just hearing her question made my thighs look soft and fleshy.

"Where's your whistle? Your mom told me to check you're wearing it."

"Oh. That." I took it out of my backpack and put it back on, feeling about five years old.

The minivan was spotless. A giant stack of placards took up the back, which Janet said were for her Lifestyle Choices presentation, a new part of her business.

"We read a lot about Cleveland—we'd love to go to the Rock and Roll Hall of Fame," I said, and showed her the travel page I'd printed out, with its picture of a giant guitar.

She frowned and glanced at her watch. "We don't have a lot of time."

"Or the International Women's Air & Space Museum." I showed her the picture.

The frown deepened.

"The Metroparks Zoo? A baby Allen's swamp monkey was just born there." Annie told Janet about her sophomore-year research on swamp monkeys—their webbed fingers and toes, their *frugivorous* and *diurnal* tendencies.

"Actually, I have somewhere I want to take you," Janet said. "A surprise." Her elbows relaxed on the steering wheel. "I'm just so happy you're here. For years your mom told me you were going to come visit, but you never did. Two Hanuk-kahs ago she promised. Then she canceled. I like visiting you in New York, but it's not the same as having you in my home." She paused. "It means a lot to me."

"My mom works really hard" was all I could think to say, but I felt guilty that we'd never visited Janet before. Since my mom hated traveling, I didn't think visiting Cleveland had ever really been a possibility.

"I keep telling her you two need to move here. You could afford a big house. We've got great schools. It's safer. You'd be so happy."

My mom once told me she'd rather stab herself in the eye than live in Cleveland. I didn't tell Janet that.

"Of course, there's the problem of Larry," Janet said. Janet and I'd never talked about Larry, though she'd met him when she stayed with us for Passover. He'd left a bottle cap on the floor that had pierced Janet's foot. She'd made a big fuss about how it ruined her expensive sock, and that thankfully she was up-to-date on her tetanus shot.

Janet glanced at me. "She's not going to marry him."

"How do you know?"

"Your mom and your dad were a couple for *ten years* before they got married. Your mom doesn't make big decisions easily. She'll put Larry off for a good decade or so, too."

"She's different now," I said.

Janet raised her eyebrows. "She's the same. Drowning herself in work—when she feels down, that's what your mom does. When she was a teenager, after our father died, she studied nonstop. She didn't work as hard when you were a baby, and when your dad was alive—she was too happy, I guess." She paused. "She and Larry haven't set a date yet. Larry will get tired of waiting and he'll be gone."

I hoped she was right. I looked out the window and felt glad to be away from my mom and Larry. Even a little distance made me feel like I could be myself more, like I could breathe, as I left my mom on one coast and moved toward Will on the other.

Those who are dead are never gone

A cemetery.
Janet's surprise was a cemetery.

Janet drove down the road slowly, along the graves. I fingered the hem of my shirt. "Why are we—?"

She craned her neck. "Just wait."

I hadn't been to a cemetery since my dad's funeral—I pushed away the memory of that gray, rainy day, our black umbrellas, my mom and me yelling at each other—that day I never wanted to think about. My mom hadn't let me bring Annie to the funeral—she'd wanted to keep it *private*.

A year ago, on the one-year anniversary of the crash, I told my mom I wanted us to visit my dad's grave. I thought that maybe if we could visit it again, on a sunny, summery day, it could become a nice place to go to, instead of a terrible memory. But my mom froze. *We're not doing that again. We need to move forward. Not back.* End of subject. I thought about going by myself, but the cemetery was two hours away, far from any train, and my mom would probably kill me if I told her I planned to wander around Westchester alone.

All I remembered about my dad's cemetery was the dank smell of the rain, the mud washing onto the paths, and the gravestones turning dark gray under the downpour. This cemetery seemed completely different. Here, everything glowed in the sunshine—blossoming trees and hydrangeas, a sparkling stream beneath a wooden bridge, grass waving in the wind.

Janet stopped the car, and we walked down a wide path to a headstone beneath the willow trees.

BRONSTEIN.
FREDA BRONSTEIN, ABRAHAM BRONSTEIN.

Freda was Bubbe 409.

"My grandparents—? I thought they were cremated?"

"I'd been carrying those ashes around from Queens to Syracuse to Cleveland and I was sick of it," Janet said, as if she were talking about a load of laundry. "Cremation is actually against Jewish law, you know, but my mother was pretty much done with religion by the time my father died. She didn't want us to pay for a burial. And the upkeep. It didn't matter to her. But you know what? After all these years I decided it matters to me. I wanted somewhere to go to."

Janet brushed off the headstone and plucked a few tiny weeds that had grown among the flowers.

I smiled at Annie awkwardly. The first stop on our cross-country road trip and we were standing in a cemetery. She didn't complain, though. She looked around approvingly. "Jewish cemeteries totally have it over Christian ones," she said. "It's so simple and understated without those phallic statues and giant tombs all over the place."

Janet picked a dead petal off a flower. "I toured a bunch before I chose this one. I like that it has a good amount of space between the plots."

I'd never imagined I'd be standing in Cleveland in front of my grandparents' buried ashes, talking about the width between plots.

I felt my chest tightening, a small seed of panic beginning—the image of my dad's grave hovering at the edge of my mind—but I willed it away. My grandparents' names were carved into the stone in both English and Hebrew, and I ran my finger across the deep grooves, their jagged edges.

"Some people—like your mom—think it's odd I did this." Janet shrugged. "But I figure, my parents were never really happy when they were alive. At least they can have some peace when they're dead."

I told Annie how my grandfather had died before I was born, and that my memories of my grandmother revolved mainly around cleaning products.

Janet sighed. "She was pretty screwed up."

Annie gazed at the headstone, at the dates of birth and death. "I can't imagine what your grandmother must've gone through during the war."

"My mom never talks about it. She's never told me anything," I said.

"You know your mom. She doesn't like talking about the past," Janet said.

"How did Freda even survive the war?" I asked.

Janet looked for a rock and placed it on the headstone. "She was around your age then. They'd started liquidating ghettos in Poland, rounding people up for the camps. Freda's father wrote to a distant relative in London and asked for help. He couldn't get the whole family out of the country, but he got Freda a place on a children's train to England with dozens of other kids."

"One of the Kindertransports? We studied those in school," Annie said.

Janet nodded. She told us how Freda's parents had taken her to the station and said good-bye. As the train moved, her parents raced alongside it, their faces crumpling. Freda waved at them until her mother and father blended into a blur of gray and brown, then disappeared in the distance.

Freda and her parents wrote letters through the Red Cross for months. Freda never told her parents the truth, that in London she lived in a boardinghouse with other girls, refugees. Mice ran across the girls' beds at night, little pricking thumps on their stomachs. She had lice on her scalp and in her eyebrows. The air raids began, and the girls slept in the basement, where the ground was covered with rat droppings.

During the day, she worked in a hat factory. Her fingers bled, and two fingernails broke off. The girls were only allowed to take baths once every couple of weeks, and each girl had to use the same bathwater. There was hardly any laundry soap, and her clothes became spotted with stains. Every night, Freda fell asleep with a photo of her parents beside her pillow, but one morning she woke up and the photo was gone. Another girl had stolen it and thrown it in the fireplace. Sometimes, girls stole things for no reason at all. Just to steal and destroy. Freda had no photos of her parents after that.

"Did she ever see her parents again?" I asked. Around us in the cemetery, everything was quiet, except for the wind whistling through the trees.

"The letters from Freda's parents stopped coming. But she was sure she'd see them when the war was over. She was sure they'd come for her."

"What happened then?" Annie asked.

"When the war finally ended, she still hadn't heard anything from them. She decided to go back to their village in Poland, thinking that if her parents survived, they'd return also.

"The outside of the house looked exactly the same, but another family was living inside it. They came to the door. They denied it had ever been Freda's family's home and wouldn't let her in. No one in the town would speak to her. An old neighbor told her to leave—some Jews who returned were being killed in the open, even though the war was over.

"She never saw or heard from her parents again, and found no records of their deaths. She found records of their deportation—her mother to Treblinka, her father to Sobibor. That was all. Nothing more."

"I can't believe my mom never told me this," I said.

Janet shrugged. "Your mom took it hard when our dad died, and then our mom. She didn't know how to cope."

She still doesn't know how to cope, I thought.

We put more stones on top of their graves. I put stones on other people's graves, too. It didn't seem right that no one had visited them. I thought of my father's grave back east, neglected, no stones having been placed on it for almost two years, no one to plant flowers or pluck the weeds.

I understood why Janet wanted the graves, wanted a place to visit. I wished that I had a place to go to, somewhere to remember my dad instead of just a pillowcase in my backpack, and a faraway cemetery that held bad memories. On the message boards, people had talked about plans for a memorial somewhere in New York, but that seemed years away from ever happening.

I felt a warmth toward Janet that I'd never felt before—maybe she wasn't all prickly comments and awkward phone messages. Maybe we weren't so different after all. We both shared that yearning to be with the dead again.

After the cemetery, our trip took a cheerier turn—Janet agreed to a quick stop to see the swamp monkeys at the zoo before it closed, and even let us go to the Rock and Roll Hall of Fame for a half hour. Annie and I locked arms as we stopped for dinner at Gittel's, Janet's favorite restaurant. It was a deli just like the ones in New York, except it was a lot cleaner. Annie ordered a pastrami sandwich. I got an egg cream, which they called a chocolate phosphate, and blueberry blintzes and matzo ball soup—and while we ate, I kept staring at the orange booth across from us.

A blond girl and a boy in a baseball cap sat there, nestled together. They shared a milkshake, and the boy kept feeding the girl French fries. Her knee bobbed up and down, and the boy put his hand there, steadying it.

The boy grasped the girl's fingers and held them tightly. He kissed them. Then he kissed her on the mouth. Hungrily. *With an ardent throbbing need*, you could say.

His hand went up her shirt. Janet glared at them. All the openness she'd shown as we'd stood in the cemetery and toured the city drained away. A switch turned on, and she was Aunt Gonorrhea again.

Janet's eyes drilled into the couple. "Disgusting," she said too loudly. "*Boys.*"

I clutched my napkin. Whenever the subject of boys came up, Janet usually said the same thing, how she thought all my mother's feminist theories could be summed up in three words: *Men are beasts.*

According to my mom, when Janet was twenty-eight, her fiancé, Sam Katz, dumped her the night before their wedding. Sam had gotten his dental hygienist, Binnie Burkowitz, pregnant. Janet got a partial refund on the reception hall and the caterer, and she returned the gifts. The dress was not returnable. It had been shredded and sent to Sam in a cardboard box.

Now Janet skewered a pickled red pepper. "They only want one thing. Girls can't get it through their heads that boys have one mission: to fornicate and impregnate."

I turned around. I hoped that the sweet-looking white-haired lady at the next table hadn't heard us. Annie was suddenly absorbed in her sandwich.

Janet picked up her fork and knife and dispatched her meat loaf. "Men—and boys—are animals."

Annie wiped her lips with her napkin. "Well, I agree we're driven by biology. Humans are mammals. And only three percent of mammals are monogamous. Males have evolved to spread their genetic material around as far and wide as possible. Even animals who mate for life, like gibbons, swans, and foxes, still have outside couplings."

"Exactly. Beasts," Janet said. "I hear all the time about what teens your age are reading on the internet, and how you're 'sexting' and sharing pornographic photos." She touched the sugar packets. "You girls are too young to realize that boys will tell you anything to take advantage of you."

I tried to think of a new subject—how to distract her? Could we talk about nice pretty cemeteries instead?

She gazed at me with her most intense glasses-on-a-stalk-of-broccoli stare, then took a deep breath. "There's something we need to discuss."

She reached into her pocketbook and pulled out a letter. She put her glasses back on and adjusted them on her nose. "This arrived at my house this morning."

Long white envelope, neat black script. Will.

A letter from Will with the top ripped open. My stomach fell.

She handed it to me. I looked inside and pulled out the poem—a short one, half a page.

E—I thought you'd love this.

It was by Emily Dickinson.

I measure every grief I meet.

"Who's this from?" Janet asked me.

"Why did you open my mail?" I gaped at her.

"Why did he send you that? I found it very cryptic."

"It's a poem. Just a poem." I couldn't believe she'd opened it. Even my mom respected federal privacy laws and never opened anything addressed to me.

Janet's eyes narrowed. "Who's Will Freeman?"

I thought fast. "We edit our high school literary journal together. That's all. He's sending poems that we're going to include in the next issue. Every issue highlights famous poems."

"Why did he need to send it here?"

"Because Mrs. Peech, our faculty adviser, asked us to work on it over the summer. If you don't believe me, you can ask Mrs. Peech. She won't believe that you *opened it*."

I hoped she wouldn't try to contact Mrs. Peech.

"The postmark is from Los Angeles. Are you going to see this person while you're there?"

"No," I said. "Why would I?"

Her eyes looked huge behind her glasses. "It's not that I'm against young people exploring a dating type of relationship. It's that I believe they should be well educated about the dangers of these situations, and of course be supervised. And I don't believe that privacy should exist among young people anymore. Not in this day and age. Not with the internet."

"Some people my age barely even use the internet," I said.

Well, one person. One person in the world. And I had to fall in love with him.

She fingered a button on her green shirt. "You know, I get paid to discuss these issues with teens. It's part of my job. I expanded my business last year to include workshops with private schools. I teach about safer driving, and my Lifestyle Choices presentation was recently featured in *Cleveland Parent* magazine."

"I'm sure it's a great presentation," Annie said politely. She probably thought that would pacify Janet and make the normal side of her return. Little did she know.

Out came the iPad from Janet's bag. She placed it on the table between us and opened up PowerPoint. "I'll just show you the beginning," she said. "Though it's much more effective on a large screen."

"LIFESTYLE CHOICES" flashed in red block letters on the tablet. Janet swiped through the pictures—a stock photo of two teenagers holding hands while strolling down a sidewalk, then one of a girl, alone, silhouetted in darkness.

"Unfortunately, teenagers often make decisions without thinking of the consequences," Janet told us. The screen read: "ONE IN FOUR TEENS IS DIAGNOSED WITH AN STD EACH YEAR."

The next photo: Lesions. Crusting sores and yellowy blisters around a girl's lips.

I put down my fork.

Annie's mouth dropped open.

"Herpes on the face," Janet said. "Most teenagers believe oral activity is completely safe. They're mistaken."

The oozing blisters trailed across the poor girl's cheeks, toward her nose.

Next: A crusty rash engulfed a man's cheeks like barnacles roosting on the skin.

"Syphilis on the face," she said.

Then another girl, her brown hair tied back in a ponytail, one eye red as blood.

"Gonorrhea on the eyeball."

I shook my head. I knew we'd be hearing about gonorrhea.

On Janet went, photo after photo, sore after sore, some on hairy areas that I hoped I'd never be asked to identify.

She gleefully shut the iPad off. "That's just a sample. Hopefully on our next visit I can show you the whole thing."

There was more?

"I want to protect you," Janet said. "I feel it's my responsibility as an adult to help you avoid making big mistakes. I want you to be safe." She separated the sugar and artificial sweetener packets, making sure all were right side up.

Annie and I were speechless.

The waitress stopped by our table. "Would you like dessert?"

We said, "No thank you."

"I have pie in the freezer at home," Janet said brightly.

"I'm sorry," I whispered to Annie as we walked to the car. "I didn't know she'd gone this wacko."

Annie's mouth was still half open. "I'm staying a virgin until I die. Did you see that *eyeball*?"

We drove to Janet's house. She lived in a gated development called Castle Ridge. The entire house, inside and out, looked like it had been dipped in Clorox: white stucco, white carpet, white walls, white tables and sofa and chairs. I gave Janet the bag of bagels we'd brought for her.

"Murray's!" She touched the bag tenderly. "I'm going to freeze them," she said, as if that was the highest compliment she could give to a bagel. She opened the freezer door.

It was the biggest freezer I'd ever seen in my life. It looked as if it had eaten three other freezers. It overflowed with frozen kosher dinners and foods of every kind.

"When you live alone, you have to freeze everything," she explained. Her hands swam through the boxes of vegetables. She was concerned that Annie and I hadn't eaten enough vegetables that day, so she microwaved a package of mixed corn, carrots, and peas for us. Annie and I set the white plates and napkins on the table.

While the microwave whirred, I lingered for a long time in Janet's living room, staring at the photos on the wall. She'd hung up a dozen framed photos of our family, pictures that I'd never seen—ones of my mom and Janet as kids, photos of Freda and Abraham, and pictures of my mom, my dad, and me.

"I love your Snoopy dress," Annie said as she looked at a photo of me. It had been taken when I was five years old.

"Pretty fancy. My mom got it at a thrift shop."

I felt a pang of longing as I stared at a picture of my parents and me hugging, sitting on a rock in Central Park. I must've been only two or three in the picture. The sun shone on us, bright on our beaming faces.

"Your mom and dad were so happy in those years," Janet said. "You were a happy baby."

My mom never threw away any photo albums after my dad died—she stored them in the back of her closet—but I never asked to look at them. Now I knew why: because it hurt too much. Our family sitting in Central Park, hugging. I couldn't believe the smiling, carefree kid in the photo was me. We had no idea what would happen to us.

We sat down to eat.

I stuck my fork in a rumpled pea. The food was thoroughly cooked, but everything had a slightly puckered, waterlogged feel, as if even the carrots were tired from their epic climate-shifting journey to our plate.

I thought about Will. Seeing him would sweep away all the bad feelings. When he kissed me on the street and on the roof, his kisses removed the world for a little while. His love, and loving him, seemed like an antidote to grief.

When I'd read about Lilith and Sage being swept away and swept off (there was always a lot of sweeping in romances), I'd always wondered what it would feel like in real life. I had no idea that the books never captured it entirely—that it felt so much better, more intense, that I felt it with my whole body—since the night with him, I didn't crave cookies or online message boards or books in the same way I used to. I didn't need any of the things I used to use for comfort. The thought of him had become the comfort.

I even felt less anxious when I thought about the recovery of the wreckage. The news articles had stopped for a while— we were still awaiting analysis of what the recorders said, and whether they'd retrieve the rest of the wreckage from the ocean floor. I thought again of what Will had told me: *The recorders will confirm what you already know: he wasn't scared.* Ever since he'd said that, I felt less frightened, too.

I watched Janet inspect her fork and her plate for cleanliness and signs of contamination, and it occurred to me that Janet was afraid. She was afraid of germs and diseases and sex and heartbreak, of her broken engagement, her old messy love.

It doesn't have to be a mess, I wanted to say.

It could be like me and Will.

Easy. Because that's how it had felt—easy to fall for him, easy to let the world fall away, to escape into dreams of him in the same way I escaped into books.

Loving him was easy. The hard part was how to keep it that way.

O Love, O fire

The next morning Janet looked like a giant eggplant. She wore purple high-waisted pants and a purple button-down shirt. I didn't know why her fashion sense was modeled on various vegetables. Maybe it was her way of expressing an inner hunger for all the fresh produce she didn't eat.

I'd heard her alarm go off at six, and then she'd been talking on the phone and emailing. Last night, when she'd said good night to us, she'd seemed wistful. She'd hugged me and said, "I'm so glad that you came. I wish you could visit more often."

This morning she seemed much more cheerful. As our waffles rattled in the toaster and she melted the orange juice concentrate, she grinned and whistled to herself.

"I have good news," she told us. "Your mom and I talked last night—she's been so worried about you girls—and I said, 'Do you know, I'm looking at my schedule and it wouldn't be too hard to rearrange things so I could join them.' I've got clients all over the country, so this is a great opportunity for me to see them. I've been planning it last night and this morning, and I can come with you all the way to LA. Well, I'll miss the Arizona stop since I have six contacts to see in Texas—the Texas market is a huge one for what I do—but I can take a quick flight from Dallas to LA and meet you at the bus station there as soon as you arrive."

I froze. "That's really not necessary."

She'd already bought the ticket. She showed us the print-out from Go Blue. "The whole trip will be a tax write-off, too. I've got a client in LA who lets me use their condo, so we don't have to stay in a hotel. I know your mom told me that resort is sponsoring the show and you can stay for free, but it's probably overrun with teenagers doing god knows what. The condo will be better. Your mom was so relieved to know I'd be with you most of the way. I even thought about driving you, but I can't take that much time off work. This way I can work while we travel. I even have an ergonomic lap desk." She pointed to a big black square thing on the table. "I'm sorry I won't get to see Lulu in Tucson. I always like seeing her. But you'll be in great hands there, and I'll get to hear all about it in LA."

"Fantastic," I said. I felt a little sick. I hoped to see Will every one of the three nights we'd be in LA, and as much time during the day as possible—how could that happen if Aunt Janet was with us?

Annie and I went back to our room to finish packing.

"Aunt Gonorrhea. On. Our. Trip." I sighed. "I'm sorry."

"Does she know there's no freezer on the bus?"

"She's going to show Will those eyeball pictures. He'll never go near me again."

"She'll probably make him swim in Purell."

"I'm going to shoot myself."

"Janet won't stand for that. Way too messy."

But we didn't seem to have a choice.

Janet hummed cheerily on the way to the bus station— she wanted to leave her car in her garage during the trip, so we took a taxi. We left over an hour early, since she insisted on being early for everything. After a while, as the taxi sped along, I saw something out the window.

CITY CHILI

"Stop the car!"

I said it without even thinking and pointed frantically at the restaurant. The driver followed my hand motions and turned into the parking lot.

"What are we doing?" Janet looked confused, and when she realized we were stopping for chili and not emergency resuscitation, she asked, "Seriously? The meter's running!"

"It's a flat fare," I said.

Janet muttered something under her breath that sounded like "chili-crazy teenagers," and then stewed in silence as Annie and I headed into the restaurant.

You could order a "Way"—a Three-Way, Four-Way, or Five-Way—steaming spaghetti covered with chili, onions, red beans, and a layer of neon cheese. I ordered a Five-Way for Annie and me to share—I figured we should go all out, when in Ohio.

Janet looked completely disgusted. She was speechless. I got the order to go so we could eat it for lunch on the bus.

Annie and I settled into the first-row seat, and Janet chose the empty row across from us.

"Isn't this lovely," Janet said as she settled herself in her seat. She sanitized her hands and our hands, and she sprayed disinfectant on the upholstery. She clutched her purse to her chest and glared ferociously at the other passengers as they boarded, as if daring them: *Just try and steal it*. Nobody sat beside her.

I checked my texts. Three new ones from my mom.

Are you ok? I worry when I don't hear from you.

Janet told me you're fine, but it would be nice to hear from you too.

How's it going w/Janet there? So nice of her to change her schedule and join you!

I wrote back:

Super nice.

At the moment, Janet was studiously spraying a dark brown stain and blotting it with a wipe.

It was my idea! I'm so happy she could do it.

Yay! Thanks!

I wanted to text my mom: *I would shoot myself, but instead I'll go poison myself because Janet would find that a nice sanitary way to die.*

I turned toward Janet, who had put her cleaning supplies away and was now typing on her laptop.

"You'll probably be really busy in LA?" I asked her across the row.

"Oh, very. My business is thriving. I tell everyone, the internet and its lack of rules and safeguards is the best thing to ever happen to my business. I'm hiring a staff soon, you know. The more engagements I book, the more I realize I can't do it all myself." I tried to picture who Janet would hire. A whole staff dressed like eggplants.

"It's good you'll be busy. Because we'll be busy with the show," I said. "Really busy."

"I understand," she said. She kept writing notes and typing on her laptop.

Annie was having her own texting drama with her sisters. I looked over her shoulder.

Mom just told me she worked back-to-back shifts because you forgot yours??! You promised you'd take over while I'm away. DO YOUR SHIFTS! YOU PROMISED!

Jenny and Lala both wrote back, "Sorry!" with about twelve goofy emojis.

Annie sighed and returned to her books.

I took out my lit notes—I was making a set of flash cards for Annie about literary figures—and I looked out the window. The city coasted by, and the land became dotted with barns and silos again, and I thought about how I'd describe our trip to Will, how I'd tell him about my worried mother, Annie's sisters, Aunt Janet's disease talk, stopping for chili, and the cows and cornfields—and I realized I wasn't only living the trip, but also taking notes for the tales I'd tell him afterward.

There was one sentence I couldn't get out of my head, though.

They only want one thing.

I looked over at Janet. Her voice had invaded my brain.

Will didn't only want one thing. He wasn't a beast. (Although, if I was completely honest, maybe there was something a *little* beasty about him—his arms, strong and wide and bracing, the weight of him as he kissed me.)

Maybe a little beastiness wasn't a bad thing.

We'd made out for hours, all night, but we didn't do it. Why didn't we?

A part of me wished we had done it, despite Janet's pictures. Maybe it would've cemented things between us, bound him to me. *The communion of souls. The dance as old as time. The delicious paradise of two becoming one.* Maybe if we'd done it, he would've found a way to stay in New York all summer.

But how did it feel to have a *raging wild dagger* inside you, making you bleed? *A throbbing moisture missle? A flaming javelin? A heat sword?*

We didn't do it because I was scared to. I didn't need Janet's gonorrhea eyeballs to frighten me—I was already totally freaking terrified.

I was scared not only of it hurting physically, but of it hurting my feelings, or changing them, or crushing them. It seemed like such a momentous thing, too enormous to even figure out. During the night, I told him, "I'm a—I haven't—I never—" I was too scared and embarrassed to even say the word *virgin*. (Would it make me sound like a loser? Did he somehow know that the only guy in high school who'd liked me so far was David Dweener, who probably kept his *Cats* T-shirt on in bed? That I'd barely even kissed anyone ever?

Would he think I was pathetic and weird?) But he said gently, patiently, "We won't do anything you don't want to. We'll take it slow," and our clothes stayed on, I spent the whole night in his arms, and though he seemed a tiny bit disappointed, I kept thinking, We'll have time for more later. We'll have plenty of time for more.

In romance novels, sex seemed kind of ridiculous, with its orbs of flesh and manhoods, but then why, in real life, did it seem so serious? On the roof with Will, each touch and kiss made me feel more in love. Did he feel that also? Is that what his kisses meant? Would sex feel like that—an even bigger expression of love?

Would I ever have the guts to do it with Will?

I wanted to talk to Annie about it again. We'd rehashed the night on the roof dozens of times, but I never stopped wanting to talk about it. I waited till Janet had fallen asleep, the bottle of sanitizer still in her lap, and I turned to Annie and whispered, "Do you think there's really a chance of getting all those diseases? Do you think it hurts to . . . do it?"

She put down her book and checked to see if Janet was asleep, too. "Have you ever seen a video of elephant sex?" she asked quietly.

"No."

"Let's just say it doesn't look like the most comfortable thing on the planet. Their penises are four feet long."

"I'm not planning on having sex with an elephant."

"I know," she said. "My point is it doesn't look so comfy when humans do it either. I don't think it's about being comfortable or easy—it's a totally different thing. Don't worry. We've got plenty of time to have tons of sex and figure it all out. In college."

In college. Her mantra again. Sometimes I thought Annie was afraid I'd become like her sisters, wasting my life away, obsessed with boys—I loved romance novels, after all, and I'd fallen for Will, but my grades were good. I told her you could fall in love *and* get into a good college and be a success, but she never seemed to believe me.

"You should take a break from thinking about him," she told me, "and focus on the show." She tapped her study schedule spreadsheet.

I picked up the flash cards again.

She paused and gazed out the window, then turned back to me. "I'm worried about whether we even have a chance of winning at all."

"Of course we do," I said.

Her eyes shifted briefly to the floor. I thought of Annie's parents working nights and weekends at the laundromat, and her mom's shrine to Annie's success. I had to stop thinking of Will and focus on winning Annie the scholarship.

I checked the map. We'd be in Tennessee soon. One hour left to study.

Annie's phone buzzed. Her cousin had texted:

See you soon! Have SOMETHING BIG to tell you!

"What's she talking about?" I asked.

Annie shrugged. "She probably won some school prize or something. Her dad loves to call my mom and compare our grades and stuff." She rolled her eyes. "I haven't seen her in two years, but she's really nice. You'll love her. I can't wait to see her." We'd be in Tennessee for two nights before the longest leg of our whole trip—the fifteen-hour bus ride from Tennessee to Texas.

She went back to American historical trivia, and I made a stack of flash cards about feminist philosophers. She had her own method for memorization—she'd translate whatever she read in textbooks into her own shorthand. Right now she was memorizing suffragette history. I peeked over at her notes:

1848 LMott & ECS = 1st pblic mtg. 1866 LS & SB
= AERA. 1869 WY Trtry = 1st rt vote.

"It's like a mad gibberish," I said.

"It works," she said.

In northern Tennessee, we stopped at a rest area with a gas station and a shop called Lammy's SpeedyMart. They sold live crickets and pie milkshakes ("Drink Your Pie!")—and romance novels. After looking through the racks I picked up one called *American Amour*. It was about a Revolutionary soldier named John Peter LeVere who falls in love with Dorothea, the daughter of a British officer. I stuck it in my backpack and then joined Janet and Annie at a picnic table. We'd already eaten our chili on the bus (Janet had pinched her nose at the smell), but we were hungry again. We ate the freeze-dried strawberries that Janet had brought from home.

When we got back on the bus, Janet checked her watch. "We're making good time," she said. "For a nine-hour bus ride it's not as bad as I thought." She took a moment to glare at the other passengers.

Just pretend she's not there, Annie had said. I took out *American Amour* and turned to page one.

"You're not still reading those," Janet said. "I thought you would've outgrown them by now." When Janet had visited us over Passover last spring, she and my mom had mocked my romances together. Of a cover featuring Gurlag, she'd said, "He looks like he needs his shots. You'd have to take him to a veterinary clinic, not a doctor's office." My mom had laughed. "In my day, in high school, I read mostly Shakespeare," Janet had said.

Now Janet told me, "I don't know if it's wise to read those in *public*. You don't want people to think you're not smart."

I squinted at her. "I want people to think I like boys with rabies who won't get their shots."

"Hysterical," she said.

PART FOUR

TIME DOES NOT BRING RELIEF

Time does not bring relief; you all have lied
Who told me time would ease me of my pain!
I miss him in the weeping of the rain;
I want him at the shrinking of the tide;
The old snows melt from every mountain-side,
And last year's leaves are smoke in every lane;
But last year's bitter loving must remain
Heaped on my heart, and my old thoughts abide.
There are a hundred places where I fear
To go,—so with his memory they brim.
And entering with relief some quiet place
Where never fell his foot or shone his face
I say, "There is no memory of him here!"
And so stand stricken, so remembering him.

—Edna St. Vincent Millay

Real

L adybug!" Annie's cousin Grace cried as we stepped off the bus in Nashville; she raced toward Annie and enveloped her in a giant hug. I'd expected Grace to look like us—another person of the dorky persuasion—but she was gorgeous: tall and thin with long tanned legs. She'd tied her satiny ponytail with a green ribbon that glimmered like Christmas wrap.

She explained that Ladybug was Annie's nickname from third grade. A ladybug had landed on top of her head one day and stayed there for their entire lunch period. I'd never heard this story before. I hadn't met Annie until fourth grade, when her family moved to our neighborhood of Sunnyside, Queens, from Jackson Heights.

Grace saw my whistle; she frowned, looking like the hosts of makeover shows do when they're about to dump someone's entire wardrobe in the garbage.

"I have to wear it—my mom is kind of crazy and—" I started to explain with a nod toward Janet, but Grace had already skipped off, arm in arm with Annie, ponytail swinging. I shoved the whistle into my backpack. As soon as I could, I was going to throw that thing in the trash.

We climbed into Grace's parents' SUV; Grace and Annie sat in the middle row. I sat behind them, next to Janet and the family dog.

Annie and Grace had seen each other only a few times since the Youngs had moved to Tennessee four years ago. "Do you remember Mrs. Lee from church camp?" Grace asked. "And her kid with the ratty knee socks?" They giggled. Grace said something in Korean and they laughed even harder. "So what's the big news?" Annie asked her.

Grace looked coy. "I'll tell you when we get to the restaurant."

Janet seemed relieved to be off the bus and in the Youngs' giant clean car. "Thank you so much for hosting us," Janet told them. "This is such a wonderful opportunity to expand my business to the South." I pitied the poor teens of Tennessee. They had no idea what was in store for them.

We drove to Shawnee, the town where Mr. Young worked for a data storage company; Grace's family had moved here for his job. Giant oaks shaded the streets, and kudzu covered the hillsides, lush and thick. We stopped to pick up Grace's boyfriend, Nick, on the way; he'd be joining us for dinner. He lived in a giant white house with columns in front. He had a shiny, porcine-pink face and blond hair cut so short you could barely see it. He squeezed in beside Grace and pinched her butt.

Her parents didn't see; they were absorbed in a conversation, and Janet was busy checking email on her phone. Apparently Nick found their obliviousness encouraging, because he leaned over and kissed Grace. *Slurped her* would be a more accurate description—he attacked her face like a squeegee tool. I tried to exchange looks with Annie, but she was staring out the window, studiously ignoring the display.

I missed Will. He didn't kiss like a squeegee tool. He was the opposite of a squeegee tool.

When Nick's hands finally released Grace, her eyes drilled into me, scrutinizing, as if asking, *Don't you wish you had this?*

Was she trying to make me uncomfortable? Because it was working. I looked out the window.

When we reached Grace's house, we gave them their gifts—Grace applied the lipstick in the hall mirror with a satisfied smile, and her parents oohed and aahed over the cookbook recipes for black-and-white cookies and Junior's cheesecake.

Grace's mom showed us to our rooms—Janet had a guest bedroom on the top floor, Annie would sleep in Grace's queen bed, and I'd sleep in Grace's brother's room—he was away visiting relatives in Korea. As Janet unpacked, Grace, Nick, and Annie and I sat on the porch and watched the sunset. Vines dripped from the trees, and everything glowed as if it had been dipped in honey.

"So," Grace said, holding Nick's hand, her gaze moving from my face to my hair (had it turned frizzy in the humidity? Was it a Jewfro all over again?). *"You* got the idea for this whole trip because of a guy, right?" Her tone was skeptical, almost accusing.

I nodded.

Annie gave me a *Sorry—maybe I shouldn't have told her* look.

Grace tilted her head. "The guy's your boyfriend, right?" she asked me.

Boyfriend was too much of a leap. "Kind of," I said. My voice sounded weak. I tried to sound more certain. "Sort of." Why did she make me so nervous?

"How long have you guys been together?"

"Um—" I shrugged. "A little while."

I couldn't say the truth. *Actually, I'm not exactly sure if I'd use the word "together." We kissed on a street corner and made out in a roof garden and now we write letters.* It would be too humiliating to say it out loud to her. All of a sudden, I felt like a fraud. What was I thinking, going on this trip?

Annie rescued me. "He's an amazing guy. He sends her famous poems. She got one yesterday. In the mail."

Grace considered this. "Sending a poem is so—" I thought she was going to say *romantic*, but she said, *"Weird.* Why doesn't he text or email it?"

"He's . . ." How to explain it without making him sound even weirder? "He likes . . . regular mail," I said.

She looked at me as if I'd said he liked to parade around in eighteenth-century knickers and a waistcoat while shouting Heigh-ho! and Odsbodikins!

Grace leaned on Nick's shoulder. "I don't think I could put up with a *kind of* anything myself. I mean, you love each other. Or you don't. If Nick and I never texted or emailed and lived thousands of miles apart, I'd just worry whether it was *real.*"

Well, your *real* has a face like a raw ham, I wanted to say. But I didn't say anything. Annie changed the subject.

A few minutes later, we got back in the car and drove to Pop's Happyland, the Youngs' favorite restaurant. Inside were rustic wooden tables and sawdust on the floor. I sat as far away from Grace as I could. Janet passed her sanitizer around, and Mr. Young ordered plenty for everyone to share: wings 'n' waffles, chicken-fried steak, biscuits and gravy, cheese grits, mac and cheese, red beans and rice, and fried okra. I told myself to forget Grace. At least the food was delicious.

I ordered iced tea and the waitress asked, "Sweet or unsweet?"

"Um . . . unsweet?" I'd never heard the word *unsweet* before. I'd never heard of chicken-fried steak either—I pictured a chicken wearing a chef's hat, throwing a steak into the deep fryer.

We'd been eating for five minutes when Grace whispered something to her father. He grinned, and they sat back in their seats.

"Grace has something important to share," Mr. Young said.

Had Nick given her syphilis on her eyeball?

Grace took a breath. "My dad wanted me to wait till dessert to tell you, but I can't keep it to myself anymore." She spoke slowly. "You're looking at one of the Smartest Girls in America."

I almost choked on my biscuit.

"You didn't tell me you auditioned!" Annie raised her eyebrows.

Grace smoothed her hair and beamed. "When you told me about the show, I thought, Why not? My dad said I should give it a try. I never thought I'd get picked. I've been waiting all this time to tell you. I wanted it to be a surprise."

Mr. Young tore into a chicken wing. "It's a great opportunity. Only in America can you get a college scholarship from being on TV."

Annie looked taken aback, and a small storm began to brew inside of me.

"You'll have some tough competition," Janet said, smiling. She patted Annie on the shoulder.

"I know *you're* going to win," Grace told Annie. "I just thought it would be fun to get the free trip. We fly out in three days—my dad's my official companion. My lifeline. We're getting there early so we can meet with a media consultant and a buzzer-skills coach. I guess these kinds of shows are all about the buzzer skills. You guys are staying at the Mirabelle too, right?"

"I have a client in LA with a lovely condo," Janet said, "so we won't be needing the hotel room. We'll have a kitchen there, and we can do laundry, and there's even a swimming pool."

My neck was too frozen to move.

"I can't believe you're going too," Annie said. "When Eva first found out about the show, *I* didn't even want to do it. Now I think I'm more excited about it than she is. Did you hear about the internship stuff?"

They chattered about MIT and Princeton, and Annie folded her arms in a way I'd seen lots of times before—her competitive *You think you might beat me but you are so, so wrong to even try* look—and I tried to stifle the inappropriate things in my head. I wanted to say, What are you doing on *our* show? Annie is *my* best friend. *Mine.*

Like a three-year-old.

They kept talking, and eventually I calmed the voices in my mind.

I couldn't stop thinking about what she'd said about Will and me, though. *Real.* I thought about it through dinner, the drive home, and while eating the entire box of Goo Goo Clusters that Mrs. Young had given me. I thought about it as I spent the night staring at wet bikinis and boobs, women with their mouths half open, grains of sand clinging to their lips—Grace's brother had plastered the walls of his room with an entire *Sports Illustrated* swimsuit issue. It was a cave of soft porn.

Annie and Grace were in Grace's queen bed. Their giggles floated down the hall.

My friendship with Annie had always felt solid and permanent, but now I could see all its holes—in just two years Annie would go to MIT. Grace would probably go there, too. Annie would have her new school and her summer internships and I'd be at Queens College, living at home. In two years it would never be the same with us again.

What did I have that was solid? That was real?

I listened to Will's mix for a while, and then I took out his letters and poems and touched the paper and ink. I couldn't shake this tiny seed of doubt in me—what if it wasn't real with Will? What if when I got there, he didn't feel the same as I did? What if *it* didn't feel the same?

Women always had these worries in romance novels, I told myself. They never felt secure until the last chapter.

I checked the clock. Grace and Annie laughed again. We had another whole day in Tennessee—when we'd planned the trip, we'd thought an extra day here would be fun.

I missed Annie. I wanted to talk to her and tell her everything.

I picked up my phone. No emails, no messages, except from my mom. I checked the message board. No news. Just the usual stream of old grief. I stared at my phone's screen as it blackened and went to sleep. I saw my face reflected in the blackness and felt so lonely all of a sudden.

I turned it back on and listened to my mom's voice mails. *Just checking in. Glad Janet's there but I'd still love to talk to you. Call me. Please call. Call soon.*

I dialed home; she answered on the first ring. It was the first time we'd spoken since I'd left, though I'd texted her dozens of times and sent her photos of the views out the bus window. (*Looks kind of nice!* she'd said.) This was only our second night away, but it already felt like I'd been gone for ages.

We talked about the weather, and a new Indian restaurant that opened down the block, and if Janet had reminded me to put on sunscreen, because windows didn't block the full spectrum of UV radiation, and whether I was wearing my whistle. I said I was, I was, I was.

"Are you okay?" she asked. "You don't sound right."

"I'm fine."

She was quiet for a moment. "It's not too late to come back, if you want. You're not that far away."

"I'm fine," I repeated.

"I'm serious. Call anytime day or night and I'll get you." Her voice cracked a little.

"Mom. What's wrong?"

"Nothing."

She sounded strange. Was she just worried? "I'm totally

being safe and careful," I assured her. "And Janet's here. You don't have to worry."

She was quiet. "I just miss you," she murmured. Her voice was hoarse, unnatural.

We said good-bye, and then *I* began to worry.

What was she eating while I was gone? Was she back to takeout containers and breakfasts of yogurt eaten standing in front of the fridge? Larry never cooked—he'd eat hot dogs three times a day if he could. I'd given her my Fresh Direct password. Had she already forgotten it? Who was making her omelets on the weekends? What if she forgot to double-lock the apartment door? One time she left her keys in the lock all night; I found them in the morning when I left for school.

I fingered my horseshoe necklace, feeling the angled edges of its tiny stone.

Sometimes when she was out late and I was alone in the apartment, listening to the rain drum on the window ledge, I'd wonder what it would be like to have it happen all over again.

It could happen so simply, just another phone call, my phone vibrating on my lap, *Hi, hello, I'm so sorry but I have some terrible news.*

A car accident. A mugging. Just last week a man had been killed two blocks from our apartment, struck by a car when it careened onto the sidewalk.

When you picture tragedies happening, it's always like a

Technicolor movie, everything too bright, glaring, loud, with screams and a thumping soundtrack. In real life it's nothing like that. When the bad news comes, it's so flat and regular and dull, the world so noiseless, so everyday, piercing you with its normalcy. My mom heard about my dad from my aunt first, who'd seen the crash reported on TV and knew my dad was flying that night. My mom had wordlessly stood up and picked up her date book with my dad's flight information inside it. She walked into her bedroom and calmly called the airline. They wouldn't give her a concrete answer until they could confirm the passenger list. She came back to me on the couch, and she didn't tell me what was happening, she didn't want me to know, she watched TV with me and she held me tight and I didn't know why until the morning. How quiet everything was, my bedspread the same muted shade of pink, a sunny morning in New York, just like any other morning. What the movies don't tell you is that the glaring colors and thundering music are only inside you.

To touch him again in this life

I can't believe I have you the whole day!" Grace said to Annie over breakfast on the porch of the University Café the next morning. Nick sat beside us; he guzzled his iced coffee with a loud slurp. Janet had gone to Nashville to meet with a client, but Grace's parents assured her they'd keep track of us. Which apparently meant letting Grace do whatever she wanted.

I'd hoped we'd go to the Grand Ole Opry, and showed Grace the travel pages we'd printed out, but she rolled her eyes and said she had much better plans for us.

Now Nick and Grace stepped outside to smoke a cigarette while Annie was in the café's bathroom. Grace had told us she was trying to quit, but that didn't seem to be working so well. I watched them. Nick's tentacles entangled her like ivy, going places where no tentacles should go.

They returned to the table, and Grace's red nails disemboweled her cinnamon bun. "I hope you brought your bathing suits." She grinned.

We hadn't. Grace lent a beige one-piece to me. She was

about five inches taller than me so it sagged everywhere, especially in the butt and the boobs, and she gave me flip-flops that were two sizes too big. I looked like I was wearing a grocery bag and a pair of flippers. She'd lent Annie a black bikini that fit perfectly.

At the local quarry the water was a fairy-tale blue. Annie and I couldn't swim, and Grace had only one kickboard. "You go first," Annie said, handing the kickboard to me.

"That's okay." I shook my head. "I'd rather sit on the shore and read for a while."

I wrapped a towel around myself, hiding my body in the grocery bag. I held up the book I'd bought at Lammy's SpeedyMart: *American Amour.* "Don't worry about me. I've got this." I turned to my dog-eared page in the middle.

While I sat on the rocks and read, Annie and Grace swam and Nick splashed them, making giant whoops. I ate an egg salad sandwich that Mrs. Young had packed for us, with eggs from her neighbors' chickens and dill from her garden. It was one of the best sandwiches I'd ever eaten, and I felt happy to be alone, reading, with thoughts of Will casting a brightness over everything, like the sun. There hadn't been a letter from him in Tennessee, but the doubts I'd had about him last night disappeared this morning.

Will put down his bowl of mutton stew. "Eva, never doubt my love for you," he told her. "It is as strong as my belief that we

*will become an independent nation." He finished the last bite of
her johnnycake and carried her to the hayloft.*

Eventually, Annie, Grace, and Nick came back onshore to
eat lunch and dry off. Grace blotted her hair with a towel and
glared at my book's cover. "Can you please put your man titty
away? It's giving me a headache."

American Amour had a particularly bad cover: pink foil lettering and a long-haired, bare-chested, glistening leviathan
on a horse. His nipples were the size of dessert plates.

"I can't believe you read that crap," Grace said.

"It's not crap," I said.

"*Grace*," Annie warned her. "Come on."

Grace shrugged. "Sorry. I just never liked that stuff. I
always thought it's not . . . decent."

I didn't know how having your boyfriend's octopus tentacles up your hoo-hoo in public was considered decent either,
but I didn't say anything. I didn't want to have a confronta-
tion. We were leaving tomorrow, I reminded myself. I could
endure Grace for one day. (And then maybe murder her when
we got to California.)

They finished eating and drying off, and we packed up
our things; we took turns changing out of our bathing suits
behind a rock. We climbed back into Grace's car, and Nick
drove us down rural back roads.

A small plane flew overhead. Whenever I heard one, I did

this thing where I pretended it wasn't happening; I didn't listen; I focused on a country music song on the radio and shut the world out until it passed.

We drove by an open field, and Grace touched Nick's arm and whispered to him. They turned a corner, and we drove for several miles until we reached a fence.

"Nick's brother works here," Grace said. Nick drove us past the gate. There they were, in the distance: tiny brightly colored planes, lined up like toys, with a larger prop plane behind them.

A giant sign read:

MEYER'S SOARING— THREE GLIDER RIDES, GET ONE FREE.

Cold seeped into my chest. I couldn't move.

"Ed started the business last summer," Nick told us.

"We can go for free!" Grace trilled.

Ed stepped out of a wooden booth and greeted us. He had a mustache so thick, it looked like a mouse was napping on his lips.

"Y'all ready to glide?" Ed asked. He placed his hands on his hips.

Annie searched my face. She pulled Grace aside and they talked for a while. I watched Annie fold her arms and stare at the dirt.

Annie returned to me and said, "We're not doing this. We're going to go right home—"

"What did you tell her?" I asked.

"I didn't say anything about your dad. I said you have a phobia." She shook her head. "She doesn't get it."

Grace came over to us. "A lot of people use glider rides as a way to get over their fear of flying," she said. "Ed and Nick take tons of people out like that, and you wouldn't believe how much it helps them. They've cured them all."

I didn't look at her. I was afraid if I did, I'd fall apart.

She walked back to Nick and Ed, whispered something to them, and shrugged. *That girl is so high-maintenance*, she probably said. *She's bringing everybody down. She won't let Annie have any fun.*

Grace was the easier friend. She required less. Annie would rather take this trip with her.

"No, it's fine," I told Annie. "I'll just wait. I'm right in the middle of my book, at a great part. . . . I'll stay here and read. You should go."

"No. I'm not going," Annie said.

"I'm serious. Really—you should go."

She searched my face again, trying to see if I was lying.

I didn't want her to go. My insides screamed, *Don't do it— you could die!* But I couldn't say that. Grace already hated me and thought I was a crazy person. If I said how I really felt, Grace would laugh. Everyone would laugh.

"She's waiting for you." I nodded at Grace, who was leaning

against the booth, talking to Nick and Ed, looking impatient.

"You ladies flying or not?" Ed called to us.

Annie glanced at me one more time.

"Go." I nudged her toward them. Then I turned and walked toward Grace's car.

Annie looked back at me; Grace touched her arm and hurried her toward the glider.

I stood by the car alone. I should've said the truth. I should've said: *You're going to fly in a plane that looks like a toy, without a motor? ARE YOU FREAKING KIDDING ME?*

It was crazy. Grace was going to kill my best friend. And I was going to stand there and watch it. Why didn't I have the guts to say the truth?

They were in the glider already, with Ed in the leader plane. He kept checking his phone. He was probably Googling how to fly a plane. He looked like he hadn't washed his hands or brushed his teeth in years—I wouldn't trust him to fly a plane in a video game.

The motor started. Words caught in my throat: Don't do it. *Don't—*

They took off.

I couldn't watch. To the left of me, a forest surrounded the field. I looked toward the car, but I couldn't sit and read. I had all this excess nervous energy. I needed to move. I turned and started running. Why had I said she should go? I was such a lying idiot. What was wrong with me?

I ran. Pine trees. Their needles covered the ground, a

brown carpet winding around the evergreens.

I stopped and leaned against a tree, panting. I heard the motor rumbling, and I tried to pretend it wasn't happening, but I couldn't—my skin started to lift off me as the sky shook. I pinched my thumbnail, watching it turn white.

I slumped down. Any new hurt dug up the old ones, unburied them. After my dad died, one of our neighbors shoved a card under our door in an orange envelope. Three kittens sleeping on a clock. It said: *Time heals all.*

Aside from making a line of funny sympathy cards, someday I want to make ones that just tell the truth:

> *Sorry to hear he died.*
> *Now you're going to feel miserable forever, pretty*
> *much.*
> *GL with that!*

I turned on my phone. I had service.

I checked the message board.

There were eighty-two new ones. Fran wrote the first. It was a link to a newspaper article. From this morning.

Bodies in Airplane Crash Are Recovered from Ocean Floor

By HUMPHREY COLES

A recovery team removed the remains of four victims from the wreckage of Freedom Airlines Flight 472, which crashed in the Atlantic two years ago, from a section of the fuselage that had been wedged in the ocean floor.

The bodies were brought to the surface from a depth of approximately a mile and a half, Frank Longbrown, the chair of the National Transportation Safety Board, said. The remains will be rushed to a laboratory in New York, where an attempt will be made to identify the victims within two weeks. The genders of the victims were not yet certain.

Longbrown raised the possibility that more bodies might still be recovered. He said "much is unknown" about how many victims remain in the wreckage of the jet on the ocean floor. "The retrieval process is in an exploratory stage," he said.

In the cold climate of the sea bottom, Longbrown said, the bodies may be intact but delicate.

The canopy of trees above me was so thick, I could barely see the sky. I was shivering. Freezing.

I ran. I kept running until I didn't feel my feet anymore.

Don't fall apart. Don't fall apart. Don't fall apart.

It didn't change anything. First the wreckage. Then the flight recorders. Now they'd found bodies. It didn't matter. He was dead. So what if they finally found the rest of his body? *So what so what so what so what so what so what?*

It mattered. It mattered more than anything in the whole entire world.

It mattered because I cared what he felt, whether he spent those last seconds screaming. It mattered because I didn't want the Greek myths to be true, to think that like the dead warriors in Hades, he was trapped forever with his body smashed beyond recognition. Or strapped into his seat. Forever.

I kept running through the forest, pounding the questions and fear into the ground, trying to shut the feelings off, close them down. I ran until I could barely breathe. Then I stood still and steeled myself. I did this literally, as I felt my insides crumbling—I pictured steel girding my body, pylons up my ribs, along my arms, bracing me, holding me up, metal around me.

I reached the airfield.

T hey landed safely.

Grace said, "That was so much fun!"

Annie bit her lip, and I could feel her eyes on me, but I knew if I said anything, the slightest peep, the steel would collapse, dissolve in front of all of them.

"Nick and Grace want to have another ride," Annie told me.

I nodded. I watched Grace and Nick get back into the glider.

Annie brushed her hair out of her eyes. "I'm sorry Grace is such a . . ."

She left the phrase hanging there. "She's just jealous of you," she finally said.

"What?"

She gazed at her feet. "Because we're doing this. Having this trip she's not a part of."

Then she moved closer to me, grasped my hand. "You'll always be my best friend," she told me as we walked back to the car.

We never said that to each other anymore. We used to say it

all the time, in fifth and sixth and seventh and eighth grades, constantly, *You're my best friend*, and then for some reason we'd stopped. I guess because we felt we'd gotten too old for saying those kinds of things, too mature to need the reminder.

I squeezed her hand back.

Nick drove us back to Grace's house quickly, and after he parked the car, Annie and I hung behind in the garden. Grace and Nick disappeared inside.

I showed Annie the article once they were out of sight. I watched her read it on my phone, the corners of her mouth turning downward.

Hold it together. Stay calm. Try not to be so thin-skinned.

"'Much is unknown.' Who writes this shit? Who *says* this shit? I'd like to shove his 'unknown' up his goddamn 'exploratory stage,'" she said.

I laughed. We both laughed. The sun hid behind the late-afternoon clouds.

She hugged me. "It will be okay. Whatever they find. I know it will be okay."

I tried to believe her. It would be so wonderful to believe her. I felt like two different people again, the one standing here with my best friend and the other girl who had a black hole growing in her chest, hollowing out her stomach, sucking away everything good.

He was dead already. Why did it feel like he kept dying again and again?

Sweat ran down my neck.

"Let's walk," Annie said. She took my arm, and we headed down the road. I tried to breathe. She kept my arm wound in hers. "It's so green here. Look at it." She waved at a meadow filled with wildflowers. "You can actually step places where thousands of people haven't already stepped today. Imagine walking along every day and not smelling pee and garbage."

I laughed and began to breathe again.

"I like the country," Annie said. "At least I think I do. Maybe I even like it better than the city. Not that I want to move here, but—I like smelling flowers instead of garbage."

"Me too," I said.

We kept walking.

"It'll be okay," she told me again.

I nodded. The farther we went, the better I began to feel.

We passed a stone wall and a dirt path alongside it. We took the path into the woods. I thought of how when I was a kid, I spent ages gazing at Edward Gorey's and Maurice Sendak's illustrations of trees and forests and felt this shiver of excitement and mystery. Earlier, as I ran through the forest near the airfield, I'd been too panicked to look around. Now it was different, being with Annie.

"Sometimes I feel like I'm always wanting something, you know?" she said as we stepped over a fallen log. "Good grades. Academic prizes. To win this show. Sometimes I feel like, What if I could just stop? Maybe I should just go to some college in the middle of nowhere and chill out."

I nodded. "I know." I'd never heard her say that before, but I knew how hard the pressure was for her. I wished we could both stop all our endless yearning.

After we'd walked for a while, we came across a run-down, abandoned cabin in the woods. It was missing its roof.

"Look up there," Annie said, pointing. There was an old, tattered treehouse. "Gurlag's house. He's followed you here. He's going to swing you up there on his vine and show you his meat sword."

"I think in that series it's called a manroot."

"Both sound so appealing. I picture a manroot as kind of looking like a long, crooked carrot." She wrinkled her nose.

"We should move here and start our own vegetable farm specializing in organic manroots."

"We'll make millions. Screw this scholarship. The TV show. It's our new plan."

We kept walking along the path, and I started to feel like myself again. Then my phone rang.

"Where did you disappear to? We're worried sick!" It was Janet. "I see that you're far from the house. I have the Locate My Kids app on. What are you doing there?"

"We just went for a walk," I said. "That's all."

"Well, come back soon please. It's nearly dinnertime."

I hung up and sighed. "Janet."

"We can hire her to work on our farm with us. She can

keep the manroots and meat swords disease-free," Annie said.

"Sounds idyllic," I said.

When we returned to the house, everyone was drinking iced tea on the porch. Janet was dressed in pale beige from head to toe today, like a stalk of cauliflower.

"By the way, this came in the Youngs' mail this morning while you were out," Janet said, and picked up an envelope beside her. She handed it to me.

His name, his handwriting. She hadn't opened it. My chest pounded.

"Another poem for the literary magazine?" Janet asked.

Help me to shatter this darkness

I excused myself to the bathroom. It was the only place I could think of to be alone.

I sat on the edge of the tub with the envelope in my hands. Just holding it made me feel better. This was what I needed, a letter from Will.

I leaned against a fluffy green towel and tore it open.

Eva—

I just got off work. I've been helping set up my dad's new show at LACMA along with his four assistants. Moving things and answering phones and stuffing envelopes addressed to Herman Therbinder IV and Bunny Burmeister-Boddington (no joke) and other rich people, inviting them to the opening reception and to donate more gobs of cash.

I'm sitting in a coffee shop in West Hollywood right now. The guy making the coffee keeps blathering about his screenplay.

I wish I had something better to say but this

summer isn't going so great. All my dad and I do is fight. When we actually speak about something besides his show, he criticizes my mom. Last night we got in a huge fight about how he thinks my mom squandered the money he sent, how she made mistakes with her business, and all the things she did wrong while raising me. I can't even sleep in the same house as the man. Last night I slept outside in a tent. I thought when I came out here it would be different. We could start over. What a stupid dream.

My friend Jon in Seattle has a job for me up there. It's building houses. I think I'm going to take it. I don't know if I can stand another day of my dad's bullshit. Jon told me to just leave tonight. I might do it.

Will

This could not be happening.

I'd get to California in five days and he wouldn't be there.

The heat, which had seemed like a warm blanket in the morning, now felt like it would choke me. Why hadn't this letter said what I thought it would? I thought he'd say: *I can't believe you're coming out here. I can't wait to see you. My dad and I are having a hard time but I'll stick it out till you get here. Seeing you will help.*

My T-shirt grew damp with sweat. The letter was

postmarked from four days ago. Just a few days after the letter he'd sent to Cleveland.

For the first time, his mysterious side—disappearing at lunch, not caring if his phone was working, saying he didn't want people *to find me*—pissed me off. All I wanted in the world was to see him again. Why did that have to be so difficult?

Someone knocked on the door. Annie. I showed her the letter.

She read it and then handed it back to me. "Just call him. He might not have meant what he wrote. Or he could've changed his mind after he sent it."

My mouth felt dry as I dialed Will's cell phone—dead, of course. It went straight to his voice mail. I tried his father's house. Nobody picked up. I left a message. *This is Eva Roth. Please tell Will to call me.*

"What if he doesn't get the message?" I asked.

Annie thought for a minute. "Come with me," she said. We left the bathroom and quietly went up the back stairs to Grace's brother's room. Annie searched the desk until she found a spiral notebook. She tore out a blank page. "Write to him, then. We'll mail it as soon as we can. FedEx it overnight or two-day or as fast as they can get it there."

I paused. "What do I say?"

"Anything. Just tell him how you feel."

I picked up the paper and took out my pen. I scribbled his

name at the top. I started to write without thinking, and the words came out on their own.

Will,

I'd give anything to have one more day with my dad. One hour. Everything ~~sucks~~ ~~sometimes~~, but you have to stick it out and give it a chance. Talk to him about it. Tell him how he's making you feel. Tell him you need to spend some time alone together. When his show is over, you guys can take your own trip together, have time to connect.

Stick it out and things will get better. I promise.

We'll be in LA in five days. ~~I'll see you then.~~

Maybe you can call my cell phone? I'd love to talk. Please call when you can, or text or email me.

As soon as the words were on the page, I felt a little better. I wanted to say more, but I wasn't sure what. Writing the letter and knowing he'd hold this piece of paper in his hands felt like it would solve things, though. He wasn't really thinking of leaving before I got there. It was his misery from his dad talking. He didn't mean it.

Seattle wasn't too far. Even if he did go, he could come back to LA to see me.

He'd get my letter and it would change his mind.

Hope. There it was again in me, trilling out.

And Rosamunde Saunders's voice was back too: *Girl, send this damn letter and go get your man.*

I didn't want to hold anything back. I didn't want to pretend. I wanted him to read this letter and know how I felt. To put a seal on things, a certainty.

The truth.

I scribbled at the bottom:

I love you—
Eva

The words looked stark against the page. I'd never said those words to a boy. I'd never *felt* them about a boy. I folded it up and put it in the envelope before I could change my mind, and Annie took it downstairs and asked Mr. Young to mail it overnight.

PART FIVE

A COMMON LANGUAGE

the more I live the more I think
two people together is a miracle.
—Adrienne Rich

Kissing in America

We left Tennessee in darkness, at five o'clock in the morning, for our fifteen-hour bus ride. We'd said good-bye to Grace and her parents as they stood at their front door, bleary-eyed, and then went back to bed.

Annie and I claimed our first-choice front row; Janet sat across from us, behind the driver.

"Next stop, Texas," Janet said. "I've always wanted to visit Texas. You wouldn't believe how interested they are in my programs. At my meetings yesterday I was given three more contacts to see in Dallas. I'm assuming rates of STD—"

"It's too early to talk disease," I told Janet. "No gonorrhea till after ten a.m., ok?"

She made a quiet huffing noise and went through her settling-in routine: spraying the armrests and upholstery, laying a large cloth napkin on the top of the seat back (to avoid catching lice), and then stretching all her muscles as well as she could in the small row.

Annie flipped on the light above. She began to read a book she'd borrowed from Grace about American first ladies.

"Grace has read every biography of every first lady ever published." She sighed. "I'm so behind."

"I heard Grace practicing questions with her father last night. They're extremely well-prepared," Janet said.

Annie wrote a note on an index card. "Do you think we'll be ready?" she asked Janet, and showed her our study spreadsheet, with its check marks for every topic we'd covered so far. Janet put on her glasses and surveyed it all thoroughly.

"I'm not sure. I'm happy to help you, though. I was a history major in college. Summa cum laude," Janet said.

Annie looked up. "I could use help with history."

"I was also captain of the debate team. We used a buzzer in my day, and if I do say so myself, I was pretty good at it."

Annie put down her pen. "So what are your tips?"

Janet shook her arms, loosening her muscles. "It's all in the wrist flick." She slapped an invisible mosquito on her lap. "See?"

We practiced, looking like crazed women enthusiastically hitting ourselves.

The bus hummed as the sun rose; the road ribboned ahead. Annie and Janet kept slapping imaginary insects while I compiled facts about nineteenth-century novelists. For breakfast, we ate the corn muffins that Mrs. Young had packed for us.

All morning I checked for a voice mail, text, or email from Will—no word—and the message board. No news. Nothing new in the papers either. Trees and farms whirred by out the windows, and I decided I'd try to not think about it too much until I saw him. I knew that when he got my letter, he wouldn't go to Seattle. And if he was here right now, I knew what he'd say: *They'll find your dad and he'll be peaceful. He's resting in peace. Annie's right. It will be okay.* He'd understand. I'd be able to tell him things, the deepest things, just as I did in the roof garden.

But there was also this tiny voice in the back of my mind, this dark place that kept telling me: Everything, in fact, will *not* be okay. The very worst thing you imagine, your biggest fear, *does* happen, it happens to people every day. Parents die, children die, babies die, animals die, love is lost in a thousand ways every second. No one is ever safe.

What are the odds? our neighbor Mrs. Neegall had said, a hand over her mouth, when she found out how my dad died. *Well, don't worry*, she said. *Lightning never strikes twice.* But she was wrong. Lightning could strike twice, three times, or ten. When you're on the wrong side of the odds, the odds are meaningless. They don't protect you or give you comfort. The mask's been pulled off your eyes. You're never immune to disaster.

My phone came to life. My mom was awake on the east coast. She texted me:

Please keep your phone on! If you turn it off, the Locate My Kids app doesn't work & I can't see where you are.

MARGO RABB

I didn't turn it off.

You had it turned off just now.

We're just driving thru places w/no service.
You know where I am. On the way from TN to TX
w/Janet & Annie.

It makes me feel better to see you on the GPS.
THX FOR KEEPING IT ON!

She also kept inventing excuses to check in. An hour later,
she wrote:

Looks like the weather's really hot there!

It's summer. Hot. The 2 kinda go together.

Drink lots of water! You don't want to get
heatstroke. Janet told me you're wearing your
whistle! Thx!

I was tempted to blow the whistle right now, which I
wore tucked under my shirt when Janet wasn't looking.
*Emergency! I'm trapped on a bus and my crazy mom won't stop
texting me!*

Then she wrote:

I'm sorry I sound worried & keep asking you to
check in. I'm just not used to being away from
you. I really, really miss you.

I knew I was supposed to say *I miss you too*, but something kept me from saying it. I could feel her strings wrapping around me, wanting me to come back, to tie me down and have me live in our Queens apartment forever.

We stopped at a Minit Mart, and Annie and I bought chips to go with the peanut butter and apple sandwiches that Mrs. Young had made. The Minit Mart had a sign that said "Get Your Ammo Here."

Janet brought out bags of freeze-dried blueberries, and we sat at a picnic table (Janet wiped it down with a sanitizing cloth) at the edge of the parking lot.

"I'm glad I'm here with you girls," she said. "This bus line is not as bad as others I've ridden. I'm actually getting quite a lot of work done on my new presentation. Though all this sitting is wreaking havoc on my sciatica." She placed her foot on the picnic table bench and did several stretches. She wore light brown today, and looked like a potato doing yoga. A group of truckers walked by and stared at us. When she finished her exercises, she told us she had appointments to confirm in Texas, so she walked up the hill behind the parking lot to try to find better cell phone service. We watched her raise her phone in the air.

I took out my book. I only had a few pages left of *American Amour*. I finished it before Janet rejoined us for lunch—Dorothea and John Paul got married on horseback—and I put it away in my backpack so I wouldn't have to hear Janet call it a ridiculous fantasy, or whatever she might say.

The story was a fantasy, but the feelings were real, I thought as we got back on the bus. That yearning, the sparks, the enormity of love—I felt those exact things with Will. The thrill of what it felt like to be in his arms, to have him look at me as if I were the only person who existed in the world. Those feelings felt as real and true as any other feelings I'd ever felt. As real and true as grief.

As we drove on, we all lost cell phone service. On my phone a bold **E** appeared in the corner where the bars would usually be; then that disappeared too. **Searching . . .** it said, and it kept searching for over an hour. Finally, I turned it off.

Annie looked at her watch. "Grace is probably already packing for LA."

"Fab for her," I said. "I still can't believe she auditioned."

She shook her head. "She's not going to win. She's weak on art and literature—and she doesn't have the secret weapon."

"What secret weapon?"

"*You.*"

"No one's ever called me a weapon before," I said. "I kind

of like it. Like a secret literary superpower."

She shut her book. She paused. "I'm sorry Grace was such a jerk. I should've . . . I wish I'd stopped her more. It's just she's my only family member I have anything in common with. At all. And I think she was acting so weird because she's so unhappy."

I grunted.

"She hates Shawnee. She doesn't have any friends there, not really. They're one of the only Asian families in town. She told me that on Nick's birthday, his baseball teammates gave him chopsticks and a Chinese takeout menu as a joke. They think Chinese and Korean are the same thing. People always ask her what her immigration status is. If she's legal. She misses New York."

In our neighborhood in Queens, almost everybody's family was from another country—our local library had books in Korean, Spanish, Romanian, Chinese, Bengali, Gujarati, Hindi, and Turkish. Even the Jews were from Israel or Yemen or Ethiopia, or their grandparents, like mine, were born in Europe. My dad had come here from England when he was seven, and he said kids made fun of his accent so much that he'd watch *The Brady Bunch* and practice talking like an American, flattening his vowels, though British terms still slipped out when he was tired or angry. *Stuff the bloody broken dishwasher.* Will's grandparents were born in Saint Lucia. He'd told me that when he visited as a kid, all he saw was a

paradise—the sugar-white beach and the jewel-blue ocean—
and it wasn't till years later that he realized what poverty his
family lived in there. His cousins' house barely had a roof.

Annie had come to America when she was five—her father
came first and sent a postcard of the White House to Annie
and her sisters back in Seoul. She thought when they came
here they were going to live in the White House. She also
thought her hair would turn blond as soon as she stepped
onto American soil.

Janet was listening to our conversation as she looked
through one of Annie's history textbooks. "Immigrants have
never had it easy," she said. "Including your grandparents."
She glanced at me. "People didn't even use the word *immigrants* back then. They were foreigners. Refugees. Everyone
looked down on refugees. They thought they didn't deserve
to be here. Ahhh. Look at this."

In the V-J Day chapter, she'd come upon a photo of a couple kissing—a GI and a nurse.

She showed it to me. "Do you remember this? It was one
of my mother's favorite photos. She tore it out of a magazine
and kept it taped to the wall above the kitchen sink for years."

I remembered Freda's plastic-covered couches and chipped
brown plates, and eating buttered noodles at her kitchen table,
its peeling white laminate with steel edges, cracks running
across its surface like tiny black rivers. She called noodles
noonies, and while I ate them she'd pour a teacup of coffee for

me (actually milk with a drop of coffee in it). I felt so grown-up when I drank it. And I remembered looking at the photo of the kiss above the sink, its fading gray picture and crumbling yellow edges.

"She said it reminded her of her first kiss with Abraham in New York," Janet said. "On the street. He took her in his arms, and she leaned back, and he kissed her till she thought she'd faint."

I couldn't believe Janet had just happily said the words *kissed her till she thought she'd faint.*

"Of course in reality, after that, this country was never all that nice to them," Janet said. "Freda called America *a hard pain in my ass* or sometimes *a pain in my hard ass*—her English was never great." She paused. "They had crap jobs and no money. But she kept that photo pinned above the sink till the day she died. She loved believing in that kiss just the same."

Cowboys on fire

That night, we reached Calypso, Texas. The bus station wasn't even a station, but a 7-Eleven with a bench beside it. The sky was inky, full of stars.

Two young men in white straw cowboy hats, clean pressed button-down shirts, jeans, and cowboy boots stood in a halo of lamplight, leaning against the 7-Eleven window.

Destry and Ewing.

Holy holy holy shit.

I'd never met a cowboy in real life. The only cowboys I'd ever seen before were the gay guys who donned leather chaps and ten-gallon hats for the Halloween parade in the West Village.

We headed out the bus door. The cowboys approached us. They nodded, took their hats off, and said hello.

"Miss Janet? Miss Annie and Miss Eva?" the dark-haired one asked. The other was blond and taller, with a sharp-looking face.

We nodded.

"Mrs. Irma Steele sent us—she's real sorry she couldn't come get you herself."

I'd forgotten that Larry's mother's last name was Steele. Larry called her a chameleon—her second husband was a Buddhist, so she became a JewBu. Her third husband was Irish Catholic, so she converted and bought a giant Virgin Mary statue for their yard. And now, her fourth husband, Clint Steele, was a Texan and a Baptist. On Larry's birthday, Irma sent him an ashtray in the shape of Texas (though he didn't smoke), a Texas star–adorned teapot (he didn't drink tea), and a Lone Star Bible (Larry was still Jewish).

We shook hands with the cowboys and introduced ourselves. Chance and Trent. Chance had the dark hair. Janet didn't shake hands; she waved hello, probably fearing cowboy germs.

"Mrs. Steele is at a meeting, and Mr. Steele's in Fort Worth at a cattle auction, so all we have is the pickup tonight. There's room for two up front, but two of you, plus Trent, will have to be in the back row," Chance said.

"The back?" Janet eyed the second row of the truck. "Are there seat belts?" She opened the door and peeked inside. It looked like a wild animal had died in there—there were black and brown stains on the seats, bits of hay all over the place, and fluff peeking out from the torn seat cover. The floor had nails and screws rolling around, dirty straw, empty tobacco tins, caked mud, and a big Styrofoam cup filled with what appeared to be liquid dirt.

"Seat belt's broken," Trent, the tall blond one, said. "Quick drive, though."

Janet turned pink. I wondered if she'd squirt sanitizer over the whole thing or if it was too far gone for her to even try.

"I'll ride in the back row," I volunteered. It wasn't a big deal to me. Annie offered to also.

Janet shook her head. "No. I'd never forgive myself if something happened to you girls, riding without a seat belt. I don't like this, but I guess we don't have a choice, do we?" She asked if there were taxi companies out here. They said no. Our options were to ride in the truck or walk ten miles. Janet contemplated this, shifting in her loafers.

"It'll be fine," I urged her. She finally relented. We let Annie have the front seat beside Chance.

They placed our luggage in the truck bed, and Trent climbed into the back row first. His long legs barely fit, even with his knees scrunched together. Janet and I squeezed in beside him. I'd never seen her face so furrowed. I smelled something unfamiliar, and it took me a moment to figure out what it was—*horse*.

Chance turned on the ignition. Janet closed her eyes as we barreled down the road. The windows were open, and my hair flew around my face. The lights from the 7-Eleven disappeared; a crescent moon hovered above, and the warm night air spun around us.

I peeked at Trent on the other side of Janet. He picked up the cup of liquid dirt and spat something into it.

Janet mumbled something that sounded like *shmegegge*, a

Yiddish word for *idiot* that my grandmother used to u.

Trent caught me staring at him and smiled. I turned away. He had a shy smile, his mouth curling ever so slightly, as if he wanted to laugh but stopped himself before he did.

The truck hit a bump. Janet placed her hand on her forehead, looking like she wanted to teleport back to Cleveland.

We turned onto a road next to a sign:

WELCOME TO CALYPSO, TEXAS
POPULATION 1,242

More people lived on my block. We bounced down dirt roads and gravel roads until we reached Larry's family's property. We drove past the trailers where the ranch hands lived, and stables and barns, and finally stopped in front of a sprawling house with a massive metal star on the front.

We climbed out of the truck. Trent and Chance lifted our bags as if they were light as pillows.

They showed us the house, which Brooklyn-born Irma had decorated. The living room: a wooden coffee table in the shape of Texas. Cowhide lamps. Texas stars on the fireplace grate. A Texas-shaped clock. A cross made from the tops of cowboy boots. "Howdy" spelled out in welded horseshoes. The bedrooms were named after heroes from Texas history: the Sam Houston Room, the Stephen F. Austin Room, the J. Frank Dobie Room.

"There you are!" Irma found us upstairs. "I'm so sorry I couldn't pick you up myself—I've had meeting after meeting for the Miss Rodeo committee and I just couldn't miss this one." She hugged us like we were old friends. Irma thanked the boys and squeezed Trent's cheek. Apparently there was a little bit of Jewish grandmother left in her yet.

"Anything else we can do to help, ma'am?" Chance asked her.

Irma asked us, "Anything you need, girls?"

To have them tell us their names were Destry and Ewing and they were whisking us away on their stallions?

We shook our heads.

"Good night, Mrs. Steele. Miss Janet. Miss Annie, Miss Eva."

We watched them leave; they walked slowly, with a man-swagger. Did they teach strutting classes at cowboy school?

Irma set out towels imprinted with spurs and saddles, and we gave her the box of chocolates that my mom and Larry had picked out—pecan and caramel turtles from a midtown shop I'd never heard of called Betty's Cocoa.

"Oh, aren't you sweetie pies," Irma said, and immediately ate three. "My favorite."

Janet went into her room, out of earshot; I pulled Irma aside. "Did any letters arrive for me?" I asked quietly. I'd hoped one might be waiting for me here.

She shook her head. "No. No letters, I'm sorry."

A minute later, Janet emerged from her room. "Does your house have an alarm system?" she asked Irma.

Irma pointed across the hallway railing toward the open living room, at the shotgun hanging above the fireplace.

Janet nodded. "I see."

It was late, and we were exhausted from traveling; we said good night to Irma and Janet and got into our pajamas. Annie and I lay side by side in the twin beds, gazing at the fan on the ceiling, the Texas star swirling at its center. Annie curled her arm around Quarky, her stuffed subatomic particle.

"*Cowboys*," I said. If you wanted to escape your dark thoughts and worries, *being* in a cowboy novel was even better than reading one.

Annie lowered her voice. "Don't get any ideas. I don't want to see you out there on horseback, shouting 'Ride me, cowboy!' or whatever they say in that series."

"Nobody ever says 'Ride me, cowboy.' And my mom already warned me not to ride a horse." I adjusted my pillow. "I can't believe they actually wear those hats and boots and it's *not a costume*."

She laughed. "Don't tell Will."

"He'd think it's funny. He wouldn't mind if I'm ogling cowboys," I said, though I wondered if that was true. Hopefully he would mind. I could overnight another letter to him: *Please stay in LA, or I might run off with a cowboy.* Obviously that was a foolproof plan.

I checked my phone. It still displayed its ever-present **Searching . . .** Weren't we all, I wanted to tell it.

I switched off the cowhide lamp, closed my eyes, and returned to the roof garden again.

In the middle of the night, I'd asked Will, "Why did you keep coming to tutoring every week? Even after you finished your college essay and took the AP?"

I wanted him to tell me that he loved me, that he'd loved me all along, just as I loved him.

His fingers stroked my hair. "Because I talked about things then that I can't talk about with anyone else."

"Books and writing, you mean?"

"And my messed-up family."

"I think mine is even more messed up." I said it into his arms. He kissed my hair. The trees rustled overhead.

I loved thinking of those hours on the roof now, even more than when they were happening—I could smell the fresh grass sprouting between the paving stones and feel the warmth of the stone table from the late afternoon sun. It had been almost too much pleasure to absorb at once. I loved replaying each moment slowly now, making sense of things alone.

Will had changed me. Being with him had made me feel strong and secure and took away the loneliness. I loved how Annie and Will didn't worry all the time. They didn't think about plane crashes and muggers and germs. They didn't tip-toe through life afraid the worst thing was going to happen to them or the people they loved. I could see my mom in a way now that I'd never been able to see her before, like pulling back after staring at the dots of a newspaper photo close up. My dad had been the one who calmed us—he was strong and optimistic and believed everything would be okay. I'd believed that too, before he died. I wished I could believe it again.

Now I pulled up the covers and stared at the ceiling. Being in a cowboy novel didn't let you escape all your anxieties, after all—they were still there, surrounding everything, like the darkness.

Annie yawned. "Good night, Mary Sue," she said.

"Good night, Miss Sage." I was glad she was here with me. She kept my stomach from turning to lead.

"You know, I think Chance likes you," I told her. "He kept staring at you."

"Probably because he's never seen an Asian person before." She yawned. "So, in your cowboy books, do the guys kind of smell like a barnyard?"

I shook my head. "They never mention that."

Horses have loved before as I love now

We woke up to the smell of frying bacon. Irma bustled around the breakfast table; she popped open a tube of biscuit dough and arranged the white blobs on a cookie sheet.

"Hope you girls had a good night's sleep." She set the table with place mats that said GIDDYUP! I'M A TEXAS COWGIRL! and PUT YOUR BIG GIRL PANTIES ON AND DEAL WITH IT. "Listen, I'm so sorry to tell you this. I planned to spend the whole day with you, but Lily Jackson just called and she needs help this afternoon with the Miss Rodeo Princess tea—Honor Travis canceled on her, so she begged me. I'm going to show you around the property this morning, but I asked the boys to take care of you this afternoon. Then I'll meet you at the rodeo. Your first rodeo! It's a small one, not like the ones in the big cities, but I think it's even better. I told Larry, 'After I take these girls to the rodeo, they're never going to want to leave.'"

As Janet came down the stairs, my eyes nearly jumped out of my head: she wore jeans. With a yellow blouse and yellow necklace—but still. *Jeans*. They actually fit her body, as opposed to the voluminous broccoli, eggplant, cauliflower, and potato pants she'd worn before. She devoured a biscuit and scowled at the bacon.

"Do you keep kosher?" Irma asked her. "That would be hard to do on the road."

"I do my best," Janet said, and shrugged. "I'm not strict when I'm away from home. I avoid pork and shellfish, of course. But sometimes you just have to make do."

"I enjoy it even more knowing it's *trayf*," Irma said with a grin, grabbing a slice of bacon barehanded.

Janet raised her eyebrows. I was afraid she might have a PowerPoint presentation on her iPad about pork products, but thankfully she didn't say anything.

After breakfast, Irma toured us around the ranch. The property stretched on for miles. The fields were dried out and yellow, and the trees were shorter than the ones we had back east—cedar, pecan, scrub oak, Irma said; they rarely grew as tall here since the land was so hot and parched. The heat was so intense that even though I wore only a T-shirt and shorts, and the air conditioning was on in the car, I was still sweating.

As Irma drove, she told us tales of how she met Clint, her rancher husband, at a blackjack table in Las Vegas; how she'd lived all over the country but her heart had found its true home in Texas; and how although she'd never ridden until she was fifty-nine, she had an inborn gift for horsemanship. Irma was sorry we wouldn't get to meet Clint, since he was away at a cattle auction in Fort Worth.

She dropped us off at the gray maintenance building. "Now I have to run. The boys'll take good care of you. I'll see you tonight."

When Irma was out of earshot, Janet said, "Four marriages," and made a scoffing noise. She and Irma had treated each other pleasantly—Irma seemed to like everybody—but now Janet couldn't wait to comment. "Meeting her gives me even more doubts about Larry," she said.

"Irma seems happy, though," Annie said. "Maybe this time she picked the right guy."

Janet gave us a *You are so young and know nothing* look. "She told me last night her husband's barely ever around. Maybe that's the secret to a happy marriage." She grinned.

I often thought Janet would be happy if she could round up all boys and men and corral them into a man zoo, where they'd be caged, allowed few visitors, and have scraps of meat flung at them every few hours.

The door to the maintenance building was open. We entered a room filled with hulking machines I didn't know the purpose of, and boxes of metal parts. In the main room was a long wooden table strewn with magazines and catalogs—*The Horse Gazette*, *Livestock Weekly*, *The Cattleman*, *Welsco Building Supply*, and *Western Horseman*. I stared at the tools hanging off the pegboard walls.

"I feel like we're on another planet," Annie whispered to me.

Trent, Chance, and a round-faced man sat at the table drinking coffee. They wore jeans, work boots, and T-shirts, and all three stood up when we entered. Trent ran a hand through his blond hair. He was so tall he hovered over everyone.

"Howdy," the round-faced man said. "You must be the ladies I've heard so much about." His name was Farley, and he was the ranch manager. He shook our hands. "Irma told me all about you," he said to Janet. "I have a safety consulting business myself."

"He invented a safety vest for bull riders," Chance said. "People all over the country wear it."

Janet squinted. "I can't see bull riding being considered safe under any circumstances."

Farley laughed. "You've got a point." He told her he was speaking at an event for teachers that afternoon, sponsored by the rodeo; he hoped Janet would join him. She didn't have any appointments until the next day in Dallas, and agreed to go with him, though she seemed wary of leaving us at first—she eyed the boys, probably wondering whether they had festering sores under their clothes. Eventually, Farley convinced her it would be a good networking opportunity for her.

"Be safe," Janet told us before she left. "Be careful."

"We'll be fine," I told her.

After they left, Trent hooked his thumbs into the pockets of his jeans. "We're just getting ready to start some chores, if you don't mind coming along."

"What chores?" I asked. I expected him to say branding, calf roping, or the other things they did in books, but Trent smiled and put down his coffee.

"Chance's overseeing insemination," he said. "And I'm feeding the cattle."

Insemination? Was that romance-novel code, like *thundersticks* and *flaming javelins*?

Chance must have seen my expression. He quickly explained that since they were primarily a breeding ranch, today he was assisting with the artificial insemination of one of their mares. "We breed mares here, stand stallions at stud, and we ship frozen horse semen all over the world."

The words *frozen horse semen* were not what I wanted to hear right after breakfast. Of course Annie, animal-obsessed scientist that she was, lit up immediately.

"What cryopreservation techniques do you use?" She spoke casually, as if frozen horse spewage was something we discussed every morning.

Chance mentioned liquid nitrogen vapors and proprietary fluids, and then he and Annie launched into a debate about heat indexes, dissipation, and several other things I barely understood. Chance had a kind, serious face, and nodded as he spoke.

"Annie's a science genius. She studies animal behavior," I explained to Trent, lest he think my friend had an unnaturally perky interest in their horses' manly urges.

"You're welcome to join them today," he told me. "Or you can come with me."

"I'll feed the cows," I said.

I hopped into the cab of Trent's pickup. The truck bed was filled with bales of hay. We drove to a fenced-in area a few miles down the property.

"Usually we only feed hay in the winter, but the drought's parched the pasture," he said. When we reached the cows, he stopped the car. "We'll just go slow and I'll toss the hay off the back. You drive." He left the keys in the ignition.

"I don't—I can't—" I tried to tell him, but he was already out of the truck and standing in the back, leaning over the bales.

"*Drive*," he yelled.

I took a deep breath. I looked out the window. The cattle were staring at me. I put my hands on the steering wheel. Maybe I should just give it a whirl—how hard could it be? Maybe I could go pick up Annie and we could drive this thing straight to LA and not turn back. I looked down at the pedals.

Trent opened the passenger door. "What's the problem?"

"Which one makes it go?"

He looked at me like I was insane.

"We don't drive in New York. I mean, some people drive." *Will.* "You can't drive if you're under sixteen at all, and when you turn sixteen you can only learn on a car with double brakes, at a driving school. It's the law." Annie and I planned to take driving lessons, but we hadn't gotten around to it yet.

"All right. I'll drive. You get in back," he said.

I climbed into the back of the truck bed. Cows were everywhere—black and white, gigantic, and smelly. They mooed and gazed at us. They almost seemed to be smiling. Trent gave me a pair of thick gloves. He showed me how to toss the hay at them—not too much, since hay was expensive and scarce, he said.

The gloves were so big that they kept flying off when I tossed the hay. Trent climbed out of the truck and got them back for me.

"Dang, you're slow," Trent said.

"People really say *dang*?"

He shook his head, got back into the cab, and slowly drove along to more cows, and I kept tossing the hay in the ninety-degree heat. I finally managed to keep the gloves on by bunching my fingers inside. Sweat ran down my forehead, but after a while I got into the rhythm of it. I pictured Destry, Ewing, and their eight cousins, Bowen, Sykes, Maverick, Hawk, Tuf, Audie, Bryce, and Tumbleweed, riding toward me in the pasture. I thought: I'm a Texas hay-tossing cowgirl.

I'm Mary Sue Lincoln and Sage Cody and Cora McMullen and all those heroines combined. As I worked, I tried to let go of all my worries about Will and whether I'd see him in LA, and I tried not to think about my dad and the wreckage, and whatever was happening in the news while we were so disconnected.

After I'd tossed the last mound of hay to the current group of cows, it was time to move forward, but Trent had stopped driving. I bent toward the back window of the cab, ready to knock on it and find out what the delay was.

He was reading. My backpack was open beside him and he held a book in his hands.

"Hey." I knocked on the window.

He held up *Cowboys on Fire.*

I hopped down from the truck bed and opened the door to the cab.

"*Why* are you reading my book?" I'd thrown my love-worn copy into my bag that morning, thinking I might get a chance to read it in honor of the occasion, but not in front of him. "Give that back," I said.

He pointed to a page.

Destry's thoughts dwelled on her ripe love-mounds and the furry nest at the apex of her femininity.

"Your bag fell over and this book came out right there on the floor. Honest." He paused and held up the cover. "I kind of look like him."

I shook my head. "No. You don't."

I felt the familiar shame heat my cheeks, my shoulders slumping, my mom's and Janet's comments about my books embedded in my brain—*dishonest and misleading*—and then I decided, then and there, watching an actual cowboy mock my cowboy romance, that I was going to stop being embarrassed by my books. I loved the fantasy and escape because I needed to believe that love didn't always end in heartache, that the world wasn't only filled with tragedies and accidents and newspapers with horrible news. The romances kept me from going into the corners of my mind that I didn't want to enter. They were bright against the darkness, and I needed bright.

"It's a good book," I said. "Actually, that one, book one, is a *great* book."

He got to his feet. "Hey. I'm going to show you something," he said.

"What?"

The almost-smile. "What *real* cowboys do for fun. Come on." We stepped outside, and he rummaged around in a large box in the truck bed, and then he walked toward me, holding a gigantic shotgun.

A chill spread across my shoulders. Was he going to shoot me?

"Everyone's got to learn how to protect themselves. Especially you—living in New York City."

"Oh," I said. "Sure. Because you never know when you might need to murder someone on the subway. With a giant shotgun."

He held it out toward me. I'd never touched a gun before. He placed it in my hands.

"It's a 12-gauge," he said.

"It's huge. Heavy." What were you supposed to say about a gun?

He went back to the truck and took out some empty beer cans. My mom would love this. If she could see me right now, she'd call the sheriff's office and try to have Trent arrested for beer-in-car possession, gun possession, driving with broken seat belts, and a hundred other things she'd think of.

"So—is it legal?" I asked. "To just go shoot stuff?"

He laughed. "Of course. We're just firing in the brush— we're not killing anybody." He paused. "At least you seem trustworthy." He smiled, went over to a small hill, found a flat rock, and set the beer cans on top of it.

A tiny lizard ran across the rock. "I'll watch you do it first," I said.

He stood in front of me, aimed at the cans, and shot them. They scattered everywhere. He fired again at a prickly pear cactus and blew off some of its leaves.

"Ready? I don't have any more cans, so you can shoot at the cactus. Easy target," he said.

He handed the shotgun to me. It felt awkward in my hands.

"So what you do is stand like this. A good stance is important.

Balance your weight on both feet." His voice was calm. "Don't lean away from the gun. Lean forward instead. No need to be shy about it. Shooting isn't passive or weak."

I leaned forward.

"Hold it like this, so the kick doesn't hurt like hell."

He placed his hands over mine, showing me. My skin froze. Was this okay? What would Will say?

He positioned the shotgun by my shoulder. "And breathe. Most folks hold their breath when they shoot for the first time, but breathing will help you relax."

I hadn't realized I'd been holding my breath, but I was.

"Okay," I said. "Here goes."

I paused. I tried to relax. It was impossible. My arms stiffened. I clenched my shoulders, aimed, exhaled, and pulled the trigger.

I flinched from the noise and the pain in my shoulder. "Ow," I said. "Did I do it?"

He nodded. "Fantastic. Great for a first-timer."

"Did I hit the cactus?"

"Not exactly. You hit the ground. Try again."

I thought of my mom again. If she was here, she wouldn't just get Trent arrested—she'd take the gun and shoot him herself.

I loved doing things that she knew nothing about.

I positioned the gun and shot again. Finally, a leaf exploded off the cactus.

I was Annie Oakley! I was a natural!

"You did good."

"I guess so. Who knew?" I asked. "But I feel kind of bad for the cactus." I rubbed my shoulder. "And that hurt."

He patted my arm. "We'll have to take you hunting feral hogs next," he said.

"Sure. I'll be a pro. Those hogs won't know what hit them." I handed the gun back to him. My hands felt strangely light without it. Weak. Spent. Trembly. I'd never before felt that type of strength. To take away a life. Because that's what guns did—wasn't that the whole purpose? To kill, or instill fear of killing. Maybe men felt that strength without guns, men like Trent, who were tall and broad-shouldered and probably could murder someone with their fists. A part of me was still shaking, not used to it, and not liking it—and a part of me did like it, to even momentarily have that kind of power.

"You okay?" he asked.

I nodded. "It just feels weird. I'm so used to being this sort of . . ." I shrugged. "I'm always the weak one. Last one picked for volleyball. Probably because I run *away* from the ball. Apparently you're not supposed to do that. I even almost failed my self-defense class. I could never find the dummy's jugular notch."

"Not so weak now," he said, and we walked back to his truck in the afternoon light.

Let's rodeo!

"Hey, Miss New York," Trent shouted from downstairs. "Hurry up."

I changed clothes—my jeans were dusty, my shirt damp with sweat—I put on a denim skirt and a black T-shirt (what were you supposed to wear to a rodeo?), and quickly fixed my hair. I checked my phone to see if service miraculously worked (it didn't), and met Trent in his truck. Chance had taken Annie on one of his chores to town earlier, so they were meeting us at the rodeo.

Trent looked me over. "Black again," he said. "You going to nun school?"

"I don't think they let Jewish people into nun school."

He glanced at me. "I've never met a Jewish person before."

"Irma's Jewish."

"Irma's got six crosses in her bathroom."

"Well, she *was* Jewish, before husband two. Or maybe it was husband three. There's no temple in a nearby town? Or a JCC?"

He looked at me like I was speaking Martian. I watched

the scrubby trees float by out the window. I was as foreign a species to him as he was to me.

We reached the fairgrounds. A banner said FORT WELLS RODEO: PRESERVING WESTERN TRADITIONS. And beneath that, LET'S RODEO! Cowboys were everywhere, wearing white hats and black hats and crisp button-down shirts tucked into their jeans. We walked past rows of orange, blue, yellow, and pink food stands—"Texas Taters Sliced Oooh Sooo Thin," "Shrimp on a Stick," "Ice Cold Sweet Tea," "Cherry Lime-ade," "Turkey Legs," "Calf Fries."

"What are calf fries?"

Trent said I didn't want to know.

At the gate of the arena, a man stamped our hands with a little blue armadillo. Chance and Annie met us in our reserved seats; Farley, Janet, and Irma sat beside them. Farley gnawed on a giant smoked turkey leg.

I slid in next to Annie. "You guys had fun?" I asked.

"Not as much fun as Janet. She got on a horse today." Annie's eyebrows lifted.

Janet's yellow shirt was slightly untucked, and her jeans had smudges of dirt on the knees. She placed a loose strand of hair behind her ear. "It was a small horse."

The poor animal. Janet probably threatened it with photos of hoof-and-mouth disease if it bucked.

"I had phone service in town today," Janet said. "I spoke to your mother. She specifically told me that she doesn't want you getting on a horse."

"There goes my rodeo career up in smoke," I said.

"A loss for horsewomen everywhere," Annie said.

Irma laughed heartily at this, and then excused herself to see a friend who worked in one of the stalls. "Be back in a few," she said.

The air smelled like oiled leather. When I'd read about rodeos in my books, I'd thought that people didn't *really* rope calves, wrestle steers, and ride broncos and bulls for fun.

But they did: the gate swung open; a horse bucked and thrashed while its rider held on for dear life. I gripped the railing in front of us.

Holy holy holy holy cow.

Literally.

We watched team roping, steer wrestling, and barrel racing; Janet soon had her fill of the smelly arena and went outside with Farley for fresh air. Trent saw someone he knew, and they walked off toward the beer stall. Then Annie and Chance left to get food. Annie invited me to come with them, but it seemed like they might want to be alone.

I sat by myself in the empty row. I took out my phone. Still no service. I put it back in my bag.

When I was around other people, keeping busy, I felt so optimistic, but when I was alone, dark thoughts poked their tendrils in. *You'll never hear from him. This whole trip was for nothing.*

My stomach rumbled. I got up to get something to eat.

I wandered past the turkey leg, popcorn, and calf fries stalls, and booths that sold jewelry and scarves, souvenirs, and cowboy hats, and I stopped at a corn dog cart. I bought one.

It was the first corn dog I'd ever eaten. The outside was soft, sweet, crumbly; the inside salty, juicy, and rich. I loved it. I ate the whole foot-long thing. Everything was big here, larger-than-life. I passed a stand that sold huge bottles of bluebonnet perfume in fluted glass decanters like a genie's house. I picked one out for my mom and put it in my backpack.

I thought of a game we used to play when I was really little, one of the rare times she was as openly affectionate as my dad. She'd say, *How much do I love you?* I'd say, *A teeny tiny bit*. She'd laugh: *No! My love for you is bigger than the house, the whole city, all the people in the world, the entire universe.*

In our texts, I'd told her bits about the trip but nothing real, nothing about the things that were going on inside me. Now, I wished that when I'd texted her yesterday I'd told her I missed her. I felt this lump in my chest and I realized that it was this primal missing, this inexplicable longing for the clink of her perfumes, the steam rising out of her coffee cup, her padding around the apartment in the mornings. I missed her and wanted to run away from her at the same time.

As I left the perfume stall, someone touched my shoulder.

It was Irma. "I've been looking all over for you! I need to show you something." She led me to a booth filled with racks of western-style shirts, dresses, and pantsuits.

"Sheri Jo, this is my granddaughter-to-be," Irma said to the woman behind the cash register, who had dyed red hair and sparkly green eye shadow.

Sheri Jo grinned. "Heard *all* about you." Her nails were painted a red so dark it was nearly black.

"She spent the day with Trent today. Cute one, isn't he?" Irma asked.

Sheri Jo nodded. "Cuuute."

"I have a boyfriend," I said. For some reason, it felt important to point that out, whether or not it was exactly true.

"Oh, who cares about *that*," said Irma. "You're too young to have just *one*. Trent has a whole bunch of girlfriends."

"A whole bunch?" How many was that? Four? Five? Sixteen? Did he keep them like livestock, in different stalls in the barn? It wasn't jealousy that I felt. (Was it?) No. It was envy that he probably had simple and easy relationships, with no drama, no chasing anyone across the country. Love always seemed so simple for some people.

Irma laughed, and Sheri Jo eyed me up and down. "When we're done fitting her, she's going to look *so dang good*. Excuse my French."

"Fitting me?" I asked.

"For your maid of honor dress!" Irma squeezed my arms.

"I'm surprising your mom. Whatever you do, don't tell her. It's our secret. Sheri Jo is the best seamstress in all of Texas. She's already finished my dress. Same material, so we'll coordinate for the pictures. When she's done, I'll send it to you in the mail. Or I can bring it in person." Irma beamed; light bounced off her bathroom-tile teeth.

Panic rose in me. "They haven't even set a wedding date."

"Oh, they did! December fourteenth. Larry checked December fourteenth to make sure I was free." She took out her date book and flipped to that day: "Wedding of Claire Roth and Larry Greenbeck," Irma had written, encircled in a pink heart. "Didn't they tell— Oh." She paused, her eyes grew wide, and she put her hand to her mouth. "I wasn't supposed to say anything. Larry's going to kill me!" She laughed.

Why didn't they tell me? I checked my phone—still nothing. I wanted to call my mom right now. How could she not tell me?

"I'm sure they just wanted it to be a surprise," Irma said, her teeth gleaming.

Sheri Jo wound a measuring tape around my waist.

Irma picked up a bright teal dress. "Now this is a similar style to the one Sheri Jo's going to make. We'll see how it looks on you." Sheri Jo finished her measurements, and Irma drew the curtain to the dressing area. She handed the dress to me and gave me a pair of silver heels to try on with it.

I felt sick, but I didn't know what to do besides put the

dress on. It was hideous: puffed sleeves, satiny and shiny but rough against my skin. Why wouldn't they tell me if they'd set a date? I shoved my feet into the heels.

I opened the curtain and tried to calm down. My mom had never asked me to be her maid of honor. I couldn't imagine actually walking down the aisle behind her, faking joy. What else could I do, though? When the rabbi said *Speak now or forever hold your peace*, I could flail my arms and yell *Don't do it, Mommy!* (Why did they even say that line at weddings if they didn't *want* you to speak up?) All this time, I'd been sure the wedding would never happen. But Janet was wrong—my mom planned to go through with it. I stared at myself with the teal mushrooms on my shoulders, and for the first time, the wedding seemed real. Or at least Irma's version of real— marriage for a few years. Maybe Larry would try on my mom and me like Buddhism or Catholicism or Texan, and then be done with us.

Sheri Jo pinned the hem. Irma bit her lip. "You look beautiful, sweetheart," Irma said.

The dress itched. I felt hot and sweaty. I was about to muster the guts to tell Irma and Sheri Jo that there was no way I was walking down the aisle in this thing when a tear rolled down Irma's cheek.

"Larry. *Married*." Her voice grew hoarse. "I never thought it would happen. You know him. Always behind the computer. He never dated much. I don't know if it was my failings as a mother, but I always think how Samuel—Larry's daddy—how he had so many problems, and that affected Larry, I know it did, despite every way I tried to make up for it. I wish Samuel was alive. Nothing would've made him happier than to be at the wedding of his only son."

Sheri Jo tucked a pencil behind her ear. "You could plant a tree. In his memory. At Wade Nelson's wedding, they planted a sycamore for his grandma."

"Larry's getting married in New York! There's more soil under my fingernails than in that whole city." Irma laughed with a whoop and wiped under her eyes with a Kleenex. Then she fluffed up the mushrooms on my shoulders. "Don't you just *love* this dress?" Another tear rolled out.

I nodded. I couldn't tell her now, while she was crying, that I wasn't going to wear it. I'd tell her later. Or I'd spill coffee on it accidentally on purpose. Or something.

All of a sudden, Irma's face lit up. "I know what we can do for Larry's dad." She touched my hand. "You could write a poem."

"What?"

"Your mom told me you write beautiful poetry. You could write a poem to read at the wedding. All about how your mom and Larry met at the Holocaust party, and you—"

"It wasn't a party," I said. Party made it sound like some kind of celebration, with Holocaust-survivor games and theme-park snacks. Pogrom cheese? Kindertransport crackers? What was Irma thinking?

"Whatever you call it," Irma said. "We could dedicate it to Samuel, since he was the reason Larry went to that party, I mean convention, in the first place. You could make it sad but also funny, you know? Because Samuel was funny, too."

My throat dried up. I didn't know what to say. I wasn't going to write a funny Holocaust poem for my mom's wedding, or wear a 1980s itchy prom dress. But I didn't have the guts to say this to Irma. She looked like she was on the brink of crying again. She blew her nose.

Janet appeared then, with Farley and Trent. "We didn't know where you were," she said, out of breath. "Annie and Chance are off seeing livestock, and when you weren't with them, I got worried—what are—?" She looked me over, squinting at the pincushion in Sheri Jo's hand. "What's going on?"

Irma explained about the fitting, the wedding, the poem I was going to write for the ceremony.

"Take that off," Janet said to me. She turned to Irma. "You should've asked me before you did this," she snapped. "And Eva isn't writing poetry on demand. She's not a trained monkey."

Irma's face dropped; I went behind the curtain and changed with relief. When I returned, Irma and Janet glared at each other. Janet shepherded me out of the stall.

"Your mom warned me that Irma might try to do something like this," Janet said as we walked off. "I'm just glad I was here."

I told her that my mom and Larry had set a date, but Janet rolled her eyes. "Larry set a date. Your mom hasn't agreed to it," she said.

I relaxed a little. Janet glanced toward the exit of the arena. "Do you want to stay for the rest of the rodeo?"

"I'm tired," I said. I wanted to get away from Irma and Sheri Jo, and all this talk of Larry and the wedding. "And we're leaving early tomorrow. . . ."

"I'm heading back now," Trent said. "I'll drop her off."

Janet gave Trent a don't-try-anything stare and looked at Farley, who put his arm around Trent.

"I'd trust this young man with my life," Farley told Janet. "Most honest, hardworking kid in all of Texas."

And so Janet agreed to let Trent lead me out of the arena and back toward his truck, leaving the rodeo and corn dogs and my soon-to-be-step-grandmother behind us.

Lies

Trent didn't ask about the dress or the whole incident; we were silent as we drove back to the ranch. We stopped by the barn first so he could do his night chores.

"Need help?"

He grinned and shook his head. "You're off duty now. Next time you come this way, I'm going to put you to work fixing fences, though."

"I'm an expert fence fixer," I said. He said he'd be done soon, so I walked outside to the pasture and waited.

The air felt warm and heavy. The sky swirled with stars— so many stars—glittery dots and white wisps and planets blinking. I began to relax a little. Tomorrow I'd see Lulu, and she could help me figure everything out. My dad used to call her the Truth Machine, because when they were in graduate school together, streams of students would come to Lulu's office hours just to ask for life advice.

She could tell me what to do about Will, the news about my dad, and the wedding.

At least we'd have a break from Janet for a couple of days

in Arizona. My shoulders relaxed, thinking about it, though we had another epic bus ride the next day—twelve hours to Tucson.

For now, I wanted to enjoy our last moments in cowboyland. Janet had mentioned renting a car for the return trip from LA and driving us home, so who knew when we'd be back here again. Or if we won—*when* we won (on the bus, before we'd lost cell phone service, Annie had read a positive psychology website that said we needed *to believe* we'd win)—we could splurge on train tickets back instead.

Secretly, though, another plan had begun to brew inside me: what if when I got to LA, I stayed there? What if when I finally saw Will, it felt exactly as it had before—or even better? I could get a job. I could get emancipated. I'd read about that in a magazine once—you could get a court order to be an emancipated teen and live on your own. I could stay in LA and finish school out there. I could have a whole new life. I could use the money I'd win on the show—$10,000, or maybe even the whole $50,000. It was possible.

After a while Trent came outside and stood nearby. We leaned against the wooden railing along the pasture.

"The books are right about Texas," I said. I felt like a different person in the country; I could feel my soul unfurl, this opening up I'd never felt before, this quiet. "There's something mesmerizing about all this space. The giant sky."

I felt like I'd never been farther away from my old life.

My mother had a framed cover of *The New Yorker* in her room, which pictured a map of America with New York, the Pacific Ocean, and almost nothing in between. Now it was all reversed. New York seemed like a tiny, inconsequential corner of the world.

"I'll switch places with you," Trent said. "I always wanted to see the city."

"Really?"

"I don't want to stay here forever."

"Where would you go?"

He shrugged. "I've been taking classes in graphics, web design, and digital development in West Stockton. Thinking of moving to Dallas next year."

Web design? *Digital development?* "I can't believe you'd want to leave this place. It seems like such a romantic life."

"Romantic? Cow shit and no pay? Chance is into the science of it, but what I do is mostly grunt work. Not what I want to do forever."

"Irma said your family's been ranching for generations, though."

He shook his head. "Not the same now. Can't make a living like people used to. You know what town kids called us in high school? Shitkickers."

"They never say that in *Cowboys on Fire*."

He laughed. "I should write one of those books."

We headed down the path to the house. He told me how

he'd designed a new website for the ranch, and Irma's husband and Farley were getting interest from breeders all over the world.

As we walked along the meadow, I looked back up at the sky. I wondered if we'd see stars like this in Tucson. I thought of how few nights in my life I'd actually seen stars for real, even though I'd memorized all the constellations for a test in seventh grade. My dad had practiced with me. He'd spent hours gluing glow-in-the-dark stars to my ceiling in the shape of constellations, in our old apartment. I missed that old apartment. I'd cried when we left the stars on the ceiling. My mom had bought me a new set and reattached them all on the ceiling in our new place. I'd told her they weren't in the right positions and I took them off. I felt a little guilty about that now.

I saw Lyra and Cassiopeia and Ursa Major. "My dad taught me to remember Ursa Major because it's in the shape of an anteater," I said, barely even realizing I was saying it out loud.

Trent turned toward me. He paused. "Irma told me you lost your dad. She said to take good care of you while you're here."

Oh. It felt weird that she'd told him. Was he spending time with me just because he had to?

"How did he die?" Trent asked me.

"A heart attack," I said. "In his sleep." The words came out automatically, without thinking.

It had always felt easy to lie, and so much better than telling the truth. The lie was a kind of protection: my safe, peaceful fantasy of how he died. But I felt empty this time, after saying the lie, and not protected at all.

I thought of the *Stages of Mourning* book my mom had given me. It had said, *Someday, when you look back, you will be able to see how your grief progressed from Denial to Anger to Bargaining to Acceptance.* But how could you progress when the news never ended, when nothing was ever simple or certain?

On the porch, I hugged my elbows. "Thank you," I said. "It's been . . . fun. Different."

Trent gave me a gentlemanly handshake and then squeezed my shoulder.

"Ow," I said, touching that spot. "My shotgun injury."

"Sorry," he said. "Forgot about that. You did good, though. Next time you come here, you can shoot a 10-gauge."

"Okay. Whatever that is," I said.

He kissed me on the cheek. "Come back this way sometime," he said.

Something warm traveled down my spine. He put his hands in his pockets, turned, and said good night.

Upstairs, I settled in bed with my book. Annie wasn't back yet. I felt a tiny humming inside, thinking of the kiss on the cheek. Maybe Trent *liked* me. Was that even possible? Maybe he wanted me to join the other sixteen girlfriends. Before Will had kissed me, I used to lie awake at night and worry that something was deeply wrong with me, since I'd never had a boyfriend. In seventh grade, Joey Braga made a chart ranking all the girls by three different measures: body, face, and personality. I got a ten on personality, but a measly three on body and a five on face. I had braces and hadn't hit puberty, unlike many of the curvy girls in my grade. That three and five had stung so deeply that they seemed stuck in my mind forever. But maybe I wasn't a three and five. Will wouldn't like a three or five. Trent wouldn't kiss a three or five girl on the cheek.

After a while, I fell asleep. A couple of hours later I awoke to the sound of a car door slamming shut. I thought it was Annie; I got up and peeked out the window.

Not Annie. It was Janet.

Farley held her hand, and they walked to the wooden fence. Then he kissed her. I gasped. She leaned back and he kissed her again, like in a romance novel. Her arms around him—Janet!—dipping backward in a long, lingering kiss.

My mouth fell open. Janet was enacting *Cowboys on Fire*.

I watched them hold hands and wander to the porch; I couldn't hear what they said. They sat there for a while and kissed again. I kept watching. I wanted a bowl of popcorn. I imagined the Lifetime movie ad: an embittered middle-aged woman finds passion with a cowboy. I watched them kiss and hold hands and kiss again until Farley reluctantly got back in his car, sadly waved good-bye, and drove off.

After he left, Janet walked over to the fence and stared up at the moon. She looked wistful and in love. I almost wanted to say something to her—*It's okay, Janet, love is good!* But of course if she knew I'd seen her, she'd probably murder me, or at least subject me to endless iPad presentations.

Janet in love. I couldn't believe it.

I couldn't wait to tell Annie, but she didn't return until it was light out. I opened my eyes when she snuck in. "Where have you been?" I asked.

She clutched something to her chest. A giant, crumbling book. *Fairy Tales and Mythology*, with sepia covers. "We went to a used-book store."

"What?" I squinted at her. Next she was going to say they observed baboons, recited calculus axioms together, and ate cold Pop-Tarts.

"Then we got hungry, so we stopped at a Waffle House to get something to eat . . . we stayed up to watch the sunrise. Talking." Her face glowed.

"What is happening? What have you done with my best friend?" It was like *A Midsummer Night's Dream* in Texas.

"He's just so . . . cool. So different from anyone I've ever met."

"What about *We're driven by biology and I'm not wasting time with a boy till I get into MIT* and everything?"

She shrugged and looked embarrassed, then smiled to herself.

"You're not the only one to fall in love tonight," I said. I told her about Janet.

"Your aunt Gonorrhea got some?"

We stayed up talking until it was breakfast time. Irma was nowhere in sight—she'd left a note on the table, beside a tray of biscuits, saying she'd be back to say good-bye before we left for the bus.

Janet teetered downstairs looking bleary-eyed. She ate a biscuit and drank coffee as if nothing had happened.

"You had a good night?" I asked her. I tried hard not to smile.

She looked unsteady and bewildered, as if she'd just stepped off a carnival ride. She wore blue pajamas and her hair was loose and frizzy. She cleared her throat, opened her mouth to say something, and then seemed to think better of it. She devoured three biscuits, washed her dishes, then popped back to her room to get something. When she returned to the table, she handed a worn brown box to me.

"This is for you," she said. "I meant to give it to you in Tennessee, or while we were traveling, but there was never the right moment. I've been carrying it around all this time— well. Here."

I opened it. Inside was a leather-bound diary. It was blank inside.

"It belonged to my mother," Janet said. "Your father gave it to her ages ago, before you were born, but she never wrote in it. They both would've wanted you to have it. To use it." She opened the leather cover. "For your poems. Not writing for Irma, or anyone else. Just for you."

I fingered the pages, touching this thing that my father had touched, that Freda had touched. "You should keep it," I told Janet, and handed it back to her. I didn't deserve it. I didn't even write poems anymore.

As if reading my thoughts, Janet said, "Just take it. You don't have to write in it if you don't want to. Just see what happens." She placed it back in my hands.

I put it in my backpack, inside my pillowcase. Why did my dad give Freda this journal? Had he wanted her to write down her story, too? I'd never realized I wasn't the only person he gave notebooks to.

"I'm going to miss you girls, but you'll be in good hands with Lulu in Tucson," Janet said. "Don't talk to strangers on the bus. Don't let your bags out of your sight. And keep your phones on and charged at all times—you should have service on that leg of the trip." She checked her watch. "I have to get ready for my meetings in Dallas. Give Lulu my best. I'll see you very soon."

We hugged her. Irma arrived just as we were saying good-bye.

"I'll see you at the wedding," Irma said cheerily, as if yesterday hadn't happened, though she whispered to me when Janet was out of earshot, "I'll be shipping the dress to you when it's done."

The wedding will never take place, I told myself, and Annie and I thanked her for hosting us.

Chance and Trent drove us to the bus stop in Farley's sedan (Janet insisted, so nobody would have to ride in the backseat of the pickup). Chance and Annie talked through most of the ride; Trent and I were quiet, watching the scrub trees and fields of cattle flash by.

They carried our bags for us and gave them to the driver. Trent shook my hand good-bye, and Chance kissed Annie on the lips quickly—Annie seemed embarrassed in front of us. As our bus pulled away, I watched the two boys lean against the car, and I thought that real-life cowboys were better than fictional ones. And then I thought about Irma and her four husbands, and Janet and her kisses, and it amazed me how even grown-ups seemed so confused by love.

We had claimed our front seats. Annie curled up in hers and immediately fell asleep holding Quarky.

I watched hills and grass and trees float by. To go from state to state in one day—it knit the country together. I thought of how the air in Cleveland had felt crisp in the morning, and Tennessee felt swampy in the afternoon, and the Texas heat made us feel like we'd landed on Mars—but it was all one country. Before we'd left, people had told me, *Every small city in America looks the same, one strip mall after another.* That wasn't true. Each state, each town, each neighborhood we traveled through was as different as a snowflake. Even the monsoon of 7-Elevens and Circle Ks, Allsup's, Valeros, Sav-O-Mats, Minit Marts, Kwik Shops, and Speedy Farms were as odd as the random things they sold: the pie shakes, hand-knit doll clothes, live crickets, alfalfa, elk jerky, stuffed javelinas. We passed billboards that said, "Daddy Bo's—It's Pig-Lickin' Good!" and another one telling us, "It's Your Choice: Heaven or Hell." We saw signs for Roustabout

Services, Dirt Contracting, Bob's Taxidermy, and Papa Joe's Feed and Seed Store, and we watched the oil pump jacks—our bus driver called them nodding donkeys—drill in fields and even in people's backyards, bobbing up and down like giant metal dodo birds pecking the ground.

I loved to travel. I loved seeing other people's houses, the kinds of beds they slept on (Janet's pristine white Tempur-Pedic, Irma's fluffy pillow-tops); and the foods they ate, the Youngs' eggs from their neighbor's chickens, and Irma's biscuits from a tube. As every mile disappeared behind us, I felt parts of me weaving and unweaving. So many different feelings at the same time.

I loved visiting unfamiliar places where I had no memories. In New York, so many street corners and shops and subway stations and parks and bookstores held reminders of my dad—on good days they were like little keys to him, unlocking doors I could open. On bad days, reliving those memories made me feel soggy, weighed down by grief. To travel felt free from all that. Was that why my mom wanted to move to a new apartment after he died? Was it this freedom that she was looking for?

I opened the journal Janet had given me. It seemed too old and intimidating to write in, with its leather cover and yellow-tinged pages.

I thought of the times I'd written with my dad, how we'd sit in coffee shops or by Turtle Pond and how, back then, I

loved that feeling of a new page. All hope and expectation—
that's how it had felt.

I thought of how Anne Frank started all her diary entries
Dear Kitty, writing to an imaginary friend. Maybe that would
be an easier way to start.

> ~~Dear Kitty,~~
> ~~Dear Freda, Bubbe 409,~~
> ~~Dear very old book I'm afraid to~~
> ~~write in,~~
> Dear Daddy,

It came out fast.

> Last night I told a cowboy in Texas
> that you died of a heart attack. In
> your sleep.
> I feel like in my regular life I
> spend so much time pretending.
> Mommy and I pretend that you
> never existed.
> I pretend with Mommy that I've
> never fallen in love.
> I love traveling, though (I love
> traveling!), because you're escaping into
> life instead of hiding from it. For the

first time in ages, I feel like I'm me.
(Whoever that is.)

Will I ever feel like I can stop
pretending?

How do I have a life that's real?

What will happen when I go back
home after this trip? Will it be back
to the same old life?

I know these are pretty heavy
questions to ask a dead person. Look at
me, pretending even now, writing to
you as if you can read this. Pretending
you're still alive.

I put the diary back into my pillowcase. Annie and I napped and talked, and I made more flash cards for her—we were actually ahead on our study schedule, according to her spreadsheet—and when we finally had cell phone service, I checked the message board. Nothing new.

I tried calling Will. I dialed the number to his dad's house and left another message. *We're on our way to Tucson and I've got cell service again. Please tell Will to give me a call.*

I hung up. I felt good. I was glad I did it. It was the right thing to do.

This feeling lasted for only five seconds.

The bus plowed on, and I entered the Fifth Dimension of Female Existence: the Realm of the Waiting.

Lulu was the one who'd called it that. Years ago, before she'd met her husband Michael, she'd stayed with us while she went to a conference in Manhattan. There, she'd met a guy who asked for her number, and then she waited for him to call. All morning and afternoon she waited. She sat at our tiny kitchen table and pretended to drink coffee and read the newspaper. The coffee cooled; she continually read page three.

Finally, she decided something was wrong with her cell phone and called the phone company. "It's working just fine," the customer service lady told her. "You got any idea how many girls call up every day and ask me that? Every hour, every day, girls suffering all the same. I'm gonna tell you something, honey: he ain't calling."

Lulu got over him, but my mom made a lesson of it. "Right now there are women everywhere, around the world, staring at their phones, waiting and waiting. You can become one of them, wasting your time, or you can be too busy achieving world peace and solving the universe's problems to even notice whether a guy has called you back. You decide."

It had sounded like an easy choice at the time.

Now, on the bus, my phone became a live object, a hand grenade. Over the next two hours I checked my messages every minute, but there was nothing. Not even from my mom. I'd texted her and asked why she hadn't told me that Larry and Irma had set a date for the wedding, but she hadn't texted or called me back.

Annie's forehead wrinkled. "You need to put that phone away."

"Maybe Janet did something to it back in Cleveland so I can't receive calls or messages from Will. Or maybe she broke it." I held it up to the light and tapped it encouragingly.

"It's working fine. Just put the phone in your backpack and don't think about it," she suggested. "Put it away for half an hour."

"Okay. No problem." Half an hour. I could do that.

Of course I could.

Fifteen minutes would be a lot more reasonable, though.

The bus thrummed. Every fifteen minutes I checked it. I kept checking it while we rode past Las Cruces and Deming and Lordsburg, and as we worked our way through *Essential Mathematical Trivia* and *An Almanac of World History*, until I thought about taking the phone to an AT&T store to get it fixed.

I turned it off.

For a few minutes.

Meanwhile, Annie received eight texts and two emails from Chance. She only checked her phone once an hour. She scribbled notes on index cards, then shook her head. "I should turn mine off, too. I can't get him out of my head. Is this normal?"

"Yup," I said.

I kept checking it throughout the twelve-hour ride to Tucson. My mom hadn't written to me in two days—her last email had been sent the night we'd arrived in Texas. She'd written: *Just to let you know, I may be a little hard to reach for a day or two—I have a lot of work. Larry says that his mom's place is pretty far off the grid, but hopefully you, Janet, or Irma can leave me a message and let me know you're okay. Please call me when you get to Arizona!* I tried her cell phone, but there was no answer, so I called our home number.

An unfamiliar, scratchy voice picked up. "Hello?"

"Who's this?" I asked.

"Who are *you*?" the voice snapped. I said my name.

"Oh, Eva. This is Mrs. Neegall. Your mom asked me to take in your mail while she's out of town."

"Where is she? She didn't tell me she was going somewhere."

"She and Larry took a couple of nights away in the country. Upstate. A little romantic time alone. They get back tomorrow."

My mom, who hated to travel, to even leave the city, had gone to the country? Why didn't she tell me?

Two thoughts suddenly anchored themselves in my mind: *Maybe she does love Larry after all. Maybe she's happier without me.*

"She told me she had a lot of work to do," I said. "Not that she was going away."

"Well, those lovebirds are hopefully not doing too much work," Mrs. Neegall said.

I reached my hands inside my backpack and touched the pillowcase. The bus picked up speed as we headed toward Arizona, the landscape blurring until I couldn't distinguish anything anymore.

PART SIX

ONE ART

The art of losing isn't hard to master;
so many things seem filled with the intent
to be lost that their loss is no disaster.

Lose something every day. Accept the fluster
of lost door keys, the hour badly spent.
The art of losing isn't hard to master.

Then practice losing farther, losing faster:
places, and names, and where it was you meant
to travel. None of these will bring disaster.

I lost my mother's watch. And look! my last, or
next-to-last, of three loved houses went.
The art of losing isn't hard to master.

I lost two cities, lovely ones. And, vaster,
some realms I owned, two rivers, a continent.
I miss them, but it wasn't a disaster.

—Even losing you (the joking voice, a gesture
I love) I shan't have lied. It's evident
the art of losing's not too hard to master
*though it may look like (*Write *it!) like disaster.*
                              —Elizabeth Bishop

The questions

Lulu lived in a yellow cottage with giant white flowers blooming around the porch. A stone path lit by tiny white lights led to the front door; the air was hot and honey-thick. It looked like a fairy-tale house, small and welcoming. "Beats Queens," Lulu said, and it did.

She looked the same as always—dark curls spilling over her pale bare shoulders, red lipstick—except for one difference: her stomach, which was now shaped like a small round balloon.

When she'd picked us up at the station, we'd tried not to stare at it, but we couldn't help ourselves. After we'd hugged and whooped and hugged again, she'd patted her middle. "Too many doughnuts." She smiled. "I'm kidding. I'm pregnant."

"Why didn't you tell us?" I asked her.

"We've been waiting for the amnio results. We didn't tell anyone," she said. They'd gotten them yesterday: the baby was a healthy boy. "I wanted to tell you in person," she said as Annie and I dragged our luggage inside. "I know it's kind of a freak show. I'm forty-six, and they call it a 'geriatric pregnancy' when you're over thirty-five. Really makes you feel good about yourself."

She seemed happier than I'd ever seen her. She'd always wanted to be a mother, and though I never said this out loud, I always thought she seemed more maternal than my mom.

"I never thought it would happen for me," she said, "after David." David was her ex-husband; they'd gotten divorced fifteen years ago. He was a yoga instructor who, as my mom put it, started giving overly personal instruction to his female students.

She met her second husband, Michael, here in Tucson—he was a professor at the university, too. They'd tried fertility treatments for the past five years, she said, and finally, it had worked.

Now we sat on the fuzzy white rug in her living room. Michael came home from the grocery store with two pints of ice cream, fudge topping, chocolate sprinkles, chocolate chip cookies, blueberries, and iced tea. I'd only met him once, when he and Lulu came to New York after they'd eloped five years ago. He had floppy blond hair and wore black-rimmed glasses, and he had a rumbling, gentle laugh. He gave us big hugs and poured us glasses of iced tea.

"Thank you," Lulu told him. "You didn't need to do all that."

"Of course I do. Now I'm off to go pack," he told us. "Save me some cookies for the road." He was leaving early tomorrow to take a group of students on a week-long archaeological field trip. He kissed Lulu and rubbed her shoulders.

Annie and I showered and put on pajamas, and then the three of us ate New York Super Fudge Chunk ice cream out of yellow teacups as we sat on the rug. Lulu placed a bowl of the blueberries on the coffee table.

Lulu had changed into pajama pants and a maternity T-shirt that said, "Give Me Chocolate." She wore blue slippers and had tied her brown curls into a ponytail. She fiddled with the ring on her left hand—her wedding ring—which was antique silver with a giant pale purple stone. In the kitchen, the washing machine whirred with our clothes from the trip.

"So tell me about the boys," Lulu said, glancing from Annie to me. "Look at you both. You look lovesick. Starry-eyed, exhausted. Dreamy. Anxious."

"It's really that obvious?" Annie asked.

She nodded. "I've been there myself."

"I thought I was hiding it." Annie hugged her knees to her chest. "I hate this feeling. It's like a disease, pining for someone. I can't stop thinking of him." She shuddered, as if trying to shake it off. "I'm worse than an elephant."

"Please don't start talking about elephant sex again," I said.

"This is different—I never told you about this state they have called *musth*—it's kind of an elephant lovesickness—they ooze this thick liquid from between their eyes and ears, and they pee constantly. Females love it."

I gaped at her. "Thank you for that image."

She rested her head on the arm of the sofa. "I'm so tired. I can't even function."

I touched her arm. "It's not that bad," I said reassuringly, though I wasn't doing much better. No letters had arrived at Lulu's house, and I couldn't stop checking my phone. Still nothing. They watched me. After I'd sent the letter from Tennessee, I'd convinced myself he wouldn't go to Seattle. He wouldn't go through with it. But maybe he had gone after all. I picked a blueberry out of the bowl, but it tasted sour. He'd sent me letters in Cleveland and Tennessee, but why not Texas or here?

On the bus I'd come up with a reasonable explanation: He'd sent letters here, but they'd been delayed in the mail. It had sounded plausible after staring out the window at the desert for hundreds of miles. Now I wasn't so sure anymore. I wished I hadn't said *I love you*. It had seemed right at the time—fearless and honest—but now I wanted to take it back.

Dear Will, When I said "I love you" I was COMPLETELY KIDDING. I meant: I like you. That's it. See you soon.

If only I could send that.

I showed Lulu all the poems and letters from him, the whole stack, and his mix CD, and told her everything I'd written to him.

I searched her face for a reaction, some Yoda-like words of wisdom, some prediction of the future. "Do you think it's the real thing?" I asked. Grace's words were lodged in my mind like the lyrics of an awful song. "Look at this e. e. cummings poem he sent. You wouldn't send that if it wasn't real, right? If you didn't plan on seeing that person again? Will I see him again?" We were so close to California now. Two days away.

She didn't answer. She didn't say, *Yes, it's real, and this is what you must do, young Jedi*, as I hoped she would. She stood up, went to her shelves, and handed me a stack of books instead.

Feast on your life

They were all shapes and sizes: a cream-colored *The Dream of a Common Language*, by Adrienne Rich; Mary Oliver's bluish-gray *New and Selected Poems*; and a tiny thin purple one called *Letters to a Young Poet*, by Rainer Maria Rilke.

I remembered the letterpress print my mom had ordered for Lulu, and I gave it to her: it was a copy of Elizabeth Bishop's "One Art." Lulu's favorite poem. She'd written her PhD thesis on Elizabeth Bishop. She unrolled it and touched the grooves of the letters and the paper, which was soft as cotton.

"Thank you," she said.

The art of losing isn't hard to master. She beamed as she read it. "I love this. I'm going to frame it and hang it right there." She pointed to a wall behind us.

I touched the books in my lap. They looked like they'd been read a hundred times, with frayed covers and the page corners folded down. Lulu pointed to the little purple book, to page thirty-four. "Start there," she said.

I would like to beg you, dear Sir, as well as I can,
to have patience with everything unresolved in your

heart and to try to love the questions themselves as if they were locked rooms or books written in a very foreign language. Don't search for the answers, which could not be given to you now, because you would not be able to live them. And the point is to live everything. Live the questions now. Perhaps then, someday far in the future, you will gradually, without even noticing it, live your way into the answer.

Don't search for the answers. I felt like I was always searching. Literally—when I felt depressed I'd wander online, pressing links, looking for something that would make me feel better. I'd surf from friends' photos to strangers' blog posts about how to apply makeup, to the flight message board, to Googling Will for the hundredth time—and feel worse.

Lulu added more books to my pile.

"I know what you really want to do is to send him a video of yourself strumming a guitar and singing, *You've got grief, I've got grief, obviously we're soulmates,*" she said.

"I kind of do," I said.

"That's what we're here for," she said. "To stop you from doing that."

She spooned more ice cream into our bowls and pointed to the letterpress print. "You know, Elizabeth Bishop wrote that poem when she was lovesick. She'd broken up with her lover, a woman named Alice. Alice was engaged to a man at the time. After Elizabeth wrote that poem, Alice broke it off with the guy and she and Elizabeth got back together. They remained together till Elizabeth died."

I couldn't believe a poem could do that, could have that kind of power.

Lulu looked at me. "What about your poems? Have you started writing again?"

"No. I've only written one in the last two years and it's bad." I was going to explain it: *I've been busy*, I could tell her, or some other lame excuse. I thought of showing her the journal Janet had given me, but I felt embarrassed about the Dear Daddy, the stuff I'd written about pretending, and the naked need of it all. And I didn't want to tell her the truth, how despite that one page I'd filled with that letter to him, it still felt too painful to try to write more than that, and how I was afraid if I really opened the floodgates, it would all rush out like Pandora's box, ugly and embarrassing things that I didn't want to write about.

I picked up *The Dream of a Common Language*. I opened it to a section called "Twenty-One Love Poems."

"Ah," Lulu said. "Another favorite." She pointed to a poem in the middle, the only poem in the sequence without a number. It was called "The Floating Poem."

Whatever happens with us, your body
will haunt mine—
. . . whatever happens, this is.

Maybe, no matter what, everything that happened with Will and me would never end—it would be out there, floating, forever. *Whatever happens, this is.* I wanted to send this poem to Will. Or I could give it to him when I saw him.

I'd forgotten how much I loved to talk to Lulu about poetry. We never talked about it on the phone—when I called her it was always about some problem I had that I couldn't share with my mom. I decided to call her more often, just to talk.

Annie cradled the stack of poetry books in her lap. "Is there any problem that can't be solved with a book?"

"Nope," Lulu said, and smiled.

Lulu was a lot like my dad in ways, treating life like a big celebration, like the world was an enormous apple they wanted to bite. Annie and Will were like that, too.

I stared at "The Floating Poem," tracing the last line with my finger.

A good world

I'd liked Texas's giant dome of a sky, its rolling hills and endless endless endlessness; I'd liked Cleveland and Tennessee and the swirling scenery of every state we rode through—but I fell in love with Tucson. Tucson was the Gurlag of cities: different, crazy, gorgeous, and surreal.

Mountains. Red and orange and bright pink at sunset. Saguaros raised their arms toward the sky like a cactus cheer. Prickly pears sprouted purple fruit. Giant aloe plants hovered like extraterrestrials. It was so hot that my Hershey's bar began to melt from store to car, but the heat made everything seem even more foreign and adventurous: another country. Another *planet*.

I still felt anxiety simmering inside me, but I pushed those feelings down deep and tried to forget about them. I tried to focus on traveling, the view outside the window, this new place, instead. My mom had texted me: Lulu said you arrived safely-so glad! She didn't mention the wedding date. I didn't write back.

Lulu toured us around town in her sky-blue VW Bug,

named Bugalicious. She took us to the café at Hotel Congress, which was antique and modern at the same time, the kind of place that makes you feel cool just for stepping inside it; to Bookman's, the biggest and most organized used-book store I'd ever been to; to Café Poca Cosa, her favorite restaurant, where we ate *pastel de elote con mole negro*—tamale pie with melted cheese and a chocolate mole sauce—gooey, spicy, and sweet. I ate the whole thing. (*Chocolate!* For *dinner!*)

Toward the end of the meal, my phone buzzed. A text from my mom, I figured, until I picked it up and saw a new number. My heart froze.

```
Still in LA. I'll see you on Friday :) Will
```

He'd texted me.

The bright tablecloth glowed, the curtains sang, the trees on the patio danced. I practically stood up on my chair. I stared at the message for a long time, then passed it to Annie and Lulu to make sure that it was real. He was staying in LA. He'd used a smiley face. Will had used a smiley face. In man-speak, that was practically the same as saying I love you.

I typed back:

```
The taping starts really early on Friday & ends
by 5pm. See you after that? Can't wait! Is this
your new #? Did you finally get a new phone? ☺
```

Instead of the smiley face, I wished they had an emoji that said *I love you and you just made my year and thank freaking god you're staying in California.*

I showed it to Annie and Lulu to make sure it sounded okay, and then I pressed send. I stared at the screen. My future, my whole life, in one little candy-bar-shaped phone.

As soon as the text was gone, my limbs felt hollow. My mind swelled with the image of Janet's face. Which side of her would we see in LA—Aunt STD? Aunt Cowboy Kiss? How would I get past her to see Will? We told Lulu about Janet and Farley.

"What if when we get to LA she won't let me see him?" I asked.

"Don't worry," Lulu said. "You'll figure something out."

"We'll smuggle you out if we have to," Annie said.

My mind imagined things I hadn't let it picture in days: Will and me alone on Venice Beach, the Santa Monica pier, the Hollywood Walk of Fame, and at all the sights I'd read about. And I thought what a great place the world is. For two years, I'd felt like I was teetering on a high wire, not knowing if the world spun on an axis of good or one of pain. Seeing Will was the universe saying: it's a good place, and the dark days are exceptions to the light.

A good death

After dinner, when the desert began to cool, we drove to Sabino Canyon to walk in the moonlight. We wandered past saguaros, cholla cacti, paloverde trees, and groves of ocotillo. The desert was quiet, nearly empty. Everything smelled like sage and mesquite, and the rocks glistened.

We walked single file down the path; the full moon lit up everything. "So if Tucson is Gurlag, who would Cleveland be?" Annie asked.

"Definitely Sir Richard," I said. "And Texas is Destry, obviously. The bold brother with a soft heart."

Annie opened her water bottle and took a sip. "Who's New York?"

I thought for a minute. "Andy Pomp from the *Pomp and Circumstance* series. He's a megalomaniacal but endearing businessman who pretty much owns the whole world, and he seduces all these women even though he has a giant ugly scar down his face."

Lulu rested her hand on her stomach. "Too bad there aren't romances about pregnant women."

"Oh, there are. There are romances about everybody—people with no legs, and women who have sex with cucumbers and stuffed animals and—"

They stared at me.

"I haven't read those. I prefer historicals."

We continued on down the trail, and Lulu changed the subject to Elizabeth Bishop, who she was writing an article about for an academic journal. She told us how Elizabeth had traveled the world, circumnavigating South America by boat.

Then Lulu stopped talking. She gasped and froze. Annie and I peered from behind her.

At first I thought it was a rope on the ground.

A rattling—an eerie, sickening sound. The rope coiled, its head raised. We stood still, paralyzed.

The snake moved closer and we ran, screaming, barreling down the path, moving faster than I ever had in my life. We reached the car, then locked the doors and huddled inside. We grasped each other, trembling. Finally, we laughed with relief.

Lulu rested her head on the steering wheel, breathing hard. "Oh my god."

"Muggers. Ax murders. Rapists. Diseases. But never rattlesnakes. My mom never warned me about rattlesnakes," I said.

"I've lived here for years and that's the closest I've ever been to one." Lulu shook her head.

"Are you supposed to run? Or stay still? What are you supposed to do?" Annie asked.

"I think move away slowly," Lulu said. "But I wasn't thinking when I saw it. All I could think was RUN!"

She drove extra carefully, and we stopped at Donut Palace on the way home. Two bored girls in red aprons eyed us, seeming annoyed that we'd come in. Little did they know how good it felt to be alive, to buy puffy hot clouds of sugary dough, which we gobbled in the car and back at Lulu's house, sitting on the chairs and the bench in her garden.

"Everything tastes much better after you almost died," Annie said.

We're lucky, we said, and *What are the chances*, and *Nothing would've happened anyway. Even if we'd stepped on him, we would've been okay. We're not far from a hospital.* But I couldn't help picturing the opposite. Lulu pregnant, Annie and me carrying her down the trail. Phone calls, the hospital vigil, Lulu's husband grieving. Telling Annie's parents and sisters, if she'd been the one. I pictured my own mother, if it had been me who'd gotten bit. In my mind I watched her throw another ceramic pitcher against the wall.

"At least it would be quick, a snake bite," I said. "You wouldn't even know what was happening."

"Not exactly," Annie said. "Snake venom can be hemotoxic—it would be pretty slow and painful if untreated." She picked up another doughnut. "Not as bad as some other reptile or animal deaths, though—there's this giant bird in Australia and New Guinea called the cassowary, and it can disembowel you with its claws. If you wanted a good death, a painless death, you'd probably want to stay away from the animal kingdom. . . ."

Lulu clutched her stomach. "No more talk of snakes and crazy animals." She glanced around the garden. Beside us, a bed overflowed with more white flowers, their petals glowing in the darkness.

Annie eyed the curve of Lulu's belly. "What's it feel like?" Annie asked her. "Being pregnant?" The fear had stripped us bare; I felt like we could ask each other anything now.

"It's amazing and terrifying at the same time."

The corner of her mouth quivered. It was strange to see Lulu scared—she always seemed so calm and together, so different from my anxious mom and anxious me. She picked a leaf off the plant growing beside her. "This isn't my first time. When I was thirty, I had a baby who died. Stillborn."

My mom had told me about that so long ago that I'd forgotten it.

"Before it happened to me, I would've wondered how someone could miss a person they'd barely known. But you can't underestimate the depth of love a mother has for her baby. Or the depth of grief. I still grieve him. It's been sixteen years and I think of him every day."

I thought of Will and his baby brother who died, his

parents who never got over it.

Lulu brushed a leaf off her chair. She shrugged. "I never thought I could get pregnant again. I never thought I'd have this chance."

We were quiet. Lulu brought us glasses of water, and we sipped them in the garden. Annie shifted on the bench and stared at the moon. After a while, she touched the elastic hair tie around her wrist. "Is this what love is supposed to be like? Is it supposed to make you feel kind of awful?"

I nodded. "Yup. It's like a never-ending low-grade flu. Kind of like grief, actually. Do you remember that book my mom gave me? *The Stages of Mourning*. It said *Each year you'll feel better and better*. I don't know what the hell that book was talking about."

"I always think *dead* is such an inadequate word. It sounds so final for something that, in so many ways, is completely unfinal after all," Lulu said.

"It's final for my mom, though. That's why she never talks about my dad. Threw out almost every trace of him." I touched the wax paper bag where the icing had pooled. "I just want to know that he died like you said"—I turned to Annie—"a good death."

"I'm not sure what a good death is," Lulu said, looking down.

The wax paper bag crinkled beneath my hand. "I don't know if I can stand more years of feeling like this. Of missing him," I said.

Lulu took off her shoes and rubbed her ankle. "Grief and pain are natural, though. One thing I love about Tucson is how close we are to Mexico. Sixty miles away. You'll have to come back sometime for the Day of the Dead—it's a national holiday, with sugar skulls, parades, dancing, and picnics in graveyards, to remember people you love who died—it's the best holiday in the world. If we had a Day of the Dead in America, it would be sponsored by Xanax."

We laughed.

"My mom would never celebrate it," I said. "She's marrying Larry, planning the wedding as if my dad never existed."

"Oh, she thinks of your dad. She thinks of him all the time. She just has a hard time being honest about it. And one of the most painful things of all, to your mom, is the thought of letting you go. You're sixteen. You'll only be at home two more years, and that scares her."

"More than two years probably. She wants me to live at home and go to Queens College."

"Will you."

She said it as more of a statement, not a question. *Will you.*

This voice inside me—a tiny, quiet voice, a new voice (or had it been there all along?) said, *I don't want to. I want to live somewhere new, on my own. I want to go away to school.*

It didn't matter what the voice said. In reality, that wasn't a possibility. Even if I went to Queens College and lived in a dorm, my mom would probably stop by every day and make sure I had no boys in my room and was wearing a whistle. My earlier idea of being emancipated seemed ridiculous when I thought about it now. My mom would probably hunt me down and guilt me into giving it up. If Lulu was the Truth Machine, my mom was the Guilt Machine. *(Shall we talk about thirty-six hours of labor?* she liked to say. *How you were surgically removed from my belly? And how you refused to eat homemade baby food—you'd only eat the expensive store-bought kind?)* I hadn't even made amends for how bad a baby—and fetus—I had been. I'd never have the guts to get emancipated.

I looked at Annie. She kept snapping the elastic band on her wrist. "Maybe you'll see Chance again soon," I told her. "And whatever happens with him, you have this amazing future ahead of you at MIT—"

Annie shook her head. "I don't know if it will be amazing." She picked at her fingernails.

"But you're happy," I said. "You're not such an anxious person like me—"

"I just hide it well." She shrugged. "I don't know. Sometimes I think how my parents have college degrees that are worthless pieces of paper here in America, so they own a laundromat, and my sisters are disappointments who break their hearts every day . . . so I feel like it's up to me to make their entire lives worth it."

She pointed to the elastic hair tie around her wrist. "And there's this." She snapped it against her skin again, hard.

"What are you doing?" I asked.

"I read about it online. Whenever you think of a guy you want to put out of your mind, you snap it."

"Really?"

"We have one more day to study. *One day.*" She snapped the rubber band once more.

"Ouch," I said.

The art of losing

I n bed, Annie conked right out to sleep, and I went back
to my nightly routine: checking texts, emails, voice mails.
Textsemailsvoicemails. Repeat.

The air conditioner hummed as I listened to my sole voice
mail from my mom (she was back from her trip, *Call me*), and I
debated how long to stay awake to see if Will would write back.

On to the message board. I'd checked it a few times since
we'd arrived in Tucson, but there hadn't been any news.

Now there were ninety-six new posts.

Fran had started a new thread.

> I just spoke to Frank Longbrown. He wanted to let us
> know before it's announced to the media tomorrow that
> seven more bodies have been recovered and are await-
> ing identification, bringing the total to eleven. These will be
> the last bodies retrieved. They're going to leave the site
> and close the recovery effort.
>
> Fran Gamuto (husband Frank,
> daughter Lisa, 22C, 22D)

This gives me hope. I pray every day that we'll be one of the lucky ones and they'll bring my son home. Then we can all close this chapter and move on with our lives.

Erin Farwell (Malcom, 19E)

I can't stand to think that my father may be there, his body intact. . . . He needs to be buried properly, with dignity.

Aurelie (father Edward, 14B)

You don't understand the state of the bodies. They're very fragile. They won't be identified by sight but by DNA. The submarines work with a robotic crane and a cage, and they'll damage the bodies by transporting them. After two years under the sea not only would they be decomposed but the fatty tissue would become wax. They will be punctured and destroyed by the crane and cage, disintegrating in the process, and then be transported in freezer containers. It's not humane.

Jill (Jacques Bluelake, 14A)

Back and forth, back and forth, retrieve the bodies, leave them there. I read through more messages, pages and pages of them on my phone.

I wanted his body found. I knew it completely. He had to be among them, we had to be among the lucky, and in my mind I thought again, *If the world spins on an axis of good*, then he'll be brought back. The people who didn't want the bodies retrieved were wrong.

I kept reading the messages until they began to numb me, like my soul was slowly freezing, but I couldn't stop.

Then I came to this.

> I've called Frank Longbrown personally and told him I don't want to be notified if my husband's body is retrieved. I don't want to have another funeral, to go through this all over again. My daughter and I have been through enough. I hope that after this there will be no more news reports or media coverage, and we can at long last put this episode in our lives to rest.
>
> Claire Roth (husband Frederick, 8B)

I read it three times.

Four times.

Six.

If I kept reading it, I thought, it would make sense, become clear, fit into everything that I knew.

Not notified? Not *notified*?

My mind spun.

I walked out into the garden. I called her.

"Eva?" her voice crackled. I'd woken her up.

"How could you?"

"What?"

"You'll talk to strangers about him but not to me?"

"You're not making sense."

"The message board. I read what you wrote on the forum."

"Eva. Calm down. Please."

"How could you do that?" I tried to clear my voice, to talk normally. "How could you say we don't want to be notified? How could you make that decision without asking me? You never asked me anything. You've never talked to me about this at all!"

Silence. She spoke slowly, softly. "You don't understand. . . . Since he was already identified, it's unlikely they'll find anything else . . . and even if somehow they do, it's not so simple. . . . The bodies aren't the way you imagine. . . ."

I said, "You've been making decisions with other people about Daddy's body. But not with me."

"I don't want to talk about this right now—"

"You never want to talk about it. That's the problem. That's the problem with *everything.*"

The line went silent. Neither of us knew what to say. I didn't know if I should hang up or not.

"We can talk about all this when I see you," my mom said. "We can—I can explain then. In person. It's not the same on the phone—it's late at night—"

"There's no way you can explain this. Not telling me that you made this decision—that's lying. And why did you go away with Larry without telling me?"

"I didn't want you to worry." She paused, and then her tone shifted. "And you lied to me. Janet told me you've been getting letters from a boy in California. A boy named Will."

My throat felt dry.

"You lied to me about what this trip was for, didn't you? It was never about the scholarship, was it?"

I didn't answer.

"How well do you even know this boy—Will? When did you meet him? You never even mentioned him to me once."

I couldn't stand to hear her say his name. She was crushing it, the love, thumb-squashing everything good. "Why do you think I didn't tell you? You don't know anything about my life."

"I hate seeing you chase some boy. Some fantasy. I keep waiting for you to grow out of it—"

"That's why I didn't tell you. Because I knew you'd react like this." My eyes stung. Tears had started.

She kept talking—lecturing—but I stopped listening. "I can't talk anymore," I told her. "I need to go." I hung up the phone and turned the ringer off. I set the phone facedown on the garden bench. The white flowers looked ghostly now, shadowy. Cicadas sang in a shrill roar.

I thought of my dad's funeral. There are so many brutal things about death. Ugly things you don't want to remember. Memories you wish you could wipe off your brain. And normally I did—usually I pushed the memory of that day away, tried to forget it, but now it rushed in—all the worst things began to rush in.

One peace

Two years ago, six weeks after my dad died, we'd received a call. A man on the phone who said, *We've recovered Mr. Roth's remains.*

Remains? You have a body?

We've identified a hand and forearm that match the DNA of Mr. Roth.

A hand.

My father's hand.

That was the part of him they'd identified. The *remains*.

We'd had to decide if we wanted it sent to a funeral home and cemetery of our choosing, to be buried.

Our rabbi said that was what we should do. That according to Jewish law, or at least his interpretation of it, we should bury it in a grave.

I asked to wait. To see if they'd find the rest of him, the body with the missing hand. The weeks passed and nothing more was found, so we went ahead with the burial.

My mom didn't invite anyone else and we almost didn't go ourselves—she wanted to back out—but I made her promise to take me.

At the cemetery, a tent was set up beside my father's grave. It was raining. We carried black umbrellas. We walked toward the tent, stared into the hole and at the coffin waiting to be lowered inside it.

"Hello, hand!" I said brightly.

"It's not funny," my mom said. "Why do you have to make this into something funny?"

"*He'd* think it's funny. He'd laugh. He'd think it was hysterical that we're having a ceremony for his hand."

And forearm, I wanted to add, but didn't.

It was absurd. It was absolutely and completely absurd and no one ever warned me how this would feel.

Now *hand and forearm* was etched in my brain forever. I couldn't stop thinking of what it must look like inside the full-size coffin (they don't make a hand-size one; it would be inappropriate, according to my mother), and I pictured it like the Halloween pranks boys in my third grade class used to do: sticking their finger in a box, making it look disembodied, with ketchup spots.

Or like a horror movie, its bloody edge with gristle and veins, a violence. I couldn't stop my mind from thinking of what had happened to the rest of his body, to the body I loved, the chest I'd crawl up on to nap and how happy I felt there, and how that could be destroyed, how I wanted to think of him in one piece but never could.

One day in school, I was trying to write the words *one piece* and instead I wrote *one peace*.

A person should die in one peace.

A good death.

People shouldn't die with their bodies destroyed. *How you die* was never a phrase that had entered my head before.

At the cemetery, my mom wore sunglasses. She'd taken a pill that morning, something her doctor had prescribed. She asked the rabbi to keep it short.

"No," I said. "Let him do the whole thing." I sort of liked the rabbi, with his long face and maplike certainty about how we should proceed, his self-assurance. I'd already gone along with my mom and agreed not to have a real funeral in a funeral parlor, but just a graveside service, just a burial. Just.

My mom couldn't even watch the service. She kept looking off to the side. Fidgeting. Buttoning and unbuttoning her coat. The rain stopped. Sweat beaded at her forehead. She kept glancing at the taxi, which waited nearby. They'd given us an hourly rate and it was going to be an expensive fare. There'd been traffic.

"Can you pay attention?" I asked her.

The rabbi paused, embarrassed.

My mom smiled awkwardly; she looked like she wanted to run away or throw up. She didn't even recite the Kaddish, the mourner's prayer; she kept the card in her hand without reading the words.

"You're not doing this right," I said.

"Don't tell me how to do it right."

"You don't even miss him."

"Stop it."

"You don't! You didn't want to give him a funeral! Why are we the only ones here? Where are his friends? My friends? Why couldn't they come too?"

She took off her sunglasses. "Don't do this to me."

The rabbi paused the ceremony. He took us aside separately. He talked to my mom for a while, hovering by the gravestones along the trees. Then he spoke to me. "Your mother is having a difficult time. Understandably," he told me.

"Not understandably," I said.

He was patient. Maybe he'd learned how to handle mother-and-daughter funeral squabbles in rabbi school. Maybe they had a whole class called *Crazy Grievers: What to Do When Mom and Kid Fight over Burial of Severed Hand. And Forearm.*

"She feels ill. It may be the medication her doctor prescribed. She needs to go home," he said. He told me that she was going to leave in the taxi, and he'd finish the service with me and drive me back to Queens.

My mom tried to hug me, but I stiffened like I did when I was four and she tried to get me into a snowsuit. She let go and climbed into the cab. She took off.

I was alone at my dad's funeral. My shoulders curled with ten different kinds of shame, and things were never the same with my mom and me again.

We started unraveling, then. We'd been unraveling ever since.

The rabbi and I finished the ceremony, and he let me shovel dirt onto the coffin after it was lowered into the ground, but without my mom there that didn't feel right, either.

When it was over, I sat by the grave. The rabbi stood off to the side, leaving me and the hand alone. I prayed for the first time in my life. I'd never asked anything of God before—in synagogue my thoughts were usually limited to *What will I eat when this is over?*—but now I had a real prayer. Maybe because I thought He might actually be listening, that there might be some kind of direct line when you're sitting in a graveyard. I prayed: *Please bring the rest of his body back.* The words kept echoing in my mind. Other words echoed too, not so much a prayer as a one-line poem: *If he's shattered, I'm not whole.*

I didn't stay at the cemetery much longer. Maybe an hour. On the way home I sat beside the rabbi, picking at the leather seat, watching the suburbs turn back into the city and wishing I could be somebody else, giving anything in the world to be somebody else.

When I got back to our apartment my mom was asleep, and when she awoke we pretended that nothing had happened. We were still pretending.

I'd never even told Annie or Lulu about that day—I'd only told them it was awful and I wanted to forget it.

Now that memory of the funeral crushed me fully, and those little bits of thumb-squashing on top of it, push after push that built up over time until I felt like I'd been knocked to the floor. I thought of how much happier I'd felt this week, being away from my mom—how I felt like myself. I wanted to keep being free from her. I didn't want to pretend anymore.

I picked up my phone. I had four missed calls and a voice mail from my mom that I didn't listen to.

I called her back. My hand wobbled as I dialed the number.

She picked up right away. I took a deep breath and tried to level my voice. "I have to tell you something. I'm not staying at Janet's condo in LA," I said. "The show is giving us a hotel room and we're going to use it." She tried to interrupt me, but I didn't let her. "And you know what? I'm done pretending with you. I'm done being your daughter."

The words came out on their own. Just two days before, at the perfume stall at the rodeo, I'd missed her—but those feelings had been trampled away now. I wiped my face on my arm. More words came, like a boulder rolling. "I'm throwing your whistle in the garbage. I'm not answering your texts anymore. Maybe I'll stay in LA after the show. Maybe I won't come home."

I hung up the phone.

She called me back. I didn't pick up. The ringer was silent, and I watched the calls pile up, Claire Roth, Claire Roth, Claire Roth, until I turned the power off. I was done with her. We were going to LA and I was done with my mother.

Worn down love

At the bus station the next day, Lulu waited on line beside us, clutching her elbows and shifting from foot to foot. We hugged her good-bye. Her belly felt hard beneath her soft dress.

She was jittery. "Please answer your mom's messages, just for today. She's so worried. . . ."

"I can't." When we woke up that morning, Lulu already knew about the fight—my mom had emailed her. Lulu thought I should call her, but I couldn't. Lulu asked if I wanted to talk about it with her, but for the first time, I didn't want to. The feelings and anger felt so raw and confusing, and all I wanted to think about was getting to California, seeing Will, and winning the show. That was all that mattered.

She took off her sunglasses. "You'll meet Janet at the other end, right?"

I shrugged. I hadn't figured out how I'd handle Janet yet. All I knew was we'd traveled this far; we could handle LA on our own, without a chaperone.

She bit her lip. "I wish I could go with you. I don't like

seeing you take off with everything with your mom like this. Please call me from the road, okay? And call as soon as you get there. I want to know you're okay. And please try to get some sleep." She touched my arm gently.

"I will," I said.

She hugged me and Annie. "Take good care of each other," she said to both of us.

We nodded and boarded the bus; the front seats were already taken. My mind buzzed from coffee and lack of sleep. I'd stayed awake the whole night, thinking of my father's body in a freezer container like that person had described, abandoned, no one telling us, no one telling me.

Annie squeezed my hand. When she'd woken up that morning and I'd told her what had happened, she'd looked at me with an expression that I've never seen in any other friend—her eyes absorbing all my feelings like a sponge, as if it were happening to her too.

Trinkets

We found seats in the third row; Annie took the spot by the window. An old woman sat across the aisle from me, knitting a scarf. Her tangerine hair floated above her scalp like a cloud; she clutched a tote bag embroidered with jumping kittens. She'd tied various trinkets onto the scarf's fringe—plastic rings, tiny children's toys, a miniature koala. She said, "Don't forget the battery acid!" and "Who took my foot grease?"

I elbowed Annie. Seven days into our trip and we'd met our first crazy bus person.

I reached into my backpack, opened my pillowcase, and checked everything was still inside. My fingers touched the glasses and tie and T-shirt. My eyes were completely dry. I was all cried out. I'd cried the tears behind the tears. My whole face felt numb.

I'd see Will tomorrow night. No one could stop us. The words rolled around in my head like marbles, like prayer beads: tomorrow night tomorrow night tomorrownight.

As we drove through Arizona, I sensed the crazy lady's

eyes on me. "I like your pillowcase. Nice pillowcase. Nice pillowcase," she said.

Great. Anger fizzed inside me, a slow burning feeling, but
instead of saying something, I stuck to the Normal New York
City Response to Wackos Rule: Pretend They Don't Exist.

That was easier to do on a subway, where you could get
up and change your seat. We were stuck in place, and the
woman was only inches away across the aisle. The driver saw
her staring at me in the rearview mirror. He called back to
me, "Don't mind old Trinkets. She's harmless."

Harmless. Except she smelled like foot grease.

I put on my earphones and listened to Will's mix again.
At lunchtime, the driver pulled into a rest stop somewhere
in the middle of western Arizona with a convenience store
called Havalind's. A quirky-looking place with a slate roof
and shingled siding. I hoped the crazy woman would get off,
but no luck.

I left the bus to get something to eat while Annie watched
our stuff. We'd been on the bus for almost three hours, but
my legs were already feeling cramped and achy. Thank god
this was our last bus day. We still had over six hours to go
before we reached LA.

Havalind's didn't sell live crickets or elk jerky, but it had
shelves and shelves of candy. Old-time candy like Pixy Stix
and Candy Buttons, and ones I'd never heard of before: Valo-
milks, Twin Bings, Nut Goodies, Idaho Spuds. They had

British candy bars, too: Crunchies, Starbars, Twirls, Aeros, and Flakes.

On the bottom shelf in the far right corner was a box of Toffee Crisps.

I picked up two, then four, then all they had. Seven total. Back on the bus, I stuck the brown bag of candy inside my pillowcase, and Annie took her turn to get food.

The bus was nearly empty; almost everyone had left on the break. People stood outside, smoking and talking on their phones.

I reached inside my backpack and took out three bars. I walked up to the front and opened the first one. The chocolate melted on my tongue. I tasted the soft gooey toffee and airy crunchy rice as I looked out the wide window, down the highway toward California. I ate the other two. I was so tired that I felt heavy all over, as if my body were filling with wet sand.

I heard something—a rustling noise—and turned around.

Orange hair bobbed between the rows. I went back to my seat. My backpack was unzipped. I reached inside and checked that my wallet was there—it was. The pillowcase was missing.

I wheeled around. "Where is it?"

The crazy woman looked away. She shook her head.

"Give it back."

She gripped the handles of her kitten bag. Of course she

had it. She'd seen me take it out a moment ago.

"Give it to me." My voice was sharp, sharper than it had ever been.

Her eyes looked blue and watery, bloodshot. She pressed the bag more tightly to her chest.

A force outside of myself seemed to act. It happened in half a second: grabbing Larry's Swiss Army knife out of my back-pack, opening the blade, my feet firmly planted, the same stance I'd had when I'd shot the gun in Texas.

"Give me my goddamn stuff."

She handed the pillowcase back to me and screamed.

End of the line

T he driver dragged our bags out of the cargo hold and
dumped them on the curb. "End of the line, ladies," he
said. He refused to let us back on the bus.

"You *can't* do this." Annie's face turned red. "We have
tickets. We *paid*. We have to be in LA tonight!" Her voice
squeaked.

No one had seen me hold the knife; I'd put it away as fast
as I could. But Trinkets hadn't stopped screaming. A sleeping
old man had woken up, the driver and passengers came running, and Trinkets denied stealing anything. She accused me
of trying to steal from her.

Now the driver wouldn't stop shaking his head. "I'm not
dealing with this. I've known Trinkets five years. She's crazy
but she's harmless. I'm taking her word over two kids." He
picked up another one of our bags. He dropped it at our feet
like it was a mound of trash.

Annie kept arguing. "We're minors—this is against the
law—"

"Out of my face, kid," he said. "Not on my bus." He climbed

back into his seat and shut the doors. The bus wheezed its exasperated sigh and skidded off. I almost swore I could see Trinkets' gleeful face through the dark window.

We sat down on a bench inside Havalind's. Annie's eyes looked glassy. She opened her mouth but didn't speak.

I bit my lip and checked the schedule: the next bus didn't leave until tomorrow morning at nine. We had to be at the studio by six thirty.

"We can catch another bus, right?" Annie asked me. "There's one soon?"

"Um—no," I said softly.

"There must be a train," she said.

I looked online. There were no train stations nearby. I shook my head.

She looked like she might explode. "Shit. Shit. *Shit*. What are we going to do?"

"I'll think of something." I rubbed my forehead. We were too young to rent a car, and neither of us even had a license. I Googled taxi companies, but there weren't any for a hundred miles. Anyway, we wouldn't be able to afford the cost of a meter running all the way to LA.

There was only one person I could call.

Lulu answered on the first ring. "You're kidding me," she said when I told her what had happened. "If you caught her stealing, why didn't you just call the police? Why didn't you—"

"I know," I said quietly. I didn't have an excuse. I didn't know how to explain the anger, the force that had taken over me.

Lulu paused on the other end. After a long while, she finally said, "All right. I'm coming."

She had a few things to take care of before she left; by the time she arrived it was almost six o'clock. We left the air-conditioned Havalind's in a daze and headed into the hot Arizona air.

Lulu checked her watch and snapped her purse shut. "If we leave right now, we should get there around one a.m. or so. I have to make a lot of stops to eat and pee, though, just so you know."

"Thank you so much for doing this," I said. I wondered how I'd ever find a way to repay her.

She tugged at her dress, adjusting it over her stomach. "The baby keeps me up all night long anyway," she said. "Kicking and dancing and having a party in there. Might as well take a trip. Anyway, if I need a nap, we can pull off the road for a little while."

"We owe you big-time," Annie said. "You've really saved us."

The VW Bug sat in the parking lot, its pale blue paint glowing against the red desert sand.

"Let's go," Lulu said. "We have to leave now if we're going to make it."

Maps

Weeks ago, when I'd pictured myself and Annie the night before the show, I'd imagined us in our fancy room at the Mirabelle Resort, painting our nails and applying deep-conditioning hair treatments. Will would be sitting beside us, asking us questions about presidents and geography and literature, all of which we'd answer right. He'd kiss me good night—a kiss even better than the spell-casting kisses on the roof. Annie and I'd iron our clothes, go to bed early, wake up well-rested, eat healthy breakfasts, and make ourselves look sleek, shiny, worthy of being on TV.

Or at least we'd be *clean*.

Instead, my hair had turned into monkey fur. My dress for the show was a wrinkled ball in my suitcase. My nails looked like a gerbil had feasted on them. A pimple swelled beneath my cheek; it looked like a buried pomegranate seed. My stomach puffed out of my jeans, probably because I'd eaten three Toffee Crisps that day.

Annie lay curled up in the backseat, sleeping. I'd tried to fall asleep but couldn't.

Still no more messages from Will.

Lulu drove with her elbows resting on her stomach. My phone buzzed. My mom again.

"Still not picking up?" Lulu asked.

I shook my head.

We were the only car on the road. "I haven't called your mom yet, but I need to soon. I have to tell her what happened and that I'm driving you. I don't want her to worry."

"I know."

Outside, the heat seemed to radiate off the highway as we sped through the desert. Lulu hesitated. "You know how much she loves you."

I looked down at my lap. I didn't know. *My love for you is bigger than the house, the whole city, all the people in the world, the entire universe,* she used to say when I was little, but I had the sinking feeling that now she'd say *My love for you is the size of a cup of coffee. Of a sugar packet.* Or she'd say whatever *Living with Your Teenage Daughter and Loving It* told her to say.

Lulu was silent for a while. "Your mom has been working so hard because she wants to provide for you. To take good care of you. Lord knows it's hard to do as a single mom."

I'd never really thought about that—I'd thought working was her way of coping, like Janet had said. I shook my head. "I just don't understand her."

"She's complicated. Everything is complicated." She paused. "You know, Rilke was wrong about one thing. As you get older, no matter how patient you are, you don't get more answers—you just get more difficult questions."

"I want to stop feeling like this. I want to be like I was before he died." The little girl in the Central Park photo. Happy. Carefree.

She glanced at me, then stared at the road. "Grief isn't like a map you can follow. It's not a simple route with a destination. Sometimes you loop back and find yourself in the exact same place you left." She paused. "I think in her own way, your mom is still grieving her parents, too."

I told her about Freda's and Abraham's graves in Cleveland. "Before this trip, I hardly knew anything about Freda except Formula 409. All I remembered was drinking milk with a drop of coffee in it with her, and eating noodles at her kitchen table."

Lulu smiled. "Years and years ago, when your grandmother was still alive, I stayed at her apartment once with your mom. I left a T-shirt there, and when your mom gave it back to me, it had bleach splotches all over it. Your grandmother had used it as a rag to clean the bathroom."

I laughed.

Lulu said, "You know, everything is connected. Freda's pain became your mom's pain. Your mom wants to protect you from inheriting any pain."

I watched the endless sea of desert. Dead and missing great-grandparents. Freda. My dad. My mom. Me. One big rolling giant ball of grief. *Protect you.* "She can't," I said.

Sleeping beauties

I woke up to a sea of cars streaming down the highway. Pink streaks smudged across the gray sky. I rubbed my eyes; my contact lenses had stuck to them. Lulu held a giant coffee cup in her hand.

I sat up. "Where are we?"

"Welcome to LA." She smiled. She'd tied her hair into a bun and stuck a pencil through it. A few tendrils curled around her face.

Palm trees lined the highway. They looked like giant lollipops with leaves on top. I checked my messages. Four, all from my mom.

Delete. Delete. Delete. Delete. I wasn't ready to talk to her. Not now. I didn't know if I'd ever be ready to.

I squinted at the time on my phone: 6:02 a.m. "Is that time right?"

"You fell asleep around Palm Springs, and I had to pull off the road and take a nap. I didn't think I could make it all the way without sleeping." She rubbed her eyes.

"We're almost there, right? We've got to be there at six thirty. . . ."

"We should be in Burbank in half an hour." She sipped her coffee.

A groan came from the backseat. Annie had woken up.

"Good morning, sleeping beauty," Lulu chirped, glancing at her in the rearview mirror.

Annie's cheek had a bright red line down the middle of it, from the seat. A gas station receipt was stuck to her chin. She peeled it off and squinted at it.

"Where are we?" she asked.

"We made it! We're here." I tried to sound cheerful, to distract us both from the fact that we were about to be on national TV looking like shipwreck survivors who hadn't showered in a year.

"We should be at the studio soon," Lulu said.

Annie leaned to the side so she could see herself in the rearview mirror.

Her mouth dropped open. "Is that my *face*?" She flopped back down onto the seat.

"You both look beautiful," Lulu tried to assure us. "Fresh as daisies."

"This is bad," I said. "This is really bad."

Lulu said, "It's a quiz show. Not a beauty pageant."

"We haven't *showered*," I said.

"Nobody will be able to smell you through the TV," Lulu said brightly as the sign to Burbank rose in the distance.

Stage 4

The studio looked like a cluster of gigantic blocks. A metal gate enclosed the property; outside, a field of unnaturally green grass surrounded a fountain and a tiny pond. We parked and approached the small white security booth.

"We're here for *The Smartest Girl in America*," we told the guard. He checked our names and IDs against a list. Annie had emailed the production company last night and told them that Lulu would be bringing us, instead of Janet.

"Good luck to you ladies. Stage 4. Wait here. A guard will escort you in." He picked up his walkie-talkie, and a few minutes later a man in a uniform drove up in a golf cart and came out to greet us. We climbed in, and he drove us to a sound stage a short distance away.

Inside, beautiful girls were everywhere, poised and manicured and perfectly coiffed. They wore brightly colored dresses and skirts and flowery perfume.

Even after being washed, my jeans held a faint whiff of horse ranch.

"Maybe we can slip off to the bathroom, clean up a little," Annie said.

At the sinks, Lulu and I splashed water on our faces. Annie rubbed her cheek; it still looked like a miniature bicycle had sped across it. An attempt to brush my hair only made it look like a pile of dried moss. I checked my phone—nothing from Will—it was still too early to text him. I'd wait an hour and then try him. Lulu told us that she'd texted Janet about the change of plans, and Janet said she'd meet us later, after the taping. Lulu said she'd called my mom last night, too, after I'd fallen asleep, and told her where I was and that I was safe. I looked at the floor. I didn't ask her more about it.

Annie picked up her phone. "Grace is looking for us."

We met Grace and her father in the hallway. "Finally! You're here!" Grace hugged Annie. "What happened to you?" She gazed at our wrinkled clothes.

"Long trip," Annie said.

Grace didn't look too great herself. Her skin had broken out, her cheeks were bright red, and her mouth seemed pinched.

"Are you okay?" Annie asked her.

She gave us a stretched, thin smile. "I'm fantastic."

Grace's father wrapped his arm around her. "She's just a little nervous. First time on camera."

The thought of being on camera made me feel a little sick, too. My stomach turned over. I tried to keep it together.

A production assistant came by with an iPad; she checked our names off and pointed toward a large room. "It's only contestants and companions allowed now, so all other people will need to say good-bye. Your belongings will be stored in a locker during the taping, so please don't bring any valuables," she said. "It's the show's policy to prevent cheating or theft while you're being filmed."

Annie and I gave Lulu a giant hug. We thanked her for driving us, for rescuing us—for everything.

"I wish there was some way we could repay you," I said. "If we win, we'll buy you your own doughnut shop. Fresh doughnuts every morning. And night. Forever."

"Sounds perfect." She smoothed her dress. "Should I take your luggage to Janet's? She sent me a message with the address."

"We're staying at the hotel," I said.

Lulu didn't argue with me. "I'll check into the hotel then and take a nap. I'll meet you back here when it's over. Good luck. I'm rooting for you." She hugged us again and kissed our cheeks.

Annie didn't have anything valuable in her backpack, but I gave the pillowcase with my dad's things to Lulu, to take to the hotel. "Please stick it back inside my luggage, okay?" I asked her.

"Believe me, I'll keep it safe," she said.

She waved good-bye. I hated to see her go. A little kid's

voice inside of me wanted to plead: *Stay. Help. I need you.*

I took a deep breath, and Annie squeezed my hand as we entered the next room. The assistants passed out forms for us to fill out, then separated us into different green rooms for hair and makeup. "Last names A through L in Room 1, and M through Z in Room 2," a production assistant said. That meant Annie would go to Room 1 and I'd go to Room 2. Grace would be in Room 2 also. My chest slowly began to fill with cement.

"Contestants and companions, this is the last time you'll see each other until after the show," the production assistant told us. "So now's your chance for any last-minute advice, encouragement, morale boosts . . . you've got two minutes."

Girls squealed and chattered; Grace's dad, her lifeline on the show, muttered something to her about a mnemonic device to remember the periodic table. Annie and I stared at each other. My neck felt tight.

"So. Here we go," Annie said.

"Here we go." I bit my lip.

She opened her bag. "Here—take this." She handed me Quarky, her good-luck charm.

"What? I can't take Quarky."

"If you start to get a panic attack, or get anxious, or feel like you're going to faint, just hold him."

"I won't panic. We've survived a rattlesnake, a bus lunatic, being abandoned by the side of the road—not to mention diseased eyeballs—"

Still, there was a definite itchiness spreading down my arms. My back had begun to sweat.

"Take him," she said.

I held him as she hugged me tightly, more tightly than she ever had before. Then she disappeared into Room 1.

Light, love, life all tumbled

As soon as Annie left my sight, the lack of sleep caught up with me and I felt like I was walking underwater. Henry, the assistant leading us to Room 2, brought us by the set. A pink neon THE SMARTEST GIRL IN AMERICA! sign sprawled across the wall. Rows and rows of seats towered above us, for the studio audience, which would be made up entirely of teen girls, Henry told us. Black cables snaked around the ceiling, over monitors and lights.

Hundreds of lights. Why did they need so many lights? And so many cameras? Wasn't one camera enough? And why were some of the cameras so huge, mounted on black moving frames like giant dinosaurs, like oversized versions of those roaming X-ray machines at the dentist, which always looked slightly sinister to me?

"Um, where do the companions sit during the show?" I asked Henry.

"The Companion Chamber. That place is sealed," he said. "It's like a vault. Off-limits to everyone till we start. They want it to have an air of secrecy."

"Are there this many cameras in there? This many lights?"

He shrugged. "Pretty much."

I took a deep breath and tried to ignore the hot prickles on my skin. Grace tapped my shoulder. "Your eyes are bugging out. I'm kind of nervous, too. Of course today's the day my face decided to explode with zits."

Why was she being civil to me, all of a sudden? Probably out of necessity, like the people on wilderness reality shows who have to be nice to each other to survive.

Grace glanced at a blond girl in the corner. I recognized her from the audition—she'd been the one wearing her school uniform.

"I talked to her this morning before you guys arrived. Her name is Lauren. Her parents hired five tutors for all different subjects. Not just run-of-the-mill tutors—for economics she had a Nobel Prize winner coaching her," Grace said.

Oh god.

"And an acting coach so she answers confidently. And a stylist added hair extensions."

Lauren's blond hair waved over her shoulders like the tresses of a teen Barbie.

"And she had porcelain veneers put on her teeth. I wanted to get veneers too, but my dad said they were too expensive."

Veneers? Last night I hadn't even *brushed* my teeth.

Grace wrinkled her nose. "Do you smell horse?"

I took a step back. "Excuse me," I said. I held up my phone, went to the corner, and checked my messages. I texted Will.

We're here in LA at the studio. See you tonight?
Filming ends at 5pm—maybe then?

Room 2 was filled with acres of food: a table was stocked with bagels, pastries, muffins, cheeses, fruit, and cookies. I filled my plate, and then everyone took turns sitting in a swivel chair in front of a lighted mirror. Henry gave us more forms to fill out while we waited. When it was my turn, the makeup artist cocked her head, squinted at my hair, and said, "I've seen worse."

She took out a giant bottle of dry shampoo and plugged in a straightening iron the size of a sword. "Don't worry. We'll get you fixed up in no time." She took out an airbrush machine, which looked like a large motorized pen, and began to spray foundation on my face. Then she opened a tiered box that seemed to contain the entire contents of Sephora: highlighters, eyeliners, blushes, lip stains and glosses, and dozens of colors of eye shadow, which she mixed like a painter.

When she finished, I could barely recognize myself. I looked like I'd actually slept the night before. And not in a VW Bug.

"I love you," I told her. "You're a miracle worker."

Grace came over to me. I practically bumped into her eyelashes; she'd had about ten pounds of mascara applied to them. She fidgeted and kept picking under her fingernails. My anxiety had congealed into a jittery simmer, a runny glue clogging my veins.

"Hey," Grace said in a quiet voice, "there's something I wanted to tell you." She looked directly at me.

"What?"

"Annie had never told me about—your dad. But Janet mentioned it to my mom . . ." She paused, trying to finish the sentence. "If I'd known—"

I felt something in my pocket. My phone buzzed.

```
Hey! It's Will. Where are you now?
```

My heart jumped into my throat.

"Um, hold on a second," I told Grace. I turned away.

My fingers felt weightless, floating on top of the screen, but as I typed, my hands shook.

```
At the studio. Getting ready for the show. Will
I see you tonight?
```

```
Can't tonight. Free this afternoon. Can you
slip away before it starts? I can meet you
there when you're on a break.
```

"Who's that text from?" Grace asked me. "Your whole face is red."

"No one."

Her eyes lit up. "It's from him. That guy. The poet guy."

I ignored her.

Now. He wanted to see me now.

I turned to Henry, who fluttered around, collecting forms and checking tasks off his list. "Are we going to have any free time before the show starts?"

He shook his head. "No. No way."

"But I thought we don't start taping for three hours."

He shrugged. "It's the rules. We can't go through the hassle of checking everyone in and out, in and out. Sorry." He sped off down the hall.

"Jeez, even your scalp is blushing," Grace said. She blinked. It was amazing she was able to blink with all that mascara. "So Poet Guy wants to see you now?"

Not only my scalp blushed, but my arms and legs and hands and face, too. Why could he only see me *now*? Why not tonight? I felt angry at that part of him that I'd used to love—that mysterious, elusive part. Why had I ever liked that about him?

"Listen. I can help you." She checked her watch. "Eddie is the guard on duty in the booth today. I slipped away from my dad this morning and had a smoke with him out there. Talked to him for a while. He's super nice." She handed me two long brown cigarettes. "Give him these—they're Gauloises, he loves them—and he'll let you out and back in, no problem. If Henry asks where you went, I'll tell him you're in the bathroom. We have two hours before they round us up for the set, so that should give you plenty of time to get back."

I didn't know if I should trust her.

"I'm not always a total asshole." She smiled. "Just let me help."

"Okay," I said. "Okay."

I texted Will:

```
If you can get here ASAP I can sneak out for
a little while. We can meet by the fountain in
front of the studio. I'd love to see you.
```

He wrote back:

```
See you soon
```

One Art

I left the building. I walked past the sound stages, the golf carts roaming, and people walking everywhere. I found Eddie in the entrance booth and gave him the cigarettes.

"Cool, thanks," he said. "I'll let you back in, no problem. Don't worry about it. See you in a bit."

Outside the gate, I sat on the bench by the fountain. Will wasn't there yet.

I waited.

And waited.

The manicured grass looked too green, too perfectly trimmed. I stuck a toe into it. How did they manage to make real grass look completely artificial?

My entire body buzzed; I'd drunk one cup of coffee but felt like I'd drunk ten. I didn't have my phone or my bag with me—Henry had collected all our things and put them in the studio lockers.

I felt grateful for the hair and makeup. If Will had liked me before, with frizzy hair, then there was no way he wouldn't like me now. I wore the vintage black dress and red high heels my mom had let me borrow. I felt a pang thinking of her, a small sharp knot of love.

Finally, a beat-up green Cadillac from the seventies turned into the parking lot. The door opened with a metal squeal.

His hair was longer, curling to his cheekbones. He looked taller, larger, his shoulders wider. Everything about him seemed absolutely familiar and completely foreign at once.

He loped toward me and enveloped me in his arms. The scar on his chin seemed more noticeable now, or maybe I just knew to look for it.

It all rushed back, the hours in the north tower, week after week, the van ride home, the bakery, our kiss on the street, our entire night in the roof garden. Everything.

Here. Now. For *real*.

Real. The word seeped under my skin. I buried my face in his T-shirt. The same smell: sugar and soap. It must've been embedded in his pores. I dissolved with relief.

He pointed to the car. "So I got a new one." He sounded apologetic. "Cupcake-free. I'm still not used to driving without a giant pastry on my roof."

I nodded. I couldn't say anything because a thousand things crowded my throat, drowning each other out.

He touched the back of my neck. "You look beautiful. Did you do something to your hair?"

I managed to say, "They did it for the show."

We sat down on the bench. The fountain sparkled; not

a speck of dirt or a fallen leaf or a single blade of dead grass wrecked the water.

I sat right next to him but I could barely see him. Dark jeans, navy T-shirt, black shoes; I had to force myself to notice these things because after all these weeks of hoping and dreaming, I could barely absorb that he sat beside me now.

He looked up. The sky seemed bluer than it ever was in New York or Tucson or Texas or Tennessee or anywhere— maybe it could only be this blue in California.

"Nice day," he said.

"It is." Clunky words. I could practically see the words clang off the bench and onto the grass. I'd spent so much time imagining what I'd say, and in my head now those ideas all sounded stupid.

That's okay, I told myself. This is normal. We just need time to get used to each other again.

"I loved all the letters and poems you sent," I said. "And the songs—I listened to them the whole trip."

"Thanks." He smiled awkwardly, the way I'd seen him smile at Mrs. Peech when she sat too close to him, or asked him how he'd become such a wonderfully accomplished swimmer.

I said, "I can't believe you're here. I was so afraid I wouldn't get to see you."

He touched my hand, grasped it lightly—his hand that I'd held in the roof garden—then clutched the edge of the bench. "How was the trip?"

"Ohhh." Where could I start? "I shot a gun in Texas. And fought a crazy woman on the bus. In Tucson I almost got bit by a *rattlesnake*."

"Wow. You're like a superhero."

"A road-trip superhero." I smiled. "They need a cartoon about that."

"I wish I'd driven out here. Cross-country."

I thought for a second. "Come back with us—at least part of the way. You'd love Tucson. And Texas. You have time before school starts, right?" I waved toward his car. "I bet that thing could make it, even if it doesn't have a cupcake on its roof." I touched his arm. "Or maybe in December, on your break. We could take a trip."

He flinched, almost imperceptibly. A twitch of his shoulders. If I hadn't spent so much time staring at him in the tutoring center, watching his smallest move, I wouldn't have noticed it. But I'd seen him do that when he'd talked about his dad, and about Gia, just before they broke up.

"Everything feels so crazy right now." His voice was soft. He looked away from me. At the ground. The concrete, the genetically engineered grass.

"What happened? Is everything okay with your dad?"

He nodded. "I took your advice. We went out for dinner. Talked for hours. He apologized. He even planned this whole trip for us—we're supposed to drive up the coast tonight and camp on the beach. Not with my car—I don't think this one would make it—we're taking his Jeep, just the two of us."

"Tonight? For how long?"

"Four days."

"I'm only here two more days. We're leaving Sunday." I tried to keep my voice level, though an icicle melted down my spine.

"I know—I'm sorry. I tried to change things, but my dad's show at LACMA opens Wednesday, so this was the only time we could do it. He wanted to leave this morning, but I put him off so I could see you. He's had dinners with donors every night, and after the opening he goes to Italy for an artist's residency for three weeks—this was the only time he could do it."

"Maybe you can come back sooner. Tell your dad we came all this way."

"We can't."

I couldn't process what he was saying. It was too different from what I expected. A person you loved couldn't tell you they're leaving tonight and not seeing you again, not after you'd come all this way, it wasn't possible.

"I'm sorry. I didn't plan it like this." His voice sounded genuinely sad. Why was he saying this? His jeans were the same jeans he'd worn in the roof garden, a quarter-size tear at the right knee. I remembered touching those jeans, the belt loops, the soft worn fabric. He could change his mind. I could change it.

"Just stay tonight then. I'll see you after the show." I was pleading now. I couldn't help it. I wanted to sound normal, but everything I said was soggy with need.

He gazed at the fountain. His T-shirt had a tiny bleach stain on one sleeve, and I thought of the time I'd stared at him in the van, memorizing the moth holes of his black coat.

"I'm starting college soon." He spoke slowly. "I live here now. You're in New York."

"I only have two more years of school—sometimes you can skip a year and go right to college."

He looked away. "Eva—"

"I could move here. We could—I could get emancipated. Anything is possible . . . anything is possible."

Those were things I'd planned to tell him. Out loud, they sounded nothing like they had in my head.

He stared at his hands. "All this summer I was hoping we could—I don't know." He paused. "Maybe that it could happen without someone getting hurt, or that we could keep it casual. But we can't keep it casual."

You can't keep it casual was what he meant. Writing *I love you* and traveling three thousand miles to see someone wasn't keeping it casual.

"You sent me that e. e. cummings poem. And the CD. I thought—"

"I shouldn't have sent that," he said. "It was a mistake. I was thinking—" He paused. "Well."

My stomach plummeted. My insides began to crumble. Everything inside me crumbled. "You were thinking what?"

He glanced at his shoes. "I'm sorry. Even before we started this—I started this—I think I was afraid it would be a mistake if I did, because I never wanted to ruin our friendship. I never want to hurt you."

Too late.

He turned to me and kissed my forehead. It was partly a chaste kiss, and partly not chaste at all—his lips lingered too long, too softly, his hands stroked my shoulders, my back. He put his arms around me. He was saying one thing and his body said another.

He didn't mean what he'd said. Deep inside, he didn't.

His tone softened. "Sometime, in the future, we'll see each other again."

"When?"

"Someday."

Something began to move inside me, birds' wings fluttering through my blood. "They may have found my dad's body." The words tumbled out of me; I had to tell him, and telling him would bring back the old Will, the roof garden Will, who didn't hold back, who made me feel, more than anyone had before, that I wasn't alone. The Will who understood.

I told him about the eleven bodies, and the fight with my mom, and how I'd stopped answering her calls. The words kept pouring out like a waterfall. I told him I was going to contact the NTSB on my own, making the decision to as I said it. If I could travel across the country, I could call some official and demand to be notified about whether they'd found my dad. "I'm going to call them tomorrow," I said.

He nodded, his arms tight around me. "I hope you do."

For a few minutes it felt good to be in the folds of his arms, confessing. And then I hated myself for it. I pulled away. Maybe Will could only be that Will in the roof garden. Maybe we could only be us *there*. Not now, in a parking lot in Burbank, staring at too-green grass.

I sat an inch from him. *This isn't happening.*

He shook his head. "Listen, I'm not going to bullshit you. I wish things were different. I wish we could run off, away from everybody else. Away from the whole world." He paused. "But I'm starting school soon. This isn't the right time. Sometimes people meet at the wrong time."

I thought: People overcome wars and storms and pirates and diseases every day and they're still together. Time is easy. Didn't he know that? Didn't he know that tomorrow we could die, or—

"I need to feel free when I get to college. To start over. No responsibilities."

It knocked the wind out of me, stamped all my stupidity and useless love on my forehead. Was that all I was? A responsibility? Did he want to forget the whole past and start over like my mom did?

We sat there silently for a while. I thought I'd cry but I didn't. I felt numb. It didn't make sense.

I thought: we're not in a romance novel. The words fell into my head. In a romance, if a person said, *Sometimes people meet at the wrong time* on page 50, then they'd still get married by page 250. They'd have their happy ending.

He checked his watch. "You probably need to get back."

I nodded. He stood up and I walked him to his car. Walking isn't the right word—I was hovering, making the motions, footsteps, barely aware. We stood at his car door and he hugged me one last time, and told me to keep writing him letters, though I knew I wouldn't, that letters alone wouldn't be enough, but even then there was still this hope deep in me, trilling—*he could still change his mind*—hope singing out, every moment, arm in arm with the humiliation, until his car turned the corner.

Then the hope disappeared in one swoop. Only the humiliation was left.

I'd imagined it so differently that the reality felt like a slap. And now all these things sat inside me waiting to burst. He was the hook I'd hung all my dreams on, and now they fell, evaporated.

Everything ached, and I didn't know why they called it heartache when it was chest and stomach and skin and flesh and blood ache. The fountain ached. The clouds ached. I started revising every single thing I'd said to him. If I'd only said the right words. If I'd been funnier and smarter, everything would've been different.

If I hadn't tried, if I'd stayed in New York and waited for his visits—surely he'd come visit to see his mom in December—if I'd waited till December, kept it casual, not taken this trip—

I walked past the fountain and sat down in the grass, pulled up blades of it.

Why did the happy and hopeful feelings never last? Why did the things I loved not last? The emptiness and hollowness and disbelief were familiar—they dug up the old grief, split it open.

There was so much more I'd wanted to tell him, so much I'd been certain we'd talk about in the long days and nights I thought we'd have. I'd thought that the things we'd shared as we talked in the stairwell and on the roof had bonded us together in this dark space, and I could tell him anything, anything.

I'd wanted to tell him about Janet and Grace, Irma and Lulu.

I'd wanted to tell him that my grandmother said good-bye to her parents on a train platform and never saw them again.

I'd wanted to tell him about Lulu's baby who died, and how she was expecting a new one.

I'd wanted to tell him about "The Floating Poem," to give it to him.

I'd wanted to tell him about the letter I'd written to my dad in the old diary.

And I wanted to tell him about the fight with my mother and the memory of the funeral, the worst memories that I never talked about with anybody, but I'd hoped to talk about with him.

Now as I sat in the grass, I kept pulling it up in clumps, until all around me I'd destroyed a tiny patch of earth.

It was late. I didn't know what time it was. I had to get myself together. I had to hurry. Maybe the producers would let me talk to Annie before the show, and I could tell her what happened. All I wanted to do was to see her and speak to her. I stood up and walked back toward the entrance.

Eddie was gone. Someone new was there now. I told him I had to get back inside right away.

"Name?" He glanced at a list in front of him.

"Eva Roth."

He eyed me warily. I knew I probably looked like a crazy person, my eyes red, makeup smeared, dirt under my finger-nails. I wiped my eyes and tried to look normal.

He took a long time going through forms, lists of paper in front of him. "Don't see an Eva Roth here."

"I'm on it. *The Smartest Girl in America*. Look—I spoke to the other guard, Eddie—can't you call him, please? He'll let me back in, he promised—"

He picked up his walkie-talkie and mumbled a few things

to someone on the other end.

"Set's closed," he said. "They're not letting anybody in."

"They have to."

My stomach twisted. This could not be happening. He had to let me in. I couldn't let Annie down. I couldn't not be there for her. That wasn't possible.

"Listen," I said, and I tried to explain again. He shook his head. The more I pleaded, the more tired and exasperated he became, as if he dealt with crying girls outside the studio all the time, and I was the last straw. He told me I had to exit the gate or security would escort me out.

My chest thickened as if it was filling with water.

All Annie wanted was the scholarship—she had to win the scholarship. I stared at the gate again. Could I run through it? Knock the guard over? How had this happened? I'd thrown everything important away. All for a guy who didn't love me.

What had I done? Who was I? Who had I become?

"Please," I pleaded with the guard one more time.

"Sorry, kid," he said.

I went out the gate and sat back down on the grass. My hands lay in my lap. I rubbed them to get the dirt off, but it was stuck on. It seemed embedded permanently.

I thought of Freda. Scrubbing. The nonstop cleaning that had seemed so weird to me all my life now made perfect sense. She was trying to scrub off the grief. You could see it on her skin, the weight of it, in her sagging face and in the deep furrows under her eyes. And she wasn't the only one in our family to feel its weight—it was there for Janet, too, burying her parents' ashes in purchased plots, and it had been there for my mother in the cemetery. It was there for me. Grief from losing Will, grief from my dad, grief from my mom who didn't even seem to love me. Grief from what I'd done to Annie. A dirty, heavy, permanent weight.

I was afraid that what was inside me wasn't strong enough. This empty fragile nothingness. Worse than nothingness: dark places. Dark places that might never leave.

I saw now how I'd spent so much of the last two years trying to disappear—into romances and websites and movies and TV—and now I wanted to disappear more than ever before, but it felt like the locks had been changed, the keys thrown out.

How do you walk through the world, how do you continue, when you know what a dark place it is? It's like you realize you were hiding beneath a blanket, and now the blanket's blown off and you see the universe for what it really is: a place where terrible things happen, the worst things, a place where your father can fall from the sky, and the romances that saved you are lying fantasies. How do you get up each day, when you know that? When you know the truth?

PART SEVEN

THE TRUTH ABOUT LOVE

There's nothing in this world but mad love.
—Mary Oliver

Reality

The *Smartest Girl in America* set was bathed in pink light. The sign on the wall sparkled and flashed; even the podiums glittered like crushed diamonds.

I watched the whole thing from the hotel room as I hid under the covers.

The set looked much fancier and glossier on TV than it had in real life. You couldn't tell that the sign was made of particle board and flimsy plastic.

The host, Rich Cavell, spent a long time getting to know each contestant. He spent the most time with Annie. He leaned against her podium and asked about her parents' laundromat, and how her family had come to America. "And where do you dream of going to college?"

She looked gorgeous in her bright red dress, her black hair perfect; she answered each question so confidently, fearlessly, talking about MIT and microevolution and all her hopes for her future.

"Microevolution? I don't even know what that is! Har har har," Rich Cavell laughed. His hair looked smooth as melted wax; his lip curled when he smiled. "Now I hear you traveled all the way here by bus and car because your best friend, your official companion, has a phobia of flying."

She nodded. He wanted her to elaborate more, but she didn't.

"And there must be some genius genes in your DNA, because here we have your cousin Grace."

Grace's face was the color of a half-ripe tomato, part red and part green. Sweat patches spread under her arms, darkening her blue dress. Whenever Rich Cavell asked her a question, her lips opened but no sound came out. Her mouth looked like a small empty hollow. It was like watching myself during my dolphin presentation: she was having a panic attack.

"First-time jitters!" said Rich Cavell. The audience laughed.

Grace was the first contestant knocked out. Her father never even got a chance to help her.

Meanwhile, Annie became a force of nature. She kept winning. At the end of each round her eyes narrowed, growing even more focused; she suddenly looked closer to thirty years old than sixteen. Some outside force had taken her over. She must've been filled with adrenaline, or several other brain chemicals that she could surely, easily name. She slapped the buzzer so quickly, the girl beside her actually flinched. (Her mosquito-swatting practice with Janet had paid off.) She obliterated the other girls on almost every single question.

Rich Cavell [lip curling]: What are the scientific names for the human tailbone and cheekbone?

Annie: Coccyx and zygoma, respectively.

RC: Which mathematician discovered logarithms in 1614?

A: John Napier.

RC: What is the area of a trapezoid with bases of 5 inches and 9 inches, and a height of 8.6 inches?

A: 60.2.

RC [touches his waxy hair, but hair does not move]: What American sculptor is most famous for his work in South Dakota?

A: Gutzon Borglum, creator of Mount Rushmore.

Questions about geography, capitals, desert flora and fauna, reptiles, celebrities and jazz musicians, famous scientists, and what type of soil is created under weather conditions of less than zero degrees Celsius for at least two years (answer: permafrost). She even knew the first female poet laureate: Louise Bogan. *"No woman should be shamefaced in attempting to give back to the world, through her work, a portion of its lost heart"—Louise Bogan.* I'd made a notecard of that quote for her, somewhere in Ohio.

By the final round, Annie was ahead of the other girls by two hundred points. She never even needed the Companion Chamber. Then it was time for the final question.

Rich Cavell [in a glacially slow voice]: Who are the
four [pause] best-selling [leering expression] writers
of fiction [weird eye movements; obviously the man
has had botox] in the world?
Annie: I know the first is Shakespeare. I'm sure of
that. I think the next must be Agatha Christie. I
don't know the other two. My best friend knows
them. She must. I'm sure they're romance novelists.
She'll know this. She'll know!

Annie actually bounced up and down above the podium, like a bobble toy.

They flashed to the Companion Chamber. My seat: empty.

I could see the producers practically cackling, as if they'd planned it like this, all this drama.

The camera zoomed on my empty seat.

Again.

And again.

And again.

In the hotel bed, under the blankets, I say the answer to the TV: "Barbara Cartland and Danielle Steel." Romance novelists. So simple. So perfect. So easy.

The camera switches to the girl from the audition, Lauren, the teen Barbie. She doesn't know the answer, either—but her best friend does: "*Barbara Cartland and Danielle Steel!*" the friend chirps.

They flash to Annie's face. Confused. Stricken. Angry.

Even the night's talk shows pick it up. The empty seat where I should've been. They pair it with a dramatic manufactured sound, like an electronic thunderclap.

I am the Worst Friend in America.

To live is to build a ship and a harbor at the same time

Lulu turned the TV off. She'd stayed in the hotel with me since she'd picked me up in the studio lot. After watching me destroy their lawn, the guard had come over to me and said, "Kid, why don't you call your mama to come get you?" and held out his phone to me. I'd called Lulu instead.

While we'd been at the studio, Lulu had spent the day napping in the hotel room and having lunch with Janet. She'd filled Janet in on everything that had happened since we'd last seen her.

Annie was staying with Janet at the condo. Annie couldn't even stand to see me.

At the hotel, I stayed in bed. Occasionally I checked my messages on Lulu's iPad to see if there was anything from Annie. Nothing. But I got an email from my mother.

> **You're not answering my calls or texts so I hope you'll at least read this. I called the NTSB and told them I'd changed my mind. I asked them to notify me about their findings. They've identified all the bodies and**

Daddy's was not among them. Please call me back, okay? I need to talk to you. I love you. Mommy

I read it twice, three times, four. The words didn't sink in. They seemed muffled, far away. I hid deeper under the covers. I closed my eyes in the darkness, thinking that if I could burrow deep enough, then everything, including myself, would disappear.

When I woke up a while later, Lulu was reading in the chair beside me.

I felt like a shell, my insides scooped out. I didn't want to talk about the email from my mom. I wanted it, and everything, to go away.

Lulu saw that I was awake. "While you were sleeping, I swung by Janet's and got this for you." She walked over to the doorway and picked up my backpack, which I'd left in the locker during the show. She handed it to me. My phone. My makeup. My change of clothes. I had the pillowcase of my dad's things in the bed with me, and now I put the pillowcase inside my backpack again, for safekeeping.

"Call Annie. She'll understand if you explain it to her," Lulu said.

What could I say, though? *I'm an idiot and a loser and you're really better off not being my friend. I did something horrible. I'm a horrible person.*

"Just apologize. Ask her to forgive you," Lulu said.

I kept imagining how it could've gone differently: I could've reasoned with the guard more. Fought with him. While I slept, I dreamed about trying to enter the building again and again, until I finally got back in. Then I'd wake up and realize it was only a dream.

There was no way Annie would forgive me. I couldn't even forgive myself. Every time I replayed the show in my mind, I hated myself. She had every reason to hate me.

Lulu adjusted the pillows on her red armchair and looked out at the ocean. She called Michael to check in and left him a voice mail.

"You probably need to get back home," I said.

"I don't—Michael's gone on his field trip this week, and it's not every day I get to stay at a beachfront hotel. How are you feeling?"

I shook my head. Images of Will in the parking lot kept flashing in front of me. My body hunched with shame. Why had we planned this whole trip? Why had I ever let myself fall in love with him? Why did I get so carried away? What was wrong with me? I knew what was wrong with me: about a thousand different things.

"If I was prettier, this wouldn't have happened. Will wouldn't have said what he said. If I was a better person. My mom is right about me. I'm so stupid. Stupid fantasies." I shook my head again. "And I'm ugly."

She put her book down and sat beside me on the bed.

"You're not stupid. You're not ugly. I used to think during all those years I was single—there were *a lot* of them—that I wasn't pretty enough, or thin enough—until I realized I'm just fine. It's that some people don't really know how to love other people. Some bad things happened to Will in his life, and those things maybe kind of screwed him up a bit, too. We all have to cope with so much crap. And we're all kind of screwed up. You have to find someone who, despite all their screwed-up-ness, still knows how to love you the way you need to be loved."

She glanced down and laughed a little. "Oh, what do I know? I'm just a crazy pregnant lady. A crazy *old* pregnant lady."

"I like your crazy," I said, peeking out from under the covers.

As I looked at her, I thought of her husband, Michael, how he made us tea and bought us ice cream, and the way he looked at her with so much love.

She touched my arm. "You might not really fall in love again for years, who knows—and that's okay. If you really want to find love and have a life, go out there and see the world. Travel not to see a guy but for yourself. Learn who you are. How can you love anyone else unless you know who you are? Learn how to be alone." She pushed up her sleeves. "Think of Elizabeth Bishop, traveling, stopping off in Brazil and staying there fifteen years. And writing some of the most beautiful poems ever written."

I thought of my father. "What would my dad think if he could see me now? He'd be so disappointed in me. In my mom too. He'd hate how my mom's been since he died. He'd have wanted her to keep his stuff. To talk to me about him. Not to make decisions without me."

She shook her head. "He'd never be disappointed in you. He loved you. And your mom. He'd know your mom is trying her best, even if she makes lots of mistakes. As we all do." She paused. "Lord knows I do. My entire first marriage." She sighed. "Don't turn your dad into someone he wasn't. He wouldn't want his death to have messed up your relationship with your mom."

I nodded, trying to absorb what she was saying.

"You've worried so much about what he felt in those last minutes before he died—but knowing your dad, he probably wasn't thinking about himself. He was probably thinking of you. Wanting the best for you. Wanting you to be happy. Not wanting to have caused you pain."

That had never occurred to me before. I'd been so focused on how afraid he must have felt as he died, and whether he felt pain, that I'd never thought he might've been thinking of us, of the people he loved.

And to finish the harbor long after the ship has gone down

I felt better after our talk, for an hour or so—Lulu and I ordered room service, and I managed to eat a little despite the churning in my stomach—but then the dark feelings returned and I went back under the covers and fell asleep. The next morning, Lulu opened the curtains and said my wallowing period was over.

She took the bedspread off. "I can't stand to see you so paralyzed that you can't get out of bed."

Stomach bug life.

"Lord knows I wallow too. Usually with Ben and Jerry." She sat down beside me and smoothed out the blanket. "When I got divorced, I hid under the covers for two weeks. I hid even longer when I lost the baby." She hesitated, and hugged her elbows.

She was silent for a while. Then she said, "You can use it, you know. The grief. I know it doesn't seem like it now, but your dad's death has given you a different way of seeing things—it's not all stomach bugs." She rested one hand on her belly, as if steadying a globe. "Sometimes, on good days,

I treasure things. Sitting here now, I know how lucky I am."

She looked distant and gloomy for a moment. "It's a struggle every day. It's not like I wake up feeling instantly hopeful. It's millions of moments of trying. Looking forward."

Outside, in the parking lot, a construction crane groaned and trucks wheezed alongside the sounds of the sea. I told her how I always felt like I was two different people—the happy-in-love romantic with my books and movies, and the anxious, stomach bug girl. The girl I was today and would probably be forever, now. How I was afraid the stomach bug girl had taken over and nothing else was left.

"It's okay to have stomach bug days. Or 'personal health days,' as we call them at my age. Days when you have to wallow, and let yourself feel all those bad feelings. But then you have to get yourself out of it. Whether it's reading romances, or traveling, or writing—"

"I always thought my mom would help me more. She could help me get through it."

"She's done the best she could. Moms aren't the only ones who mother, you know. Friends mother. Fathers mother. We mother ourselves."

I thought of my dad's trays of tea and the hot water bottle he used to bring me on cold nights. "My dad was kind of a great mom, actually."

"He mothered your mom, too. She lost that also, when she lost him. It hit her so hard not to have that comfort from him anymore."

I'd never really thought about her loss before, that she'd lost so many of the same things I had.

"Your dad was such a joyful person—you know, you can honor him by doing the things you love, the things he showed you how to love—great food. A cup of tea. Poetry. Writing, reading books, cooking, enjoying a beautiful place. A beautiful view."

Her eyes shifted to the window. "Your dad would understand what you're going through because he loved you. Loves you, from wherever he is."

I thought of Will's little brother with his telescope, looking down on their family. I thought of my dad, looking at us from the ocean. My body felt heavy, flooded with sadness.

Lulu twisted her silver ring. "Love is never easy or guaranteed. Real love is a leap, you know. As you get older, you learn how hard it is, how hard everything is, how we never know if there's any ground beneath our feet, or if we'll be hurt or heartbroken. But we leap anyway. You have to take that leap."

still wallowed for the rest of the morning. I surfed from channel to channel, from soap operas to old westerns, but they made me feel worse. (All those cowboys just wanted to be web designers, anyway.)

That afternoon, though, I picked up the old, nearly empty diary Janet had given me, the diary my father had given to my grandmother. I glanced at the quick letter I'd written to my dad on the bus. I'd broken the seal of the journal, the blank page. I'd been afraid to write more since then because I hadn't wanted the worst feelings and memories to come out. But they'd come out anyway, flooded into my brain on their own. I felt so low now—how much lower could I go?

I opened the diary to the next page. I wrote two words. *Dear Daddy* again. I wrote a few more lines—another letter to him—well, not exactly a letter. A poem-letter. Then another. And another. I told him about the word *remains* and Wonder-boob and grief group, and Rosamunde Saunders's voice in my head, and meeting Will and being dumped by Will, and the wreckage in the news and Bubbe 409's grave and every stop on our trip—the whole story of it, the outside story and the one inside me.

Once I got going, I couldn't stop. I told him about every fight I'd ever had with my mom. And I wrote down everything Lulu had told me while I hid in the hotel bed. Words that had coasted over my mind now began to sink in. *It's a struggle every day. Your dad wouldn't have wanted to cause you pain. Travel not to see a guy but for yourself. Mother yourself. Learn who you are. Learn how to be alone.* Things I needed to learn and to remember. Writing them down made them soak into my pores, seem possible. Seem real.

I kept writing for hours. As I reached the middle of the journal, something changed on the page. I didn't know where the words were coming from—from this deep buried part of me, or some force outside myself—but suddenly, my dad was writing to me.

> *Dear Eva,*
> *It's pretty funny about the hand. And I like the part*
> *about the disembodied finger trick,*
> *with the ketchup spots. And the forearm. You have to be*
> *kind to Mommy,*
> *you know—she never found dark stuff so funny.*
> *Remember the time when you were only six*
> *and I dressed up as Bubbe 409 for Halloween? Scrubbies*
> *taped all over my chest.*

Mommy made me take them off. And you know what's
  funny, too? That I like it here at the bottom
of the ocean. It's a good place to be, in this giant
  underworld
of fallen sailors and mermaids, pirates and explorers. In
  the morning I have breakfast
with Ariel and afternoon tea with the Strauses from the
  Titanic. Dinner is with
Francis Drake and sometimes we have parties with all
  the lost souls
dancing. And do you know how quiet it is here, how the
  plankton flicker like a thousand tiny stars? Scientists
  know more about the surface of the moon
than the depth of the sea, but that's the way it should be,
  to leave something a mystery.
                                          Daddy

I looked at what I'd just written, the tiny print on the yellowed page of the notebook.

I closed the leather cover and held it in my palms.

It had been so long since I'd written, really written, that I'd forgotten what it felt like—how it changed things, shifted everything. I'd forgotten how writing surprises you—how you sit down feeling one thing and come out feeling another—and that I'd never heard my dad's voice in my head like this before, never known I could feel this close to him again, that this letter from him might ever exist. But here it was.

I'd thought the blank page was a giant slab of raw pain, but once I was inside it, it was like looking off to the side during a horror movie, realizing that all that fear isn't necessary or real.

That's what writing did, what I'd forgotten: how it unraveled the tangled feelings and wove them into something new.

I lay in bed for a long time, holding the journal, staring at what I'd written. The stomach bug was mostly gone and there was a sense of quiet. And with it came an idea.

I wrote down notes, and then I called Trent in Texas. We talked about my idea to build a website, to start a campaign to raise donations for Annie's scholarship fund. He said he could design a rough beta version, working from his trailer in Texas. At first I wanted to get something posted online as fast as possible, but he said that the better we made it, the bigger chance it would have of paying off. I wrote a draft of the content, explaining what happened with the show, Annie, and Will (changing his name), and explaining how it had been my fault we lost. I told the whole story of what led to me being shut out of the studio that day. We planned to set up a PayPal account for the donations to the fund, and to create links to all of Annie's academic prizes. I hoped that if we worked hard at this, I could make back some—or even all—of the money I'd lost for her.

"It'll take me a week to get the site live," Trent said. "I'll work as fast as I can."

The thought of posting the whole story online felt a little bit like dancing naked on a stage, humiliating and crazy at the same time—but the idea of splaying your insides out for the entire world to see is easier when you're not actually on a stage, but hiding in a hotel room under a blanket.

I sent Annie a link to the first page Trent designed for the beta site. I didn't hear back. The next morning, while Lulu was out getting breakfast, there was a knock on my door. I opened it.

Annie looked both the same and different—she wore jeans and a black T-shirt she'd worn during our trip—but she stood stiffly, her elbows sticking out at odd angles.

"Janet dropped me off," she said. "She's on her way to discuss syphilis with members of the LA school board."

She leaned against the doorframe, her arms folded. Would she forgive me? Or murder me?

I held the door open. "Come in! Do you want coffee? The coffee pods they have here are really cool." I hated how self-conscious I sounded, like I was either an extremely bad waitress or we were on some weird sort of friend date.

She shook her head.

"How's the condo?" I asked.

"It's nice. Janet's actually been really great." She shrugged.

Everything seemed strange between us now. The world had turned upside down. She and Janet had probably been painting each other's toenails while watching Lifetime movies and stabbing a voodoo doll of me.

She sat down on the edge of the bed and twisted her hands in her lap. It felt a little like it had when I'd seen Will. She was going to say it was over with us. Our friendship was done. She'd bolt like he did. Something sharp lodged itself in my throat.

"I don't even know what to say," she said.

"I'm sorry. I screwed up." I leaned against the dresser and squeezed it so tightly my knuckles turned white. "I keep thinking how I can make it up to you—"

"Was this whole trip just about a guy for you?"

"No—"

"Were you lying that you cared about the scholarship? Did you just use me because you wanted to take this trip?"

"No."

"We would've won."

"I know." I hated that this had happened. How could I fix it? "I have a check for you. I can pay you back for the trip now. I borrowed the money from Lulu." I walked over to the desk to get it. I thought it might make things easier if I paid Lulu back instead of Annie.

"You don't need to do that. I know you'll pay me back." She returned the check to me.

"I'll give you all my checks from the laundromat. Everything I earn from now on. I promise. I got so carried away. I had to see him. I couldn't not see him. I never thought they wouldn't let me back in. Not in a million years."

"I know you didn't do it on purpose. I just—" She sighed. "I thought you'd be there for me, you know?"

"I know." I squeezed the corner of the dresser again, so hard this time that my fingernail broke. "I'm going to do everything I can to get you another scholarship. I'll go on *Promzillas* if I have to."

"You're not going on *Promzillas.*"

"Then *Girls with Lots of Cats, Who Need Boyfriends.*"

"You don't have cats."

"I'll get some."

I shook my head. "I'm so sorry. About everything. Losing the money. That's the worst thing I've ever done in my life." I couldn't stop thinking about the money. It had been so much that I couldn't even picture it, *two hundred thousand dollars, fifty thousand dollars,* ha ha ha, it had even seemed like a joke sometimes, but now that it was lost, I felt ashamed to have joked about it at all, because it wasn't a funny thing—it was our futures and our freedom.

"Wait till the website's up—it'll get the word out. Maybe there are scholarships out there that we don't even know about," I said.

"I got a couple emails this morning. One from this woman who works at Girls Strive, one of the organizations that sponsored the show. She wants me to apply for some other scholarships. And I got a message from some guy who saw the show and found me online. He knows about this internal-nomination-only scholarship. I mean, I Googled him and it says he works for some education foundation, so I think he's for real. Of course, maybe it's fake and he's really some convict writing from prison."

"Possibly," I said. "See? So many opportunities. Even prisoners want to help you."

She smiled for the first time, and then hesitated and lowered her voice. "I'm really sorry about Dickhead. I mean Will."

I moved to the bed and sat down across from her, on the blanket. "Thanks. He isn't totally a dickhead, though. Maybe just five percent dickhead. Two percent." The dickhead part of him was because his kisses, whether he'd wanted them to or not, had felt like a promise to me. A broken one, though I saw now that all along he'd never intended to promise anything.

"There should be a government board that labels guys like meats, listing the degree of potential dickheadness. The chance they'll break your heart. Prime Grade A Dickhead. Mild Grade C Dickhead," she said.

"I don't regret the night with him on the roof, though. The friendship." Maybe that's what "The Floating Poem" meant. What had happened with him would always exist, apart from time. Not everything has to have a beginning, a middle, and an end. Will would always be the first boy I loved. *Whatever happens, this is.* We still were, the way Will's brother was always his brother. My father was always my father.

I thought of how I'd always admired Will's strength, how confident and sure of himself he seemed, how even in the beginning when I hardly knew him, he wasn't afraid to tell the truth about his brother. Maybe the real strength was in facing things, putting your heart out there, leaping, as Lulu said, taking chances, feeling pain, loving again and again. Maybe there were as many different types of strength as there were different types of love.

"I regret seeing him in the parking lot and losing the show—*that* I'd take back in a second," I said.

I got up and walked over to my bag. "I need to give this back to you." I took out Quarky and handed him to her. She held him in her arms.

I lay next to her on the bed. We were quiet for a long time as we stared at the ceiling, just as we had all over the country.

There's a thing in poetry called the caesura—a pause between words, a silence. I thought: That's what real friendship is, too. Someone you can be quiet with. Someone who understands your mistakes and forgives you.

She fingered the blanket. "Grace was so embarrassed about her panic attack, she hasn't even talked to me since. She and her dad took a flight after the show—they didn't want to stick around. I think she just cracked under the pressure." She turned to me. "She didn't mean to have you locked out. She told me how guilty she felt about Tennessee. How she treated you there."

I nodded. I didn't think it had been Grace's fault, either.

"I decided for the trip back I'm going to get off in Calypso and spend a week there with Chance. Is that nuts?"

"It's not nuts. I think he'd be labeled only .5 percent dickhead. Or maybe zero."

She smiled. "Want to stay there with me? And Janet? Janet's going back to Texas too."

"What?"

"Apparently she's coming around to the idea of love. Herpes aside. She's planning to 'meet with more clients' there—but I think she's really just planning to see Farley again."

"Wow. Janet in love. You guys really need to read *Cowboys on Fire*, you know."

"We can write a new book. *Cowboys on Fire with Gonorrhea*." She leaned on her elbow. "I did win something from the show after all. They had a consolation prize from one of their sponsors. Guess who the sponsor was? GE. You could pick a plasma TV or anything. I told my mom she could choose what she wanted."

"What did she get?"

"Three new washers and dryers. She's thrilled. She can't wait to replace some of the old clunkers."

"Oh god. Life is so mean," I said.

"Could be worse," she said with a small smile. She reached

out and picked a piece of lint off my shirt. There was still a gulf between us—but it was closing.

A little while later, Lulu returned. We'd planned to have lunch in the Mirabelle restaurant and then go for a walk. We rode the elevator down together.

"I have a table reserved," Lulu said. The other hotel guests clopped past us in flip-flops and towels, coming in from the beach.

We entered the restaurant. There was someone at our table already. My mother.

PART EIGHT

I REMEMBER YOU

It's winter again: the sky's a deep headstrong blue, and the
    sunlight pours through

the open living room windows because the heat's on too
    high in here, and I can't turn it off.
For weeks now, driving, or dropping a bag of groceries in
    the street, the bag breaking,

I've been thinking: This is what the living do. And
    yesterday, hurrying along those
wobbly bricks in the Cambridge sidewalk, spilling my
    coffee down my wrist and sleeve,

I thought it again, and again later, when buying a
    hairbrush. This is it.

Parking. Slamming the car door shut in the cold. What
    you called that yearning.

What you finally gave up. We want the spring to come
    and the winter to pass. We want
whoever to call or not call, a letter, a kiss—we want
    more and more and then more of it.

But there are moments, walking, when I catch a glimpse
    of myself in the window glass,
say, the window of the corner video store, and I'm
    gripped by a cherishing so deep

for my own blowing hair, chapped face, and unbuttoned
    coat that I'm speechless:
I am living. I remember you.

—Marie Howe

How did you get here?" I asked her. She looked so out of her element in the peachy-white hotel restaurant, with its pastel napkins, absurdly huge baskets of peonies, and pink tablecloths. She wore a short-sleeved black dress and black sandals. All around us were bouncy blond waitresses in white pants and floral shirts.

"I flew."

My mom had flown to see me. I couldn't absorb it.

She looked around. "It's nice here." She smiled at me. I looked away from her face. I couldn't meet her gaze.

Lulu and Annie excused themselves and said they'd meet us later. I wished I could go with them.

"I'm so happy to see you. I missed you." My mom's voice sounded both nervous and relieved. "You look good. I'm so glad—" She paused. "Please sit down."

I sat across from her and didn't say anything. I kept my backpack on my lap like a barrier between us, an extra person.

Saying good-bye to her in Port Authority seemed like months ago. I thought of how my mom looked in the photo of us in Central Park, young and happy, a different person. I thought of my mom as a teenager, studying nonstop after her father died. My mom watching Freda scrub and scrub. And I thought of my dad under the sea, looking at us in the restaurant right now, using his own telescope.

"Lulu and Janet told me about your trip. Sounds like an adventure." She smiled again, a sad smile. She rearranged the sugar packets, making sure all were right side up, the same way Janet had in Cleveland. "I wish I could've come along." Her voice was gentle.

I shook my head. "You wouldn't have liked it."

She let go of the sugar packets. Her hand lay on the table, grasping and releasing something invisible. She had a callus on the same finger that I did, from writing her lectures by hand.

I stared out the window at the beach and the ocean. California seemed as if it was on the edge of the world, a different country from the east coast and every state in between. The waitress grinned as she placed menus and water glasses in front of us. We didn't touch them.

"Come home with me tomorrow," she said. "We'll take the train back together."

I shook my head.

"You want to go back with Annie. I understand."

I fingered my bag. It was softer after having been lugged across the country, with tiny grease stains from our rest stop meals, and dirt from the middle of Texas, and a million other splotches and microscopic souvenirs from our trip.

I let go of the bag and smoothed a wrinkle in the table-cloth. My mom reached her hands across the table and tried to touch mine, but I moved them to my lap.

"I shouldn't have made the decision about the search with-out you. I kept thinking if we had to have another funeral—" She spoke slowly, then paused. "I wanted it to be easier for you this time."

I looked down. "We never talk about him," I said.

"Who?"

"Daddy."

My hands started to shake as I said his name. All the anger I'd buried for so long simmered to the top. I opened my bag and took out the pillowcase.

The silk tie, T-shirt, postcards, Toffee Crisp wrappers—I dumped everything out.

The edges of her face quivered. She stared at it all, disbe-lieving, as if I'd just taken my father out of my bag and placed him on the table.

Her lips thinned into a frown. She picked up the tie first, her mouth working, twisting at one corner. She touched the fabric like a scientist, distantly, unsure. Then she picked up the paperweight, the postcards.

"Where have you been keeping it?" She made a little move-ment with her shoulders, as if she wanted to get away from all this stuff, get rid of it as soon as possible.

I shook my head. "You would've thrown it out." The backs of my eyes stung, and I could feel the tears threatening.

The waitress walked by and glanced at our faces and all the stuff on our table. She hurried off.

My mom's mouth kept working. Then she took the T-shirt and held it, pressed it to her face. She breathed it in. She picked up the Toffee Crisp wrappers, touched the yellow lettering, the white insides. "Do you know why he couldn't stop buying these?"

I shook my head.

Her face changed; her mouth relaxed. Her skin looked soft and pale. "I never got to meet Daddy's father, but from the stories Daddy told me, I think he was a lot like my mother. Except instead of her crazy cleaning, he used to hoard food. Candy. Chocolate. When Daddy's father was a kid in England, food was rationed during the war. He hoarded sweets for the rest of his life. Whenever he traveled, he brought back tons of Toffee Crisps for Daddy. Daddy was only twelve when his father died of a heart attack."

I pictured my dad as a boy, missing his own father, losing him when he was younger than me. Here all this time I'd been remembering the carefree and happy side of my dad, but he had his own grief and worries, too. Maybe he'd felt his own father's buried fears and heartache, just as my mom felt Freda's. As I felt hers.

My mom kept holding the wrappers. "They're releasing the preliminary report next week. About the data and voice recorders." She spoke quickly. "It isn't a surprise or anything. It was a combination of things, of errors and mistakes. Computer malfunctions. Pilot errors—a string of pilot errors. Bad weather, bad luck."

I touched the tablecloth. Maybe he had been thinking of us in those last minutes. Or maybe what he felt then would always be a mystery. An unanswerable question.

"I wanted to be strong for you," she murmured. "I thought if we could forget the past and move forward—both of us— we'd be okay." She glanced down. "Maybe it wasn't the best way. But it was all I could manage to do."

Her face looked bare, unsure. We were quiet for a long time.

It's not enough, I wanted to say. Maybe the two of us, left alone, isn't enough. Maybe too much had been broken between us, more than could be fixed.

My mom lowered her voice. "Your romances are right, you know. About great love."

I looked up at the ceiling. "Please don't make fun of me right now."

She shook her head. "I'm not making fun. I'm telling the truth." She opened her handbag and took out a big cloth pouch. Silk floral fabric with a silver zipper.

She opened it and gingerly removed a baby's pink and blue

knit cap, a tiny hospital bracelet, a necklace I'd made for her in first grade out of puffy beads, a small album of elementary school art, the Urbanwords book of poems.

"I usually keep it in my top drawer, but I wanted it with me on the plane."

I looked at the stuff. I didn't understand it.

"The minute you were born, the nurse put you in my arms, and I felt like all my life I'd been waiting for you. I couldn't stop kissing your velvet skin and spun-sugar hair and tiny seashell fingernails. At night you'd fall asleep on my chest and I couldn't bear to wake you. I'd sit in the rocking chair, holding you, letting the love wash over me in waves. The fairy tales were right—there were stars and moons, my dream come true." She stared at me. "That feeling never changed. It will never change."

She'd never told me this before. Not in words.

But she had told me—she'd told me in the phone calls and texts, so many of them; in that hand on my forehead, knowing it wasn't a stomach bug at all; in wanting to keep me nearby for college; in trying to protect me from the grief and pain. I'd always seen it as overbearing, or as something I didn't understand, and maybe it didn't always take the right form, but it had been there, all around me, though I'd never before let myself see it for what it was.

My eyes hurt. Under the table, her fingers closed over mine.

No one wrote romances about mothers and daughters. There were no epic cowboy and jungle tales about mother and daughter love. Our table held a paperweight and a striped silk tie, a baby's cap and a book of poems, and our hands lay beneath it, hidden like the stitches of a quilt.

PART NINE

MAD LOVE

her wounds   came   from the same source as her power
—Adrienne Rich

Kaddish

As the sun sank toward the horizon and the city grew even more alive, we walked along the beach near the Santa Monica pier. Annie, Lulu, Janet, my mom, and me. The air was warm as bathwater; we carried our shoes and felt the sand squish between our toes. (Except for Janet, who didn't take her sneakers off.) We walked past little kids building sand castles, and people playing volleyball in bathing suits, and we watched a man with a white beard comb the sand with a metal detector.

My mom and Lulu talked and laughed and caught up on their lives. As we stood at the edge of the ocean, my mom told us that she and Larry had decided to postpone the wedding. They'd been rushing things. They weren't quite ready, not yet.

"While Eva was away, we had a lot of time alone together. I don't know if he's right for me, or if it's still too soon. And I forgot how much laundry men make. Even when they have their own apartment, all their laundry ends up at your place." My mom rolled her eyes. "I'm not ready to have a man in my life that much of the time just yet. Maybe having one *some-times* is just fine for now."

"Sometimes is definitely good," Lulu agreed.

"Sometimes *is* good," Janet said in an entirely different tone.

We started walking again. Maybe there were people in our lives who left us—like Will—but they served another kind of purpose. They made you do things you'd never have done otherwise. If I hadn't met Will, I wouldn't be here right now. None of this would've happened.

Janet watched the waves lap at our feet. "Watch out for jellyfish. Even when they look dead, their sting is a pain in the *tuchas* like you never felt in your life."

We walked for over an hour. When it was time to leave and return to the hotel, I paused at the shore. Annie and Janet stopped with me.

I opened my bag.

I thought about how honoring the dead means making a hundred little choices. What to keep, how to remember. The people who are left behind have to curate the memories. That's the job we have to do.

I'd keep the paperweight, the postcards, the real things. The things that he would want me to keep. I took out the Toffee Crisp wrappers and the receipt.

"What are you doing?" Janet asked. "There's a $100 fine," she said as I flung the wrappers and paper into the ocean.

"Oh, too late." Janet shook her head. *"Yitgadal v'yitgadash.* There go some Toffee Crisps that meant a lot to Frederick Roth, and now they're being returned to—"

The wind had picked up, and instead of carrying them to the ocean, they flew up and over us, back to shore.

"—to the beach," Janet said.

"Hey!" the white-bearded old man called, waving his metal detector. "Whatcha doing? Ya littering! Ya littering!" He ran across the beach, chasing the wrappers as they flapped in the breeze.

We started laughing. My dad would love it. It was better than any funeral he could wish for—the old man in his chase like a modern dance, the flying Toffee Crisp wrappers, the warm sand, the wind and the sea.

To leap

t almost seemed like a bus station. An incredibly clean, expensive bus station.

Women in giant sunglasses and heels tottered across the floor, little girls dragged their tiny pink suitcases, and mothers juggled babies. All these people going about their lives fearlessly. Or so it seemed.

We'd gotten there two hours early. To get used to it. To prepare. My mom was determined not to take a pill this time, as she had on the flight out. (She'd taken two.) "It's just a flying subway, really," my mom said. "A subway with wings."

I felt a familiar whirring in my stomach, my skin growing colder. We stuffed my mom's tote bag with magazines, sandwiches, juices, Skittles, Snickers, Tic Tacs, and granola bars, as if we were traveling for a week. She picked out a new bottle of perfume, though she already had two others in her checked baggage, including the bluebonnet one I'd given her. We picked out a gift, a lavender-scented household cleanser set, for Janet, who'd given us her frequent flyer miles for the tickets.

We sat and read in a coffee shop—almost like any other coffee shop—except there were planes out the window. We ordered two giant pieces of chocolate cake.

My mom closed her magazine. "I'm so freaking scared," she said.

"Me too." I laughed at her honesty; she giggled too. To everyone around us, we probably looked deranged: mother and daughter devouring cake like it was their last meal.

We walked toward the gate.

I thought of Elizabeth Bishop, traveling the world. Or Edna St. Vincent Millay, touring the country, reading to packed theaters. Or Adrienne Rich or Nikki Giovanni or Marie Howe, or all those women at once. Those women took risks, they loved and lost, they wrote about it. They took their disasters and turned them into something beautiful. That's what I wanted to do with my life.

I thought of Annie and Janet, who were on a train right now barreling toward Texas. I thought of Lulu, who was driving back to Tucson. And I thought of my mom.

She stood beside me as we faced the gate. All this time I'd been searching for true love when I already had it. *Every poem is a love poem*, my dad had said. I'd always thought he meant romantic love—but there were so many kinds of great love: mother and daughter love. Father love. Best friend love. Aunt love. Mother's-best-friend love. Friendish friendesque love. Love for the living and love for the dead. Love for who you really are, for those weird parts of yourself that only a few people understand. Love for the things you yearn to do, for putting words on a page. Love for traveling, for meeting new people and seeing new ways to live. Love for the world, for it being a hard pain in your ass. Love for the questions, for the ever more complicated questions.

I watched the display of destinations.

AMSTERDAM	BANGKOK	DUBLIN
EDINBURGH	FLORENCE	LONDON
MADRID	MELBOURNE	NAIROBI
PARIS	ROME	SINGAPORE
TAIPEI	TEL AVIV	TOKYO

Places that someday I would see.

The sun filtered through the giant windows, dappling the floors and seats and walls with diamonds of light.

I took that leap, and I was flying.

Acknowledgments

My deepest thanks to my extraordinary editor, Alexandra Cooper, and my wonderful agent, Emily van Beek. I'm grateful to the incredible team at Harper: Megan Barlog, Rosemary Brosnan, Renée Cafiero, Kate Engbring, Barbara Fitzsimmons, Erin Fitzsimmons, Megan Gendell, Victor Hendrickson, Kate Morgan Jackson, Susan Katz, Nellie Kurtzman, Jenna Lisanti, Alyssa Miele, Diane Naughton, Andrea Pappenheimer, Sandee Roston, Patty Rosati and the entire School and Library Marketing team, Olivia Russo, and Booki Vivat.

Thank you to the readers of various drafts of this novel for their wisdom and advice: Allison Amend, Dalia Azim, Judy Blundell, Shana Burg, Becky Hagenston, Jodi Keller, Dika Lam, April Lurie, Anna Sabat, Mary Helen Specht, Cecilia Ward, and Lara Wilson.

Thank you to Brian Anderson, Bob Ayres, Pinckney Benedict, Sam Bond, Patti Calkosz, Doug Dorst, Benjamin Dreyer, Valerie Greenhill, Bethany Hegedus, Shelby Hogan, Robin Lauzon, Kirk Lynn, Justin St. Germain, Stacey Swann, Nina Brown Theis, Marsha and Rich Wagner-McCoy, and Bobson Wong for the fact-checking help.

I'm grateful for the support and encouragement of Lynne

Barrett, Michelle Beebower, Sarah Bird, Edward Carey, Nichole Chagnon, Elizabeth Everett, Carrie Fountain, Deborah Heiligman, Devon Holmes, Marthe Jocelyn, Varian Johnson, Sheri Joseph, Ana Knezevic, Iva Knezevic, Mila Knezevic, Elizabeth McCracken, Linda Sue Park, Jackie Rabb, Helen Reid, Karleigh Ross, Sharmila Rudrappa, Andrea Silber, Laura Silber, Cynthia Leitich Smith, Rebecca Stead, Michael Taeckens, Hannah Tinti, Julien Yoo, and Jennifer Ziegler.

Thank you to Adrienne Brodeur at *Zoetrope: All Story* for publishing the short story that inspired this novel. I'm also grateful to the following sources of information: the documentary film *My Knees Were Jumping: Remembering the Kindertransports*; *Too Young to Remember* by Julie Heifetz; and the reporting by the *New York Times* on the crash of Air France 447 and the recovery of its wreckage.

Thank you to SCBWI for the Work-in-Progress grant that helped support the writing of this book, and to Cecilia Ward for providing a place for me to write the first draft while I had a young baby at home. Thank you to the MacDowell Colony, the Writers' League of Texas, and to Meghan Dietsche Goel, Mandy Brooks, and all of the staff at BookPeople in Austin.

Enormous thanks to Lara Wilson for the long talks about motherhood, writing, and grief, and to Dika Lam for the daily laughs (including the manroot jokes), and for keeping me going every day.

Thank you especially to Marshall, Delphine, and Leo, with all of my love.

List of Works Referenced

As I wrote this book, I started each day by reading a poem. Many of the selections below are from my favorite poems, which continually inspire me; these poems take loss and grief and turn them into something beautiful. As a reader and a writer, poetry is my first love; it captures, in the words of Dylan Thomas, how "your bliss and suffering is forever shared and forever all your own." And in the words of Rita Dove, "Poetry is language at its most distilled and most powerful." In Audre Lorde's words, which I believe can be applied to fiction as well, "Poetry is the way we help give name to the nameless so it can be thought." I'm enormously grateful for the work of all the authors included here, and I hope that readers will love their books as much as I have.

Excerpt from "O Tell Me the Truth About Love" by W. H. Auden, pp. 1, 341.

Excerpt from "If Men Could Menstruate" by Gloria Steinem, p. 6.

Excerpts from "Fern Hill" by Dylan Thomas, pp. 8, 10, 11.

"Funny grief" from "Vilify" by Sherman Alexie, p. 23.

"I dwell in possibility" from "I Dwell in Possibility" by Emily Dickinson, p. 37.

Excerpt from "March" by Mary Oliver, pp. 44, 341, 379.

Excerpts from "I measure every Grief I meet" by Emily Dickinson, pp. 53, 125, 156.

"At his touch, the scabs would fall away" from "Adolescence—III" by Rita Dove, p. 68.

Excerpts from "Wild Nights!" by Emily Dickinson, pp. 84, 254.

Excerpt from "kidnap poem" by Nikki Giovanni, p. 87.

Excerpt from *Women and Economics* by Charlotte Perkins Gilman, p. 110.

"You can't keep weaving all day and undoing it all through the night" from "An Ancient Gesture" by Edna St. Vincent Millay, p. 134.

"There is no music like this without real grief" from "Orfeo" by Louise Glück, p. 137.

Excerpt from "i like my body" by e. e. cummings, p. 141.

"Those who are dead are never gone" from "Sighs" by Birago Diop, p. 148.

"O Love, O fire!" from "Fatima" by Alfred, Lord Tennyson, p. 163.

"Time does not bring relief" by Edna St. Vincent Millay, p. 175.

"To touch him again in this life" from "The Race" by Sharon Olds, p. 188.

"Help me to shatter this darkness" from "As I Grew Older," by Langston Hughes, p. 202.

Excerpts from "Twenty-One Love Poems" by Adrienne Rich, pp. 207, 278, 279.

Excerpts from "One Art" by Elizabeth Bishop, pp. 269, 276, 291, 327.

"Feast on your life" from "Love after Love" by Derek Walcott, p. 276.

Excerpt from "Letters to a Young Poet" by Rainer Maria Rilke, pp. 276–77.

"Worn down love" from "The North Ship XXV" by Philip Larkin, p. 302.

"Light, love, life all tumbled": from "Coda" by Marilyn Hacker, p. 321.

Excerpts from "A Letter" by Yehuda Amichai, pp. 348, 353, 356.

Excerpt from "What the Living Do" by Marie Howe, p. 369–70.

Excerpts from "Power" by Adrienne Rich, pp. 371, 379.